THE ORACLE
BETRAYED

Catherine Fisher

THE
ORACLE
BETRAYED

Book One of
The Oracle Prophecies

GREENWILLOW BOOKS

An Imprint of HarperCollins*Publishers*

The text of this book is set in 11-point Galliard.

Library of Congress Cataloging-in-Publication Data
Fisher, Catherine.
The oracle betrayed / by Catherine Fisher.
    p. cm.
"Greenwillow Books."
Summary: After she is chosen to be "Bearer-of-the-god," Mirany questions the established order and sets out, along with a musician and a scribe, to find the legitimate heir of the religious leader known as the Archon.
ISBN 0-06-057157-8 (trade). ISBN 0-06-057158-6 (lib. bdg.)
[1. Fantasy.] I. Title.
PZ7.F4995Or 2004 [Fic]—dc21 2003048498

10 9 8 7 6 5 4 3 2
First American Edition

 GREENWILLOW BOOKS

THE FIRST HOUSE
OF THE STING OF THE GOD

Even gods dream.

I dream of water, of how it falls, the plop of the great hot drops on the desert, the hollow pits they make in the sand; how the parched land drinks them instantly.

I am a god; my dreams should come true. But then, water is different, water is she, and there's no control over her.

I think I have lines on my body, and great scorched places and pustules that burn like volcanoes. Or sores. Or deserts.

I puzzle myself. Am I single or double? Light or light's shadow?

And the tunnel leads up to the world and I climb and scuttle through it, and come to where you live. And one of the problems of divinity is that people expect something huge and powerful.

And an instant result.

SHE SPEAKS TO THE ARCHON

The Procession was at least halfway down the terraces before Mirany stopped trembling enough to walk properly. It was hard to see clearly through the eye slits; the mask was too big, the slits too far apart. And in the sweltering heat, the dust rising in clouds, the flies, the shimmering mirage of the road, everything was bewildering. She flipped hair out of her eyes, tight with dread, her whole body sheened with sweat. Just as the back strap on her sandal started to chafe, the Procession shuffled to a stop. They had reached the Oracle.

Rattles, drums, and zithers were silenced on one note.

In the terrible still heat, Chryse whispered, "My arms are burning."

She had oddly fair skin. Maybe, generations back, her people came from the mountains.

"Put anything on them?" Mirany said breathlessly.

"Aloe oil."

"That won't help." Her voice was tight.

Through the mask of the Taster-for-the-God, Chryse looked at her kindly. "Don't be scared, Mirany. You'll be all right."

If I survive. Behind, as she glanced back, the long ranks of troops were clanking to a halt, glittering in their bronze, their general, Argelin, grim on his white horse, and in front of them the six men that carried the Archon's litter had paused, too, lowering the golden canopy thankfully onto the track, rubbing their aching shoulders. The old man must be heavy.

But then, he wouldn't be going back.

The Speaker turned. "Mirany." The great mask she wore was the only one of the Nine with an open mouth. It muffled her voice; made the familiar name sound strange, a breathy, unfamiliar summons. As if the god was speaking then, for a moment. Until she snapped, "Follow me. Only you," and it was Hermia again, acid and watchful, and Mirany saw her eyes gleam dark through the narrow slits.

Giving the end of the garland to Chryse, Mirany stepped out, silent. She felt shriveled with dread, sick with it. The narrow path that led off the road was made of cobbles tightly placed together, and wasn't straight but wound round into the olive trees through a doorway of three great stones. On the smooth lintel the scorpion and the snake were carved, fighting their eternal battle. Uneasy, Mirany glanced up at them. She had passed the doorway many times, but had never entered it. The Speaker, already through, turned, impatient. "Quickly!"

Mirany took a deep breath, and followed.

She was in the enclosure of the Oracle.

They walked down the path. In the sizzling heat Hermia said, "Are you afraid?"

"Should I be?" Mirany whispered.

The mask swiveled. "I'll assume that was a serious question, and not impudence. Indeed you should. Yours is a dangerous honor for a girl so inexperienced."

She knew that. She had never, never thought it would be her. When Alana had died, all the girls had whispered about who would be next Bearer, but when Hermia had sent for her this morning and told her she'd been chosen, she hadn't been able to believe it. Neither had anyone else.

The terror had come later, growing all day. Now, despite the heat, her hands were so chilled she could hardly feel them, so she rubbed them together and asked the question she already knew the answer to. "Will I be doing it today? Carrying the god?"

"If he wills it." Hermia sounded amused.

Fear tasted sour. A prickling, her heart thudding, and that sickening, sweating emptiness. She swallowed a huge lump of it in her throat but it was still there, choking her, and the gold and scarlet mask was a stifling hand over her breathlessness.

Up here the noise of the Procession had faded; it was as if the path under the stone door had led them both abruptly out of the Island into another, hushed place, where only cicadas hissed in the prickly furze. Stumbling, Mirany felt a sticky strand of hair fall in her eyes. It was coming loose, like it always did. Then she thought, *All right, so you're terrified. But at least you'll see the Oracle.*

The others had arguments, in the Lower House, late at night. About whether the Oracle was a statue that spoke or a spring that bubbled up out of the ground. Whether it thundered with a roaring voice, or whispered like leaves in the wind, while Hermia went into a trance and moaned and shrieked. Too shy to join in, Mirany had listened, and thought her secret, wicked thought. Now she'd finally see. But she'd never be allowed to tell them about it.

Juniper and stunted bushes of thyme and artemisia scorched the heat with scent. The path coiled round on itself like a sleeping snake, and the underbrush stirred and crackled with the god's life, small scurryings, slither of scales, the quick green scuttle of a lizard.

Then they made the final turn and were there.

Wide circular stone steps led up. The Speaker climbed them, her shadow tiny in the high sun. The steps were worn; under Mirany's thin sandals the smoothness of them was a faint reminder of pleasure, hollowed where generations had walked. And there was a breeze up here, faint and unmistakable, cool through the softly swishing branches.

The steps led to a stone platform. In its center a huge standing stone stood angled, as if the gales of centuries had slowly forced it over. The platform was surrounded on three sides by the bent, gnarled, leafy masses of the olive trees, but to the east the view was open, and as this was the highest point on the Island, the cobalt blue of the sea glittered out there, endless to the horizon.

Mirany licked parched lips.

The Speaker took off her mask. It took both hands to manage, but when she laid down the feathers and golden smiling face, she was Hermia again, hot and irritated, her hair askew.

She looked across. "The bowl. Behind you."

It was a wide, bronze vessel, terrifyingly shallow. As Mirany knelt and her shadow darkened it, she saw the ship of the Rain Queen was cut around its brim with thin incised lines. She had to put both arms round it to pick it up, and the metal was as hot as fire. It was surprisingly light. But then, it was still empty.

"Bring it here."

Awkwardly, Mirany hefted the wide dish to the center of the stone platform and set it down. The metal made a dull, brazen clang. Below, where the Procession waited impatiently in the scorching heat, a drum banged as if in answer.

Next to the bowl was a pit. It was narrow and sinister, in the very heart of the circular sky platform, and the standing stone covered it with deep shadow. She knew at once that this was the Oracle. It led straight down, a narrow crack into darkness, down through the Island and the rocks and the depths of the sea to the place where the god lived. This was the mouth he spoke through.

Fascinated, she edged closer. The pit was black. She couldn't tell if it was empty, or flooded with some oily water; in the sun glare it looked negative, a place of nothing. A faint haze of fumes hung over it.

"Make your offering," Hermia said.

Mirany unpinned a brooch from her dress, a jeweled scorpion, its body of ruby. Her father had given it to her the day she'd sailed from Mylos; she remembered the touch of his fingers pressing it into her hand. "I'm proud of you," he'd said. His face had looked so happy.

The Speaker was watching. Hot, Mirany held the brooch out over the Oracle. "For you, Bright One," she breathed, and let it go. It flashed through sun into shadow. Far below, it rattled down and down.

Hermia put her mask back on. She raised her arms to the sky and Mirany knelt, hastily, flattening her palms on the gritty stone and crouching down so that the forehead of the mask touched the rock. It was red-hot on her skin; she jerked back a fraction, stifling a gasp.

Hermia began to speak.

The god had his own language. Listening to the fluid consonants, Mirany wondered why. Surely he could speak the normal words. But then of course, everyone would know what he was saying, and that wouldn't do. Not for Hermia, for one.

Anyway, Mirany had no doubt what was being asked for. After four months without rain, there was only one thing the whole land craved. The thing that obsessed them all, from the moment of waking with a cracked throat to going thirsty to bed.

Water.

Wordless, she spoke it to herself. *Water. Water.* It was a word that dripped and cooled and healed and gurgled. It was a torment and a dream. A god's dream. It fell from the sky, and if none fell soon there would be no flocks and no people and no one left alive, even on the Island. They were desperate. She hoped Hermia was making that clear. But then the god would know anyway, if he was real. Face down on the hot stone, Mirany swallowed painfully. *I didn't mean that*, she thought in a shiver of terror. *I didn't mean that.*

Hermia had finished. Only the hot wind hissed through the branches. Eyes close to the rock, Mirany watched the stone pavement under her fingers, waiting. Would there be a splash, a hot raindrop from the sky, then more, and more? Gathering clouds, thunder, a flapping of wind?

But the sky was blue and hot and clear and went on forever.

Then, deep in the darkness of the pit, she saw movement.

One tiny, jointed pincer groped over the rim of stone. Small grains of soil dislodged.

Every hair on her neck crawled; gooseflesh broke out on her arms. "Speaker!" she hissed.

"Keep still."

Hermia had seen.

A second pincer, edged with minute hairs. Then, with a

scrabble that made Mirany jerk backward, six more legs and a body, sand yellow, the coiled segmented tail with its deadly sting held high and quivering.

The scorpion crawled out of the pit into the shadow of the bowl.

"Now!" the Speaker whispered.

Mirany glanced at her. Her eyes were dark behind the mask.

Because this was it. This was where you found out if you could live the life of the Bearer or whether the god would kill you.

About you not existing. I didn't mean it.

The scorpion made a small run at her. Hastily, Mirany grabbed the bowl, tipped it gently, and the scorpion climbed inside.

Rigid, she said, "What now?"

Hermia's voice was acid from behind the mask, a cold amusement. "Wait," she said quietly. "We don't know in which he will be."

In all, nine scorpions crawled out of the pit. One after the other, some small and yellow, one of the huge red ones, three tiny black things no bigger than beetles, the most venomous of all. In the bowl they rattled and slid and scuttled at each other. One of the yellow ones already looked dead; they would attack and sting each other till only one was left. If they didn't climb up the rim and kill her first. One touch, that was all it would take. One brush . . .

Her hands were so cold now they seemed frozen to the

bronze. When Hermia finally said, "That's enough," relief broke over Mirany like sweat, but this was where the real torment began. She knew the Speaker was watching her, enjoying it. She didn't understand why Hermia had chosen her. Unless she knew what Mirany secretly thought. Unless the god was real and had told her.

Every step down the path back to the Procession was a nightmare. She held the bowl as far from her body as she could, hands carefully spread under the rim, but it was heavy like that, and would get heavier all the way to the City. Once she stumbled, and gasped in utter horror. If she fell, she was dead.

Back at the stone doorway, the Speaker stood and called in a clear voice, "He is with us!"

All down the ranks of the Procession, a ragged dry cry echoed her, fierce and desperate. Soldiers clashed their spears against the great shields, the Temple servants and scribes yelled. The litter bearers heaved the Archon's swaying palanquin onto their sore, padded shoulders. With a wide-eyed glance at Mirany through her blue mask, Chryse led off with the rest of the Nine, and behind them came a hundred little girls; rank after rank of white arms strewing the pale petals of poppy and eucalyptus, crushed underfoot, and as they came past they turned their heads and glanced at her, all of them, consumed with curiosity, even Rhetia, who had wanted it to be her.

Mirany stood stiff with concentration. Sweat was drenching her. Her eyes were fixed on the scorpions, their restless climbing over one another, the terrifying balance of tilting and tipping that would keep them in the bowl's wide base. Already the muscles of her arms ached.

After the girls came the Archon's litter, swaying as the men worked out their rhythm, slowly striding down the rough uneven surface of the road. Fan bearers beat at the clouds of flies that tormented them; streams of sweat cracked the dust on their faces.

Mirany swallowed, or tried to. Her throat was hoarse with thirst.

Argelin rode up, his horse nervous, side-stepping. He flicked an inquiring glance at Hermia; she nodded briefly. Then she gestured to Mirany; they both stepped in behind the litter, and walked.

The road down to the Underworld must be like this. Sweat was blurring Mirany's sight; behind her the cacophony of the trumpeters and drummers was loud as pain, the sacred rattles and the endless rhythmic clash of spears on shields a harsh racket, and far ahead, like a ghostly echo, the clapping hands of all the people, waiting on the bridge and the desert, lining the shimmering route to the City of the Dead.

And the scorpions slid and rattled on the polished bronze; they made angry runs and shuffled and their quivering tails stung at one another again and again in a maelstrom of fury. Tiny drops of venom splashed the bowl. Mirany walked without raising her eyes, her feet stumbling in potholes, her whole body so tense that she was a mass of concentrated energy, eyes and hands and the gently tipping, balanced bowl. And for a second the god was in her, and she knew she was a great power, and that she held the hemisphere of the world there, with all its puny, squabbling creatures, lifting some, casting others down, queen of life and death. And then two of the hateful things scrabbled up opposite sides at once, and she stifled a scream and flipped them back, and was Mirany again, scared witless, inches from death.

She only knew she'd reached the bridge because the sound of the wood rumbled ahead; then her feet felt the road become smooth planks, and giving one rapid glance to the side of the bowl, she saw the sea, far below, through the slats. Waves pounded a rock.

Not far now. Half the scorpions looked dead, lying still, but you couldn't be sure, because suddenly one would revive and come scuttling up toward her, and the bowl was so heavy now she had to clutch it against her chest, and her hands were slippery, and it rose and fell with her panicky breath. Under her chin, the scorpions fought their vicious war.

The desert! Sand on the track, and on all sides, close, people. They clapped the rhythm of the Procession, threw flowers, herbs that were crushed as she trod them, whole wreaths of laurel and bay onto the Archon's litter. Risking a glance, she saw that the old man was peering out through the curtains.

He was watching her. Through the beautiful grave mask

that covered his face she could see his eyes, fixed on her, and for a moment they exchanged a glance, and their terror was shared.

Then he turned away, and opened the hangings. He looked out at his people from behind the face of gold and scarlet, turning from side to side, hands raised, blessing. And the people roared and wept and ran alongside, and the soldiers pushed them back, and goats bleated somewhere, and the sun blazed, and the air was choked with dust.

A scorpion had reached the rim; one pincer touched her hand. With a convulsive sickening shudder she flicked it back, biting her screech silent.

The City of the Dead.

At its entrance, in a great empty square, the ziggurat waited.

A sacred mountain, high ledges of cut stone, the steps up to it so steep she had to grit her teeth to think of it. "Don't let me drop you," she whispered. "Let me carry you up."

The god was in the black scorpion, the tiny one. As it crawled over the red one's body she was sure.

The Archon had climbed from his litter. His tunic was white and he raised his hands and everything went quiet. Except Mirany's heart.

"Today," he said, "I-who-am-the-god will leave you. Today I will drink in the garden of the Rain Queen. I will speak with her. Today my mind and hers will be one. This was why I came to you as a child, why you fed and clothed me all these long years. You have suffered a long time. Your flocks are dying, your children are parched, and still the skies stay empty. But for my sake, because I ask her, she will send you rain. Because the god is in me, I will send you rain."

No one cheered. Only the drums and rattles went on, a constant throb. Then the Archon turned and began to climb the ziggurat. The Speaker pushed Mirany after him.

Legs ached, breath came hard. Hers, and Hermia's, and behind his mask, the old man's. Up and up, step by high step, into the sky, into the hard blueness where the kites already gathered, dizzy circling spots. Her muscles were knots of pain, an agony. She felt she would never be able to straighten her arms again.

On the top, chest heaving, spots before her eyes, she clutched the bowl. Two scorpions fought for life.

The three of them stood high in the sky. Then, to her amazement, the Archon removed his mask. It was the first time she had ever seen his face, and it was strangely unlined, and pale, as if the sun had never weathered it. He was flabby, well fed, his head bald, a stern kindness about him, like someone's uncle. Stiffly he lay down on the bare, hot stones and closed his eyes. He never said a word to either of them.

Mirany crouched and laid the bowl beside him. The relief was so tremendous her knees felt weak. Behind her the Speaker moved hastily away to the lip of the platform.

And instantly the Archon's eyes snapped open, and his hand caught Mirany's. "Take this," he mouthed, urgent, barely making the words. "Keep it secret." A crumpled scrap of papyrus was pushed at her; instinctively she grabbed it. His eyes were palest blue. "The Island is full of treachery," he breathed. *"Be careful*. Stay alive!"

As Hermia turned he lay back, eyes tight shut. Then, even before Mirany could scramble up, he lifted his hand, and placed it, deliberately, into the bowl.

Below, all the drums stopped.

The world was silent.

She couldn't tell exactly when he died. It was so noiseless, so still. After a while, breathing hard, awed, she saw the tiny black scorpion come crawling up across his arm; it clung a moment to his face, its tiny pincers working in the air. Then it clambered over his tunic, fell off, scuttled into a crevice in the stones, and was gone.

The whole land waited.

The desert, and the pitiless sea, and the Island.

Below, the people stood baking in the hot sun, Argelin's soldiers in a great defensive square round the base of the ziggurat. Only the flies buzzed, settling on the Archon's face till Mirany crouched and waved them off.

Finally Hermia came close, knelt, looked at the dead scorpions in the bowl, then touched the old man's neck, felt for his breath.

Without looking at Mirany she stood and cried out to the people, "The god has left us!"

There was a ripple, then a roar of sound. Gongs, chimes, rattles, drums. Cries of lament.

Mirany stood exhausted, every muscle aching, shivering, burning, parched with thirst, the parchment crumpled small in her fist. The old man's face was slack, unoccupied. He lay without moving.

Someone shouted. Noise erupted like a thunder of joy. Hermia turned quickly, and Mirany's gaze followed hers.

Far to the east, on the very rim of the world, was a gray cloud.

SHE ENTERS THE UPPER HOUSE

That afternoon the skies darkened; the gray cloud spread and a bleak wind whipped over the sea, flapping all the awnings and canvas store covers down the steep winding alleys of the Port. The fishing boats came in, the last sailing for the safety of the harbor as fast as it could, small white waves breaking at its prow. Gulls screamed a warning overhead.

As Mirany folded her spare tunics and put them into the bag, the wind came rippling through the dormitory, whispering through the gauzy hangings around each bed, and the skirts of the watching girls.

No one was saying much. She knew they were jealous, and also that they were glad it wasn't them. Not for this office. Until Chryse glanced out at the sky, and jumped up. "It's raining! It is, look, look at it!"

She ran and leaned on the sill, holding her arms out, and

the others followed. A few large drops pattered on the floor.

Not much for an old man's death, Mirany thought.

To her horror Rhetia turned on her then. "I suppose you think you brought the rain, don't you." She frowned angrily. "I can't understand why the god picked you. You, of all of us, to get to the Upper House! Little mumbling Mirany, too scared to say a word!"

Some of the girls giggled. Mirany pulled the bag tight with a jerk of the cord. She wanted to floor Rhetia with some acid, brilliant remark. But she knew it would all come out wrong. Instead she gave a weak smile, hating herself for it.

"I suppose there are easier ways to serve."

"There certainly are!" Rhetia was openly scornful. "And you won't last long. Six months is the longest anyone's survived as Bearer and that was a woman called Castia, years ago, and they say she was tough as nails. Not a twitchy little mouse like you."

Mirany glanced at Chryse, who pulled a face. They both knew Rhetia came from the best family in the Two Lands, and fancied herself as Speaker one day. She'd been in the Lower House two years, and was already Cupbearer. It should have been her who moved up, and they all knew it. She was furious.

"Lady Mirany." The steward, Koret, stood at the door. "Will you come with me, please?"

She picked up the bag. Chryse looked ridiculously tearful, the others sullen, resentful.

"See you all later," Mirany whispered. Then she followed the man out, and was glad to go.

Beyond, far out to sea, a faint drizzle was falling, where it was useless.

As she followed Koret down the steps to the courtyard, she knew Rhetia had been right. There were only nine of them in the Temple, five in the Lower House and four in the Upper, and they were all more senior than she was. Each of the Nine had a title, and you moved up only when someone died or left, as they all had to leave when they reached thirty. It was rigorously ordered, or so she'd thought. First you were Embroideress-of-the-God's-Clothes, then Taster-for-the-God, then Washer-of-the-God, then Cupbearer, then Keeper-of-the-Flame, then Anointer. By that time you were probably in your twenties, and too old, but if you were lucky, you got to be Watcher-of-the-Stars and learned how to calculate the exact moment of sunrise, moonset, all those things. Which left the Bearer-of-the-God, and the Speaker-to-the-God.

Crossing the courtyard where the doves flustered and flapped in their niches, she thought back over her year here. It had hardly been promising. Her father had schemed and plotted and bribed to get her in, and her name had been on the list since she'd been born, but even when the letter with news of the vacancy came, and her father had gone whooping through the old colonnades of their decaying house, she had felt only dread. Of being stared at. Of having people bowing and calling her lady. Of having to talk to people.

Still, it hadn't been that bad. Duties were light. As Embroideress she'd had no idea how to sew, but the work-women did all of it anyway. Life was easy: books to read, playing games, swimming in the secret pool at the foot of the curved steps in the garden. The best food, plenty of water—the Temple always had to have enough. But she had only been Embroideress.

Until, last week, Alana felt the touch of the god.

It had been quick. One minute the dark-haired girl had been standing rigid, the next the bowl had fallen with a clatter that had terrified them all. There had been one scorpion, and the girl's crumpled huddle. That sudden. That fast. Once, she remembered, Alana had loaned her a white stole. Now she was dead. And Mirany was Bearer.

It was a huge honor, unbelievable, terrifying. But why, why her?

Koret opened the door to the Upper House and stood aside to let her go up. He was a tall, silent man, his head shaven, a wide collar of gold and lapis lazuli around his neck, with the sign of the god picked out in garnets. The girls joked about him, but not when he was in earshot.

The terrace up here was wide, floored with speckled marble. On the right the arches of the loggia pierced the white walls, tendrils of grape vines trained up and around them. As Mirany's sandals tapped on the cool stone she passed statues on tall plinths, the stony pale gazes of previous Speakers, staring out over the sea, Koret said. "The last door, lady."

She knew. It had the god's image on it in gold, and the word.

BEARER.

He bent politely in front of her and lifted the latch, pushing the door wide. She walked in.

It was an airy room, bigger than the ones downstairs, white and empty but for the bed in its billows of mosquito netting, a single table, a chair.

Anything that had been Alana's had been hastily cleared. As if she'd never existed.

Turning, she managed to say thank you without it being a whisper, and at the same time saw that the rear wall was painted with the same designs as the great animals of the desert, the monkey, the crocodile, the ibis. Their eyes were red garnets. They watched her, glassily.

Koret bowed. "When the gong rings, the Lady Hermia will see you." He paused, his eyes giving her a swift, almost furtive look. Then he went out silently, closing the door.

Mirany sank onto the bed. Some of the girls thought Koret was Hermia's spy. She wasn't sure.

The Island is full of treachery.

She looked round, quickly, then got up to check the two windows. One looked down into the Temple gardens. Parched flowers wilted below it. The other, in the side wall of the building, amazed her; if she stood on the stone seat under it, she was poised far above a sheer, smashed cliff face. Far beneath, a colony of seabirds plunged and screeched; scrub grew on the cliffs, a few bushes hanging precariously out, some scrawny lemons with tiny fruit. A thread of goat path zigzagged suicidally down. It was so high it made her dizzy, and exhilarated. The sea went on forever; she stared out at the cloudy horizon, thinking that surely she might see her own island of Mylos from up here, perhaps when the storm cleared, or at night, when the beacon was lit.

She turned, sitting down on the cool seat. Then she put her hand into the pocket inside her tunic, and pulled out the parchment. This was the first chance she'd had to look at it closely; it was splintered and cracked, an old piece, and it broke as she opened it. The writing was very small and had been done in haste, in letters so faint she was barely able to make them out.

> *I have seen you from my window. I know you are from Mylos; it was my island, too, before I was brought to be Archon. Because of that I will trust you. There's no one else, and I will be dead soon.*

Something rustled, outside on the terrace.

Instantly she stood, heart thudding. After a second she crossed to the door and opened it a crack, and peered out along the marble loggia. Only the statues stared back; between them the doors of the other rooms were closed.

She closed hers, and stood with her back against it.

> *Listen, girl. The Speaker is corrupt. The god is speaking to us but she cannot hear him. The things she*

*tells us are not the messages the god sends. He is angry,
so he holds back the rain. The Oracle is being betrayed.*

*Two things you must do. Find the new Archon. The
Speaker and Argelin will choose the one they want and
he will not be the choice of the god. You must stop them.
Second. In my palace is a musician. Oblek. Talk to
him. He knows.*

*Do not be afraid of the god. He will not hurt you.
He has chosen you. Burn this. Stay alive.*

She stared at it in dismay, read it again, and again.
Down the corridor, soft and shimmering, a gong rang.

In panic then, she ran, fumbled with the incense
burner on the table, flipped it open. Breathless with terror
she fed the parchment in, holding it hurriedly to the red-
hot ember until a small blue flame flickered round its edge,
turning it till the whole thing was alight; but it burned
slowly, reluctantly.

The gong rang again.

She threw the note on the floor, stamped it out, gathered the cracked mess and flung it hastily down the cliff.
Her fingers were black. She wiped them quickly, straightened her hair and went.

Closing the door, she saw some fragments still lay on
the floor, the breeze drifting them. But there was no time
now.

The Speaker had a suite of rooms in the Upper House, with

a private courtyard full of climbing roses. As Mirany opened the cedarwood door and peered in, the sweet smell of petals drifted after her. The room was empty, but on its stand by the unlit brazier the mask of the Speaker smiled down at her with its empty eyes.

After a moment she crossed the floor and stood under it.

The god is speaking to us but she cannot hear him.

Mirany bit her lip. The old man was naive. It had probably always been like that. Hermia would listen at the Oracle, and no voice would come. So she would say what she wanted to say.

Things would happen that she wanted to happen. The Speaker ruled the Island, and the Island ruled all the Two Lands, from the Sunrise to the Mountains of the Moon.

Because there was no god in the Oracle at all.

The mask was looking at her. She stepped closer.

It was pure gold, with scarlet embossing and ibis feathers and small gold discs that hung and turned on their threaded wire. Coiled snakes had been delicately incised on its cheekbones. Its eyebrows were black, perfect arches and the mouth was an oval darkness; it was open, and the breeze was coming in from the sea and making a noise through it, a tiny, high-pitched whisper.

She listened, despite herself. Brought her ear closer to the mask's lips.

A tiny, faint, dry whisper.

Saying nothing.

And reflected in the gleaming gold, distorted and still and unsmiling, she saw Hermia, who had come in behind and was watching her.

Mirany turned so fast the mask clattered and nearly fell off the stand; she had to grab it tight. Her heart leaped. Her face flushed.

"So," Hermia said. "Still jumping like a scared cat."

She was a tall woman, her nose long and straight. She wore her hair swept up in an elegant style, fastened with dozens of small gold pins. Her tunic was red, floor-length, pleated into hundreds of tiny folds that swished round her bare feet.

Mirany stood very still, prickling with sweat. "You wanted to see me."

The Speaker sat casually in the chair by the window and smoothed her dress. Without any warning she said, "I was surprised when the god gave me your name. Astounded, in fact. The lowest of the Nine, a new girl, no presence, no self-confidence. But when the Oracle speaks, there is no room for doubt, though your first year has been a disaster. All that homesickness . . . "

Mirany licked her lips.

" . . . which seemed to obsess you for weeks, your general timidity . . . " She shrugged. "I was expecting anyone else. Even Chryse."

Chryse! She would have wailed in horror. With an effort at boldness Mirany looked straight at Hermia. She was lying. She had to be. Coldly, deliberately. The Speaker had chosen her, not the god, and with that a thought struck Mirany, sharp as truth. They wanted someone shy, who wouldn't make trouble. That was why they'd picked her, and not Rhetia.

Hermia took a pomegranate from a bowl and began to cut into it with a small knife. "I have to say, though, you did far better than I had expected. Some girls faint. Some become hysterical. You did neither."

Mirany whispered, "Thank you."

"Your duties. Today, with the Archon's death, the ancient funeral process has begun. His body must be escorted through the nine houses to his final resting place in the City of the Dead. This will take nine days. Each day the whole of the Nine must be present, and the god, if he presents himself in any form, will be with us." She flicked a piece of peel into a bowl. "A busy time for you."

Carefully Mirany kept her fingers still. They still ached from carrying the bronze bowl.

"On the ninth day the new Archon will be appointed. A boy ten years old, without stain, without sin, perfect in body, sound in mind. At the moment of the old Archon's death the god entered his soul, for the god does not die. The search for this boy begins at once; General Argelin will send out searchers as the Oracle directs us. Meanwhile we must do our duty to the dead. You and Rhetia will go to the Palace tomorrow and fetch the prepared clothes for his body, and then the soldiers will seal the buildings." She smiled distantly. "Can you manage that?"

Controlling her worry, Mirany nodded.

"Good. That's all."

Walking along the loggia, Mirany paused, leaned on the sill, and stared out to sea. The drizzle had stopped. Already the cloud was breaking apart; out there the water glittered in the fading light, its wave tops catching faint pink glints as the sun set over the hills. It had hardly rained at all. Nothing had changed. Tomorrow would be hot again, and dry.

She thought of the old man with a pang of sadness. He had seemed so calm, so resigned. He had died, and for what? All his life he had been masked and kept holy, never speaking to anyone, rarely leaving the Palace, a living prisoner, and then they had killed him, and what use was it? His death wouldn't bring the rain.

It was all wrong, and she knew it.

She turned, and went into her room, pulling her clothes angrily out of the bag.

It was only then, as she turned to the bed, that she saw the fragments of the note were gone. Instantly she whipped the netting up, knelt on the floor and felt for them desperately, scrabbling on her hands and knees.

Nothing.

Someone had been in here.

Someone had gathered up the half-burned scraps and taken them away.

He Encounters Wild Beasts

The alleyway was dark and it stank. A slit between the dim shapes of high mud houses, it led down into a quarter of the Port no one in their right senses would enter after dark.

Unless they were desperate.

Standing here, where there was still some moonlight, Seth looked around furtively. Something dark and doglike slunk into the shadows, and from a house over the narrow alley a flicker of lamplight passed a window with a grille across it.

Nothing else. No one about.

Maybe they thought he wouldn't have the guts to come down here. They'd be wrong.

He lifted his chin, set his shoulders, and walked into the alley.

After three steps he was in blackness. Rats scuttled away; the faint drizzle of the day had done nothing to soften the baked dung that tripped him, or wash away any of the filth flung out of the houses; rotting stalks of vegetables, rags, a dead cat, flyblown and foul.

Cutthroats, he thought, and took out the long knife from his boot and held it tight, his thumb comforted by the wickedly sharp blade. The night was hot, the wind unable to pierce the steep, intricate labyrinth of streets and hovels above him, and the air lay like a weight on him, a mix of stenches, spices and jasmine and camel muck and smoke.

High up in the palace of some city merchant, music was playing.

At the end of the alley he edged out into a tiny square he had never seen before. The moon lit one side of it, the leaning houses, their doorways deep in shadow. The other side was a blackness, except for a tiny patch of light.

With a face looking out of it.

Seth paused, breathing deep. Probably the man couldn't see him here, but in this place ten others might be watching right now, and he'd thought earlier that someone had been following him as he came out of the City. He pulled the long mantle up over his head, wrapped it round so only his eyes were visible, and crossed to the door.

The doorkeeper peered through the grille. "Who are you?"

"That's my business. I'm looking for someone called the Jackal."

Something like a grin split the man's bearded face. "So are half of the soldiers in town. He's not here. Get lost."

Seth nodded. "But they don't know the word *Sostris*."

It meant something. The man's grin faded; he looked round, said something to someone behind him, listened for an answer. Then Seth heard the bolts and latches of the door being shot back.

Hastily he shoved the knife into his boot. It would be worse than useless.

When the door opened, a wave of hot air came out like a sirocco from the desert, cloudy with the sickly sweetness of opium. Glad his face was covered, he pushed past the doorkeeper, picked his way down two steps, round a corner and into the den.

It was airless and gloomy. Even the oil lamps burned with a greasy blue light. In corners men sprawled, smoking long, curved pipes, or chewing unspeakable food from dirty bowls. In the middle of the room a cauldron hung from the rafters, smoke curling up from it into heady clouds from the pipes, forming a thick haze that made the roof invisible. A few women, one or two of them almost pretty, peered from round dim hangings. It was rowdy, a mix of noise and argument and the rantings of those that lay in corners, talking to themselves nonstop and at high volume, their minds gone with the drug, or the terrible eternal thirst that tormented them.

Everyone who could still focus stared at Seth.

He licked his lips, looked round slowly. Taking his time.

They were easy to spot. There were two of them, sitting at a table in the corner, and they seemed the only people in the filthy den with whole minds. They were watching him, too. One waved a hand.

He crossed between the opium wrecks.

"What do you come about?"

"Sostris."

The two men exchanged a glance. Then one tapped the empty stool, and Seth perched on it warily.

"Uncover."

It wasn't a request. Sourly he unwrapped the mantle from his face. The smaller man grinned. "Pretty boy."

"More than I can say about you," Seth growled. The man was red-bearded, had one eye and broken front teeth and a nose that had been smashed in too many fights; he breathed noisily, his words oddly distorted. He wore a gold chain round his neck and a striped coat, gathered with a belt with three knives stuck in it, each larger than Seth's. He had not bothered to cover his face.

"Are you the Jackal?"

The red beard laughed and spat.

"That's me," the other one said quietly.

As Seth turned, he knew his mistake at once. The taller man wore no gold. His clothes were dark and his skin a smooth olive, unremarkable except for his eyes. They were narrow and long, strangely almond shaped, like some animal's, and Seth shivered as he looked at them. The man's face was half-covered with a hood, but he looked younger than the other, well fed. A stray strand of hair hung down, long and straight. Fair.

Seth sat back, stretched his legs out, and looked straight at him. If he showed fear, this man would kill him. This man had already killed, many times. He was sure of that.

The Jackal waved a regal hand and a woman came and poured something clear into a dented metal cup in front of Seth. He tasted it carefully; then, despite himself, he drank every drop, fast. It was water. Pure, and cold. Priceless in this drought.

"A sample of my wares." The man leaned forward, chin on hand. "Now, tell me about Sostris. How much do you know?"

"All that you need." Seth took the jug from the woman, poured another cup and drank. He had not known how deep the thirst had seared into him. He felt like the desert, dry as sand, as if he would never get enough water. Then he put the cup down and looked at his hands. They were shaking; he laid them flat on the table, carefully. "I work in the City of the Dead; my job is fourth assistant archivist, in the Office of Plans."

"Exalted," the red-bearded man lisped, picking his teeth.

Seth fixed him with a glare. "Enough for your purposes. I have access to the plans of the tombs of the twelfth-dynasty Archons, from the north gate to the mausoleum of Hytemheb in the corner by the southwest well. I can get you the plans of the tunnels drawn by the engineers who dug them centuries ago. I can provide the texts that warn of the traps and pitfalls set for . . . thieves."

The Jackal smiled a slight smile. "This sounds adequate. And the price?"

"Water. A large amphora every day, left outside a house in the potters' quarter. The red house, on the corner of Straight Street. Starting tomorrow, without interruption, until the drought ends. Clear clean well water, no tainted muck." Too late he realized that telling them where Pa and Telia lived meant they'd always have a way of getting at him if things went wrong. But the Jackal was laughing a soft laugh.

"You'd do better to ask for gold or turquoises, my friend. In these days such things are less scarce than water."

"You know where to get it."

"Do you think even I can bring water out of the sky? I leave that to the Rain Queen. And like all women, she's fickle. But yes, I can supply you. At others' expense."

That meant it would be stolen. Seth kept the guilt out of his face. If it meant Telia would have water, that's all that mattered. Suddenly all he wanted was to get out of here. He knew if he stayed longer his confidence would go, and they'd find out he was almost too scared to think straight.

He wrapped the cloth back round his face. "It's agreed then. The tomb of Sostris."

"The richest tomb of the Archons." The Jackal's strange eyes surveyed him curiously. "All the treasures of the early dynasty, of the scorpion's son on earth. Whole rooms of gold and a thousand servants of silver, and a thousand horses of ivory, so they say." His voice was a whisper, but even in that room of cackles and delirium and groans, it sounded sharp, intense, as if the words cut the air like diamond. "What a thing to sell, for a loyal servant of the dead. Don't you fear their revenge?"

Seth stood up abruptly. "I've said I'll get the plans."

The bearded man laughed sourly, his eyes unfocused, and the Jackal stood, too, and he was a tall man, taller than Seth, and slender. "I am a predator," he whispered, his fair hair swinging forward. "One who prowls tombs at night. I conduct the dead to their afterlife. In the darkness and shadows I am intimate with bones and skulls and the wrappings of ghosts. I have no enemies except dead men. Do you understand?"

All too well. Seth nodded.

"Good. Now, when the late Archon's body reaches the Third House, two days from now, you will bring the plans. Not here. We will get a message to you."

"How?"

"In the way of wild beasts. Secretly."

Without another word, Seth turned. He crossed the den and at the door looked back, through the stifling opium haze. The table where the two men had sat was empty.

Outside he dragged in deep breaths of air, coughing and retching. Even the stench of the alley seemed wholesome now; he plunged into it, running swiftly, his jerky shadow flickering beside him along the walls of the houses. He might be followed; he dodged back into lanes, around the empty cobbles of a market, then slipped into the warren of streets that plummeted down to the waterfront, their precarious tenements almost meeting over his head.

There were more people about here. He slowed, walking, not to be noticed, stepped back into a doorway as a litter flanked with torches was heaved up steps, then he made a detour into the labyrinth of the potter's quarter and knocked at a small door. His father opened it and said, "Well?"

"I've got some. It'll start coming tomorrow. Get it in before the neighbors see."

"How did you get it?" Pa's thin face looked sour.

"A favor. Don't ask."

As if dried up with worry, his father only nodded. He even seemed beyond relief.

"How is she?"

"Asleep. Come and see."

Seth hesitated, then said, "Quickly then. I'm late already."

Telia slept on the floor in the back room, on the mat that had once been his. She was four, small even for her age, her black hair cut straight across her eyes, restless now. A glister of sweat dampened her forehead. For a moment Seth bent over her, touched her; then he turned and went back out.

"You could stay," his father said acidly.

"I've told you, I have to be back. With the Archon's death there'll be chaos. Nine days of mourning. The tomb to be made ready, all its contents listed, checked, double-checked. It's a lot of work."

But the door was already shut in his face.

He got out through the west gate easily, though as a precaution he wrapped the mantle round him and staggered.

"You've had a skinful." The soldier was one of the Port guards; he steadied Seth with a sour laugh. "Pass?"

He took time fumbling for it, but the guard gave it barely a glance and was certainly unable to read anyway; the sign of the god on the top was enough. He slapped Seth on the back; Seth almost stumbled with the impact.

"A lot of use you'll be tomorrow. Stay on the road. There are jackals about."

Seth raised a hand without looking back. Sweat chilled him. *The god knows*, he thought.

Out here in the desert the air was cooler. He paused, far down the paved road, and breathed deep, and on each side of him the dim land lay silent, a dark falling and rising of sand and rock, where nothing moved. Above, the clouds had cleared; the moon was high, almost full, and he could see how it glinted out at sea, and on the topmost pinnacles of the House of the Nine on the Island.

But not on the City of the Dead.

The necropolis rose up like a black wall in front of him, a parapet of darkness, pierced by ominous pylons and the great yawning mouth of the snake that was its gateway, and along its top the wall was crowded by rows of identical

seated images of dead Archons, hands on knees, calm, gazing eternally out at the horizon where the sun would rise.

Hollowed into that great citadel were the labyrinthine
offices of the tomb makers, the workshops of goldsmiths,
sculptors, ebony workers, carvers of marble and chalcedony
and lapis lazuli. There were the squalid living quarters of the
twenty thousand slaves that dug and tunneled and built and
died in the service of the dead. There were the secret chambers of the embalmers, and herbalists, the surgeons of
death, the smell of their unguents and oils making some
corridors too pungent to enter without fainting.
Honeycombed into this structure like cells were the storeroom of artifacts, the furniture makers' stores, the drying
rooms for papyrus, the paint-patched arches of the artists,
the barrels of stored water, and the thousands of scribes,
scribes just like him, unimportant, overlooked, keeping
notes, records, lists of payments, wages, contracts, debts,
invoices, bills, plans, and reports; or spending their lives
laboriously scratching the histories and the sacred texts that
each Archon as he died would take as his library down into
the dark.

Weary now, Seth made himself walk on. He was a
nobody, forced to plot and lie to get on, but one day, he
would be overseer, and more. He'd get to the very top. To
the Island.

Only no one must find out about the Jackal. Tomb robbers were staked out in the desert for the vultures to pick at
and the ants to eat. His punishment would be worse. His

eyes would be put out. And then he would be led down into the darkest levels far below the tombs, into places so old they were forgotten even before the Archons came.

And he'd be left there, for the dead to take their revenge.

He breathed in sharply, clutching a sudden stitch in his side.

By the time he reached the snake gate, dawn was coming. The eastern sky was pale, and high on the wall the first Archon's basalt face was flushed with rosy light.

"Good night out?" the gatekeeper asked, sucking a pebble to keep his dry mouth moist.

Seth glanced at him in disgust. "None of your business."

He walked in, head high.

The guard spat at his shadow. "Cocky little brat," he muttered.

THE SECOND HOUSE
OF MUSIC

I've realized that I am young.

I was old, not long ago—worn and anxious and unbearably weary, but that's gone and I've become young again. It's happened before. Gods do this, I suppose. Shed their skins like a snake.

I am young and rather frail. My body is small, but inside that my self is even smaller, a corner of a chattering mind, a glint of light caught only sometimes, when I turn.

I don't think my body knows yet that it contains a god; this bruised body with sores on its mouth. It longs for water. The way up to its surface is a long one; I send words but they are echoed and broken and come out as fragments.

Gods shouldn't have such problems.

Perhaps words are not enough. Because somewhere, out in some room, if there is a room, I can hear music. Flutes. That, too, is a thing that comes from deep down, along the veins and breath and metal pipes and the fingers on the stops and then out, into others' ears and minds.

Maybe I'll travel along it, and fly all the way to the sun.

She Seeks the Musician

Nothing interrupted the sunrise Ritual, not the Archon's death, not the failure of the rains.

Standing at the back of the group, Mirany watched, glad to have nothing to do, though in the year she had been here the Ritual had become automatic, a calm, regular repeating of movements and words.

The only difference today was that there was a new Embroideress, a tall, fair-haired girl who knew the words already and said them far more clearly than Mirany had ever managed. She smiled to herself sadly.

The statue of the god that stood in the Temple was seen by no one else but the Nine. It was said to have risen from the sea after a great earthquake centuries ago; the one that had split the Island from the desert and made it holy. The statue was of a young man, beautiful, olive skinned, his eyes watchful and slightly puzzled. It had amazed Mirany when she'd first seen it. The god came in many forms: the scorpion, the snake, the sun. In his shadow self he was his own twin; he was darkness and his venom gave death. He was the Bright Lord, the Archer, the Lemon Grower, the Mousegod. People thought the Archon was the God-in-the-World, that the god lived inside him. But this, this was something else. Looking at him now, while his marble hands and body were incensed and washed by Persis, she thought, *Is it you, then, that speaks from the Oracle?* And immediately the worry that had kept her awake most of the night came back, the worry about the letter and the disturbed fragments. Most of it had burned. Surely most of it had. She'd been an utter fool not to make certain!

They were dressing him now. The soft white tunic was fresh every morning; the precious water perfumed with roses, the wreath of flowers plaited every sunrise. Music played, softly, from the room beyond.

Finally Ixaca stepped back, and the food was brought.

On three silver plates it was laid at his feet; fruit and honeycakes and bread and olives. Rhetia, as Cupbearer, carried the wine, only the best vintage, a brimming cup, placed on the small table with the rest.

Every evening it was all removed and thrown away. The god had eaten and drunk the spirit of it; no one else could touch it.

Mirany moved her foot, drawing a small circle in the sandy dust. What would they do if he did eat it? What would they do if he came down from that pedestal? For a moment she almost grinned at the thought: Chryse's panic, Rhetia on her knees, Hermia struck dumb with amazement.

And what about her? She'd be the most astonished of all. Because, after all, they believed in the god. It was her secret, her terrible sin, that she didn't.

They must never find that out.

When the Ritual was over, Hermia came over and said briskly, "This is the key to the Archon's private chest. Bring clean clothes and sandals; the steward will have them ready. Rhetia will go with you."

Mirany's heart sank. Then she thought, *Are they keeping a watch on me?*

The tall girl was waiting at the doorway of the Temple; together they went out, through the men's courtyard and the women's courtyard to the great outer portico, and on each side people stood back respectfully, their heads bowed, hand to chin. Mirany had never got used to it, and it embarrassed her, but Rhetia swept on without noticing.

Barely an hour after sunrise, the day was already hot. Small lizards darted over the stones of the wall.

"Shall we walk?" Mirany asked quietly.

"The Nine don't walk. I've ordered a litter."

There was no change then. Mirany was higher than Rhetia now; she could give the orders. But they both knew she wouldn't.

The litter was waiting at the foot of the Cadmian steps; a stuffy, dark box hung with scarlet curtains. Inside were two padded seats and a scatter of petals on the floor, left from the last user. Rhetia looked the bearers over critically. "Take us to the Palace of the Archon. *Don't* lurch and don't go too slowly."

Then she climbed in.

The four men glanced at one another, tying the bindings on their hands and shoulders. Mirany knew the journey would be hot and heavy and totally unnecessary; the fact that she was young and fit and could easily have walked filled her with a sick sort of anger, at herself as much as anyone. She wanted to say something kind, but it came out as a pleading smile. She ducked under the curtain quickly.

As she sat the litter swung up, jolting them. Rhetia swore under her breath.

The journey was quiet. There were few people on the Island this early, and as they crossed the bridge Mirany lay back and parted the fine curtains to look down at the sea as it lapped the rocks far below, its depths as blue as the sky. A dolphin swam, farther out, and then another, a whole school of them leaping out of the water.

"How do dolphins drink?" she wondered aloud.

"How should I know?" Rhetia snapped.

After the rhythmic thud of the men's boots on the bridge, the road through the desert was silent. Flies gathered in a cloud around the litter; the bearers ducked their heads and were bitten, their hisses of annoyance muted out of respect. Rhetia moved restlessly on the couch. Finally she burst out with, "I *still* can't believe they chose you!"

Mirany sighed. Desperate to change the subject she took out the key and looked at it. "I suppose it's like being chosen as Archon. You don't want it, you just have to live with it." She looked up. "His death hasn't helped things, has it?"

"Of course it has."

"The rain didn't happen."

"Maybe that's what the god wants. Anyway, even if there isn't any, the Temple will be all right."

The Temple will be all right. Mirany stared at her in disbelief. "What about the people in the Port? What about the animals and crops?"

"The Temple is more important," Rhetia snapped. "Everyone knows that, even you. They'd give their last cup of water to us, all of them."

It was true, and it silenced her. For the rest of the long, swaying journey through the desert, she couldn't say another word.

The Archon's Palace was just outside the Port, a white, oddly small facade, with a few of the rarest trees around it, a small garden of herbs, and fountains, now dry.

When the litter stopped with a particularly sudden jolt, Rhetia jumped down and glared furiously at the bearers. They were sweating and winded; one had crouched in pain, but that wouldn't have stopped her making her feelings only too clear. Suddenly Mirany couldn't stand it anymore. In a clear, hurried voice she said, "Thank you. Go into the kitchens for water. Tell them you have the authority of the Nine."

They looked at her in surprise. The leader mumbled something, but Rhetia had grabbed her arm and turned her wrathfully. "You may be Bearer-of-the-God," she hissed, "but don't take liberties with me! My family is better than yours and I've been here longer than you."

Chilled, Mirany pulled away. Then she saw the men waiting by the dry fountain.

There were two of them, the steward of the Archon's house, a swarthy, sweating, fat man in an ornate robe, and behind him a scribe, probably from the City, no older than she was. Before she could move, Rhetia had snatched the key and swept forward, head high, her pleated tunic rippling. Miserable, Mirany followed.

"Holiness." The steward bowed, and after a second, the scribe bowed, too. "We have everything ready here, the rooms cleared, the apartments purified, as the Speaker ordered. The personal goods of the late Archon, may he be blessed . . . "

"Thank you." Rhetia swept past him; he had to turn quickly to keep up. "Lead the way. That's all."

Mirany trailed behind her, embarrassed. Rhetia spoke to everyone as if they were slaves. *It would be nice to be that confident*, she thought enviously.

The scribe was two steps back. At the door she turned and waited for him. He seemed preoccupied so he didn't notice and almost walked into her. Instantly he stepped back and bowed. "I'm sorry."

"It was my fault." Her voice was small. Her face red.

She turned away and walked on quickly, like Rhetia.

Inside the house it was clear that whatever "purified" meant, it had been carried out thoroughly. There was nothing at all left in any room: no furniture, no statues, everything was white and bare and smelled faintly of a peculiar scented oil that she had smelled in the City.

Rhetia went through all the rooms like a small whirlwind, glancing at them haughtily. Then she said, "The personal effects?"

"In the Archon's library, holiness."

The library was empty too. As Rhetia unlocked the only thing left, a small chest of cedarwood, Mirany stepped back and said quietly, "What's happened to everything?"

The scribe had dark, curly hair; his face was handsome and she thought he knew it. He gave her a surprised glance, and when he answered, his voice had lost some respect. A tiny change, but she sensed it. "Removed, lady. Everything in the Palace will go into his tomb. Listed and carefully packed away until the Day of Gathered Goods."

She should have known that. She felt humiliated.

Silent, they watched Rhetia open the chest.

If this was all that was left of a man's life, Mirany thought, it wasn't much. Four tunics, some sandals, a painted image of a woman ("His mother," the steward said hastily), a small wallet containing some dried leaves and a dessicated sea horse, a book with writing in it, three gold rings, a scarab brooch, and a purse of gold coins, useless, because the Archon had no need for money, having only to ask for whatever he wanted. The steward murmured, "The coins are for the poor. It was his request."

Rhetia rummaged through impatiently, then took an elaborately embroidered tunic and sandals and snapped the box shut. "These will be sufficient. The rest can go in the tomb." She turned and walked to the door. "Mirany."

It was an order, an unspoken command.

Maybe the scribe knew that; a small smile of scorn curled one corner of his mouth. With an effort Mirany drew herself up. "You go," she said quietly. "I have a few other things to do."

Rhetia stared. "What things?"

For a moment Mirany's mind was a total blank. Then words came into it and she said them, as if the voice was barely hers. "Errands which concern the god."

It was enough and Rhetia knew it. Any sort of question or demand to know what exactly she meant would have been impossible with two outsiders looking on, so she just gave Mirany a sour glare and said, "I'll tell the Speaker this then."

"Yes," Mirany said softly. But her courage had ebbed like water into sand.

It was too late. Rhetia was gone, carrying the clothes, and the steward behind her, puffing and talking and assuring her everything was in order, that the arrangements would be carried out.

His voice faded in the echoing rooms.

Mirany turned. The scribe had a stylus out and was making a list, quickly and methodically, of all the objects in the chest. Without looking up he said, "Yours was the only key?"

"What?" She came over.

"Someone else has opened this, lady. The lock has been forced and then closed again. Look."

There were marks, she could see now. A deep scratch in the ivory. She knew then that the Archon's goods had been searched. Probably the whole house had been searched, but the old man would not have left anything behind. *Burn this,* he had written. He'd been careful. But there was something left. Or rather, someone, and she knew with a sudden desperation that she'd never find him without help.

She said, "What's your name, and who are you?"

Still writing, the scribe glanced over. "Seth, lady. Fourth assistant archivist, Office of Plans. We're dealing with the Archon's funeral arrangements."

"What happened to the servants?"

"I'm sorry?"

Impatient, she said, "The servants here. There would have been lots, wouldn't there? Where are they all?"

He put the stylus away. "Each Archon has a staff of two hundred to look after his every need. At his death they all go with him. The new Archon will have a totally new staff."

"Go with him?"

He raised an eyebrow, looking at her in surprise. "Die," he said.

She'd known that. Why didn't she concentrate? *Was it so they wouldn't pass on secrets?*

She said, "Could you find one of them for me before that happens?"

He looked up. She knew then she might have sounded too eager, so she walked to the window and looked out, trying to sound bored and faintly irritated. "A musician the Temple has heard spoken of highly. We need new people. I believe his name is Oblek."

Before he could answer, the steward looked in. "Will you need me anymore, holiness?"

"The lady is looking for a musician named Oblek." Seth had said it before she could object.

The steward paused. He took a white piece of rag from his robes and mopped his face, and his eyes were small and black and looked at her with sudden, frightening curiosity. "Indeed? Well, you won't find him here, lady. He was arrested. Last night."

"Arrested?" She came forward, jolted into fear. "Why?"

"For safekeeping, I should think. Argelin's men came for them all. Anything else?"

He was a lot more offhand since Rhetia had gone. She shook her head, then said quickly, "What about you? Will you . . . go with him, too?"

In the doorway he paused and said, "Yes," without looking back. Then he sidled out.

The scribe was watching her sidelong.

Shocked, she turned, tried to think. So they'd got Oblek. Maybe it was just what always happened when an Archon died. But perhaps they'd read his name on the note, the wretched scraps of the note that should have been burned! It was her fault. She had to get to him.

She looked up quickly. "Listen," she said. "Do you know where prisoners are taken?"

"The cells, under the harbor guardposts. But you can't go there, lady."

She drew herself up, tried to look calm. "I'm one of the Nine. I go where I wish."

"Yes, but . . . "

Already at the door, she turned. "Will you come with me?"

It should have been an order, imperious, but it was more like a plea. Would she never get things right!

Seth rolled up the parchment and put it in a small wicker basket on his back. There was ink on his fingers. He rubbed at it thoughtfully. "Why should I?" he said. His voice sounded almost arrogant.

She stared at him. "Because I say so. And because I might need help to get him out."

He Sees an Opening for Advantage

She was a mousy little thing, he thought. Jumpy. Had no idea how to behave. For a start she kept waiting for him to catch up, though the regulations were that he should walk three steps behind and never speak unless she spoke to him.

Maybe she didn't even know that.

And as if they'd give her one of the Archon's servants just for the asking! He should have stayed out of this. Rich little girls were trouble.

Seth reached into the wicker basket of scrolls and pulled out a stoppered flask of water; he uncorked it and drank a cool mouthful.

The priestess had noticed; she watched him sidelong. He didn't know whether to offer her any or not—it might be seen as an insult either way. Anyway, it was his whole day's ration. He put it back.

When they'd come out of the Palace, the litter had gone; he'd been horrified but the girl had just started walking patiently to the Port. Now they were both footsore from the dusty road and almost at the gate. Neither of them spoke. She seemed shy, and he was tired from last night and worried. He didn't have time for this. He only had two days to get the plans.

But even if he found them, there was another difficulty. He couldn't just hand over the plans of Sostris's tomb to a man like the Jackal. The thieves would disappear with them; he'd have no guarantees of the water or anything else, and if they were caught and the maps were found on them it would be the end for him. He wasn't that stupid. No, it was risky, but the only way to make sure Telia got the water was to make sure the Jackal still needed him. It was tricky. If they thought he was holding out, they might just kill him anyway. . . .

He realized the girl had asked him a question.

"What?"

She looked upset. "I said, did you know the Archon?"

He stared at her. "Lady, nobody knows any Archon. He never comes out of the Palace without wearing his mask; no one is allowed to talk to him but the steward of his house and then only about everyday things. He speaks to no one all his life but the people and the god."

Walking on, she said, "It must be a lonely life."

Seth shrugged. "He has everything he needs, food, drink, clothes, all of the best. There are many in the Port who'd change places. And if he's lucky he never has to give the only payment they ask of him."

"But this one did."

He shrugged.

She pushed the brown hair off her face. Then she said, "I was there, when he died. I carried the god to him."

A shudder crawled down his back. He'd had no idea she was that important. The other one had seemed far more full of herself.

They were at the gate. The girl didn't seem to have a pass. She just went up to the barrier and said, "I am one of the Nine. Do you know me?"

The barrier went up instantly. Both guards bowed, nervous.

Seth walked in behind her. "Impressive," he said.

Her face was faintly red. "I can't really get used to it. Where now?"

"The waterfront." His heart sank as he thought of taking her to such a place. Stinking of fish, crowded with swearing sailors and mouthy fishwives, thieves, merchants. He stopped, looking at her clean white tunic of fine, expensive linen, the gold necklace she wore. "Maybe we should take a few of the guards with us."

She looked at him oddly. "They're Argelin's men."

"Yes, but you can—"

"No. We'll just go by ourselves."

He thought of the knife in his boot and swallowed. It wasn't much. If he let one of the Nine get mauled by some greasy sailor, he'd be out of the City without his ears and begging here himself tomorrow.

She didn't seem to realize that. Once they'd got down the precipitous lanes and steps to the harbor, she walked quickly, looking round with interest, as if she didn't get out much, dodging the camel muck and a backing wagon, the piled boxes of shrimps and whitebait and slippery, slithering squid. The stink and the salt and the screams of the gulls seemed to enliven her; she turned, smiling, and said, "It's like home!"

"Home?"

"Mylos. Out in the Heklades. We lived above the harbor."

He nodded. He supposed she missed it, but then she had the Island, and who could want more? He went to catch her arm and then stopped himself, and said instead, "This is the place, lady."

At the back of the Portico of the Traders rose a large, dark stone facade. This was where the soldiers' guardroom was, and where General Argelin had his headquarters. It was not a place Seth had ever been inside, or wanted to be.

The girl was uneasy, too. In fact, as she stopped and stared up at it, she seemed scared stiff. Suddenly she turned, grabbed him, and hustled him behind a stall.

"How do I do this? What if they won't listen to me?"

Seth stared, then shrugged. "Do it like your friend did. But they have to listen. You're one—"

"Of the Nine. Yes." For a minute she was silent, then she said, "I need your help. You know about these people."

Suddenly he saw his chance, and grinned with the surge of excitement in his chest. "If I do, will you get me promoted?"

"Promoted?"

"I'm only fourth assistant archivist. The pay's terrible. If I was third . . . second . . . I'd get more."

"Oh, I see." She didn't. She hadn't a clue. "Well, if I can. I mean, yes, of course. If you help me get the musician out. *Without Argelin knowing.*"

They looked at each other. What was going on here, he thought, and all his sense of self-preservation made his skin prickle and sent tiny warnings of energy down his back. He didn't want to get mixed up in anything with Argelin. All this for some musician?

"Without him knowing? I thought it was for the Temple?"

"It's secret," she murmured. And then she said what she'd said to the other one. "It's an errand for the god."

Seth raised his eyebrows. Well, he respected the god. And presumably she must know what she was talking about. Also, being in on any secret was power, being able to blackmail one of the Nine if he needed to would be only too useful. "All right," he said. "It's agreed. Now, for a start, you need to look haughty. Like your friend. Don't speak unless you have to; I'll do the talking."

Mirany shook her head miserably. "You don't understand! I can't! I'm no good at it. I hate it when people even look at me!"

"You'll just have to pretend."

"I *can't!*"

He sighed, impatient. "Lady, do you want to do this or not, because I've got plenty of other things to waste my time on."

She went red. Then she calmed, making herself breathe deep, picking at the gold chain. "Yes," she said finally. "Yes."

"Then follow my lead."

He began to walk, then turned instantly and waved her in front. "Sorry. But try and look like you're better than everyone else. As if they're all dirt."

In front of him, he heard her sigh. "That's not so easy," she muttered.

At the door he stopped her and went in first. "The Lady Mirany," he announced in a loud voice to the first guard he saw. "On the errand of the god."

It was a big room, and his voice echoed. People turned and looked. The guard stepped back, confused, hand to chin.

The girl came in, out of the sun.

She looked very small and pale, but she gazed round calmly enough and said in a voice that was almost impressive in its quietness. "I want to see one of your prisoners. Where are they kept?"

It was direct, he had to give her that. He'd have spent at least five minutes working up to it. But maybe she had something, because an officer pushed forward and came over straight away, not too high ranking, just an optio, but that was probably enough. He bowed.

"We had no warning of a visit, lady."

Mirany smiled, and gave one glimmer of panic at Seth, who said smoothly, "This is not an official or religious occasion. The Lady Mirany is here on behalf of a servant of her family, who seems to have been . . . detained, by some oversight. She wishes to know on what grounds, and whether she may speak with the man." He had dropped his voice and drawn the officer to one side; there was no point in the whole place hearing their business. Though it would get back to Argelin sooner or later.

The optio was a gray-haired man. He looked shrewd. "What's the man's name?"

"Oblek," Mirany said quietly. "A musician."

There was a list on the wall; the officer faced up to it as if he could read the names only with difficulty, but Seth had already seen it, halfway down. "This man," he said, tapping the parchment. "Cell five."

"Five?" The optio paled slightly. "There must be some mistake. Those are the . . . " He glanced at Mirany. "At least . . . Forgive me, lady, I'll have this seen to. The prisoner will be brought to the Temple. This very afternoon . . . "

Mirany frowned. She was nervous; her fingers flexed together but she said, "I'm sorry, I really am, but I want him now. I've come here to take him away. I'm sure you understand that the Temple and the service of the god are more important than anything else. This man is required to play in the Temple, and I'm not leaving here without him."

The last part was almost petulant, and her voice had

sunk to a whisper, but the words were clear. The optio looked round, as if desperate for someone else to pass this on to; to follow up, Seth murmured discreetly, "She's the new Bearer. I wouldn't keep her waiting."

The optio made a snap decision, turned, and yelled. Two guards presented themselves. "Get the man from number five. Bring him here."

"Number five?"

"Do it."

The men turned. Seth saw the glance pass between them.

They waited. The optio fetched a chair for Mirany and she sat in it, or on the edge of it, glancing round warily. Soldiers came and went, looking sidelong, a sort of rigid respect coming into their bodies as they passed her. She made a small, frightened face at Seth. They were both tense; if the general came in, Seth thought, he'd have to play things very carefully. Duck right out.

Then the guards were back. And the musician was with them.

Somehow, Seth had been expecting a young man. But if this was Oblek he was hardly worth the trouble. Paunchy, balding, obviously the worse for drink, or badly hungover. His old blue tunic was filthy, and he scratched as if he had lice. His face was weatherbeaten and oddly ugly.

Mirany hesitated for only a second. Then she jumped up. "Oblek! Look at the state of you!"

If he had wits they were scrambled. He blinked,

scratched, and said slowly, "Who are you?"

Seth turned on the optio fast. "Has this man been beaten? What was his crime?"

The optio laboriously fingered the parchment a sweating clerk had scurried up with. "Well . . . he was beaten for drunkenness. He was found in the Archon's wine cellar. In the remains of it, I should say; he seems to have been working his way through every bottle."

"With the old man's blessing, may the god love him," the man said grimly.

"And is that all?"

The officer licked his lips. "Yes. But all the Archon's servants . . . "

Seth knew they had to get out; Mirany was already on her feet. "You," she said quietly to the musician, "will come with me. You've been requested for the service of the Temple. Do you understand?"

He looked at her sourly. "I understand, lady."

"Thank you." She nodded at the optio, turned, and walked out.

Oblek went after her unsteadily, but before Seth could move, the optio had grabbed him. "What do I tell Argelin? Number five is special."

"Why?"

"They're for the Archon's tomb!"

"One won't be missed."

The optio looked uncomfortable. "If Argelin finds out—"

"Your problem," Seth said quickly. "Tell him about the girl; let him sort it. He's more than friends with the Speaker, from all I've heard."

He went quickly, running down the wide steps.

Outside the sun was glaring. Heat hit him like a wall, and the light was dazzling, a white glint on the sea. The racket of the harbor and the stink of the fish sizzled in the air. Swallows screamed between the narrow houses, high overhead.

The girl and the ugly man had vanished into the crowd. He ran after them, round a corner and straight into a meaty fist that shot out, grabbed a handful of his tunic, and hauled him painfully into a doorway.

Mirany was there, looking terrified.

"I want to know exactly where you live," Oblek snarled. "Right now."

She Hears What She Never Thought to Hear

A thin, weary-looking man had opened the door; now Oblek shoved past him, flung back the curtains of the three small rooms, and looked into each, then rapidly surveyed the roof, the outhouse, the courtyard where a little girl sat playing languidly with date stones in the shade.

"What is this?" the thin man demanded. He looked like Seth's father, Mirany thought. Suddenly tired and terrified of what she had done, she sat collapsed on a rickety chair. The child smiled at her.

"Shut up." Oblek sat, too. "Get me some water." His voice was a rasp.

Mirany saw Seth nod; his father went reluctantly to an amphora that stood in a stand in the coolest room; he brought a cupful and Oblek drank it at once, thirstily, noisily, spilling great drops onto his stained tunic, and then waved the cup impatiently for more.

They waited for him. It was as if no one dared speak before he had finished; his small eyes watched them expressionlessly over the brim, and when his thirst was finally quenched he wiped his mouth with a great sigh, and belched. Then he put the cup on the stained table deliberately. His hands were pudgy, his fingertips remarkably broad.

"So. Is this Argelin's big idea? That I'll talk to some smarmy little pen pusher instead of him? He must be sunstruck." He swiveled, scornful. "And you, trying to make out you were one of the Nine! He could have picked someone a bit more convincing."

Mirany bit the edge of a nail. "You're right," she said quietly.

Seth had been standing, tense, holding Telia. Now he said, "She is one of them. She's the Bearer."

Oblek snorted.

"It's true." Seth looked at his father, who went over and picked up the little girl and took her out; Mirany saw how he and his son glared at each other. Then Seth sat down, but before he could speak, she said quietly, "I came to find you because the Archon told me to. At least, he wrote to me. He said you knew."

The big man sucked his teeth. He was looking at her hard; finally he said, "Knew what?"

"About . . . " She glanced at Seth, awkward. "The betrayal of the Oracle."

Something changed in the man's face; a new alertness came into his eyes.

"He wrote?"

"A note. The day he died."

"Where is it?"

"I burned it." She shrugged unhappily. "Most of it. I think someone might have read the fragments."

"So you've got no proof."

"No. But I am one of the Nine. Well, at the moment . . . I don't know what will happen when they find out what I've done." She looked so appalled Seth almost felt sorry for her; instead he went and fetched water for her and himself. As he handed her the cup she smiled shyly. "Thank you."

The musician watched. "This one. You trust him?"

Mirany sighed. "I don't really know him, but—"

"Then we go." Oblek was on his feet; Seth didn't move.

Calmly Seth said, "I know too much already. And if Argelin has found out you've escaped, and you're really this important, he'll have men out looking for you. You're safer here."

"Please," Mirany muttered. "Sit down!" She felt sick at the thought of going out with him on to the streets. He terrified her; she felt she'd unleashed some sort of demon, had taken a step she should never have taken. As if he guessed, Oblek grinned.

Slowly he sat down.

For a moment there was a sort of silence. Flies buzzed and a bee fumbled in the tiny blue flowers of some pungent herb growing in a pot on the wall; from the street the never-ending noise of the Port rumbled and banged and yelled.

The heat was glaring; Mirany felt the sun burning her arm; a trickle of sweat touched her forehead. She edged the chair into the shade.

"Are you the girl from Mylos?" the musician said suddenly.

"Yes. In the note—"

"He came from there. He talked about it all the time, would have loved to go back. But they kept him in their cage of pleasures. All his life, smothered, his every whim fetched, all he could ever want. Except freedom." His voice was low now, almost tired. Then he said, "The god knows, I loved that old man. He and I, we'd drink and we'd talk, night after night. He told me all about how they found him, when he was only ten, and how his mother bought new clothes and boasted in the village about her son the Archon, and then they never let him talk to her again. Never. Sometimes he saw her in the crowd, through the eyeholes of the mask. Ten years old." Maudlin, he shrugged. "Got anything to eat? Wine?"

"Later." Seth leaned forward. "How could you talk to him? He was forbidden."

"No one can go through sixty years silent." Oblek's scorn was bitter. "You wouldn't last six weeks, pen pusher. When I went to the Palace he was already fifty years the Archon; it had warped him, made him strange and half-crazy, old before his time. But he loved music. And I can play, lady, just as you said. So I played for him late into the night, when everyone else was asleep. Night and day were the same to him. He'd lost the rhythm. He ate and slept and wandered the rooms as he wanted. He didn't live in the world, not of the living or yet the dead. He had the god inside him, after all."

It was long past noon. Mirany thought suddenly of the ceremony; the Archon's body already lay in the House of Music, and she would have to be back before dark. "They'll be playing for him now," she whispered.

"Not like I used to play." But Oblek rubbed his stubbly beard and filthy neck, then spat into a corner and said, "If I could trust you . . . "

"We got you here."

"And I don't know why."

Mirany shook her head, impatient. "Because he said to! Because there'll be a new Archon, and we have to make sure he is the one the god chooses, and not—"

He nodded, blunt. "Argelin. Right." With one more doubtful stare at Seth, the musician folded his arms. "All right. He knew they would kill him. Was waiting for it. He'd started to question their plans, look too closely at the taxes, the way things were run, the way Argelin takes bribes from the rich and rides roughshod over the poor. I told him to keep shut but he sent for Argelin. They argued. 'What can you do against me, old man?' I heard the general say. 'Even a god has to know his limits.'"

Seth felt cold. "But the Oracle said—"

"Oh yes." Mirany nodded acidly. "Hermia came out of the sanctuary and she was white. She had to sit down. Then she said the god had spoken and told her if the Archon was ready to die there would be rain."

Oblek laughed. "She lied. The skywatchers—the ones in the City of the Dead—sent a confidential report to the Temple a week ago that rain might be expected, but not much. Don't you see, that was her excuse. Her and Argelin. They killed the Archon, and the rain came. He hated them, he would never trust them, they were always afraid of what he might say. The people liked him. So now he's dead and they put their own choice in. Some boy they can control."

Seth almost whistled. He was surprised at the girl, though; she nodded as if it was all nothing new. "And the Oracle?"

Oblek shrugged, stubborn, "Get me some wine first."

In the end Seth went and fetched some, pale yellow stuff and probably sour, because Oblek downed it fast and made a face. "God!" Then he leaned forward and said rapidly, "The Archon told me, late one night, that the Speaker is false. She betrays the Oracle. The answers she gives to people's questions, questions they pay gold and silver for, she makes them up. That's why the merchants from Talla were told not to trade; Argelin has his own spice route; he didn't want the competition. And why the army was told by the Oracle to attack Chios; it's a nest of rebels. Argelin wanted it, so the Oracle said yes. The god is angry and that's why there's no rain. He speaks and she can't hear him. She's lost the power, if she ever had it."

Mirany shook her head, and then saw they were looking at her. Confused, she stood up.

"Look, I have to get back. I'm late already. We'll talk again, about what we have to do, but—"

"We?" Seth stood at once. "Lady, I'm not part of this."

Oblek stiffened.

Meekly Mirany said, "You know too much. You said it yourself. I'm willing to pay for your help."

She took one of the gold chains from her neck and held it out. "Keep him safe. This will pay for food and water."

"My father and sister live here! Think of the danger to them!"

"The soldiers won't look here."

"I'm not thinking of the soldiers!" Seth's voice dropped. "He's some drunkard—"

"There's nowhere else, until I can get him onto the Island."

Reluctant, Seth took the gold. It felt warm from her neck.

Oblek snorted. "Hermia will finish you first."

"Me?"

"They must suspect you. Why else choose you for Bearer? You'll be dead in days, girl, because you carry the god through the houses of mourning, and he destroys his own. Useful for them. As for hiding out here, yes, I'll do it for now, until it's time for my revenge." He poured more wine and gulped it down.

Cold, even in the heat, Mirany turned and walked into

the dimness of the house. At the door to the street Seth pushed in front of her, looked out cautiously and said, "No one."

"I'll be back as soon as I can. Please keep him safe."

"Him!" Seth scowled. "It's my family I'm worried about."

She nodded unhappily. "Yes, I know. I'm sorry. I'm sure he's not too dangerous, not really. I swear I'll sort things out. It's just the third house is entered at sunset and I've got to be there."

"Good luck," he muttered.

Flustered, she ran quickly down the shimmer of the street.

Seth glanced round at the houses and doorways, saw no one he didn't know, and closed the door. His back against it, he wiped the sweat from his face. Then he took a breath and walked back into the courtyard. "Seems I'm stuck with you."

Oblek had finished the wine. His eyes were small and his voice bleary.

"Don't worry. I can't stand you, either," he mumbled.

She crossed the bridge at a run. The Nine never ran. It was undignified; Hermia might be watching now, from the terraces of the Upper House.

Breathless, Mirany slowed, clutching her side. Ridiculous to be worried about being told off for running. It was treachery she was involved in now. But no, no,

Hermia was the traitor. Hermia had betrayed the Oracle. But then, if there was no god anyway . . .

Mirany shook her head. The path was steep and the procession yesterday had scuffed it up; dust and loose small stones worked their way into her sandals.

By the time she came to the doorway to the Oracle she couldn't stand it; she sat carefully on the path and pulled the left shoe off, brushing her grubby foot hastily with her hand.

Something moved, just beside her.

A snake.

She leaped up with a gasp of fear; the small green slither zigzagged back instantly, a jerk of terror as instinctive as her own.

For a moment they looked at each other.

Then it flowed under a stone and was gone.

Mirany breathed out, and bit her lip. Leaning on the stone lintel of the Oracle, she pulled her other sandal on, and said shakily, "I suppose that was you then, Bright One?"

Small fragments of sand slid from the stone's edge.

As she straightened, the answer came, quiet and small in the corner of her mind.

No.

Mirany stood still. Perfectly still.

Every part of her stopped. Even her heart, she was sure.

She turned slowly.

The doorway to the Oracle loomed dim and strange against the darkening sky. Up at the Temple a fire was burning; the smoke drifted down here, sweet-smelling and sharp. Rosemary was in the air; her skirt must have brushed it.

For a long moment she could not even think, would not let herself know that she had heard it, but the echo of the small word seemed to reverberate silently inside her.

"Who said that?"

The gong rang, high and soft in the hot still air. She was late.

She stepped away, then almost at once turned back, walked to the Oracle entrance and stood there, one hand on each of the great stones.

The small path coiled in on itself before her, into the leafy dark.

And the voice in her head said, *Mirany. Come in, Mirany. Come to the place where I am.*

THE THIRD HOUSE
OF THE OPENING OF DREAMS

Water is powerful.

I've begun to realize what it can do. It seeps and percolates and drips and gushes, can even rise through rock, over centuries, over eons.

My landscape and my body are formed by water, its caresses, its violence. Gouged and smoothed. Carved.

Where the water is the animals gather, the people come and build. Without water, they die. They have a story, the people, about the Rainwoman, that long ago the god and his shadow fought over her, that darkness and light were in conflict, that day attacked night.

And what did the Rainwoman do but laugh at them, and when they saw neither could win she spread her wings over them, and her wings were the sky, and the rains fell and fell.

I heard this in the marketplace, where an old man was telling the children.

My mouth was sore, and I felt my fingers and they were thin and frail.

For a moment then, I knew who I was.

Until the girl spoke to me.

She Hears the Sun's Voice

The path seemed darker than before. Olive branches meshed over her head; small moths brushed against her.

Mirany walked as silently as she could, and the path coiled in on itself like a sleeping snake, and at its heart was the holy place.

The stone. The dark hole.

Breathless, a slight pain in her side, she waited, a little way off.

There was no god.

It had always been her greatest fear that she would give away what she thought. Her father had been so thrilled at her coming here, at restoring the family's reputation, that she had never had the heart to explain to him. She was odd, she knew that. Everyone believed, or said they did, that the god spoke through the Oracle, and what the god said was true.

But from the time she had first met Hermia, she had known that couldn't be right.

Because surely if you heard a god you would be different from other people. You would shine, your heart would be full of joy.

And why would the power that made the world hide in a hole in the ground?

Now, trembling, she licked her lips and listened.

The voice had been so faint; as she thought of it, it grew dimmer inside her. She had imagined it. She had turned the breeze from the sea into words. The creaks of the trees, the leaf rustle. There was no god.

Come closer.

She stepped inside. It was all wrong. There should be attendants; there should be incense and chanting and she should be masked, and rock back and forth, and cry out in strange, convulsive voices, as Hermia did. She should have drunk the infusion, be carried in to breathe deep the fumes of the Underworld.

Talking to a god shouldn't be this simple.

She crossed to the Oracle, and crouched slowly.

Then she said, "Who are you?"

There *were* fumes. They shimmered in the purple twilight; the moths avoided them. As if something hot was down there, the haziest smoke. She saw that crystals glinted in the rock at the lip of the hole; accretions of quartz and a yellow powder like sulphur.

You know who. I am the god. If I had a name, I have forgotten it.

"Only the Speaker knows the god's name." She was whispering. In fact her lips were so dry they made no sound at all. "How can you be speaking to me? Where are you?"

Did gods laugh? He made some sound like that, quiet, and strange. A deep, subterranean rumble. *I am in many places. But one of them is new. One of them is the smallest and most precarious. I haven't been here long.*

Mirany knelt on the jagged rocks. Behind the grove, up in the Temple, the gongs were ringing.

"Do you mean the new Archon?" she said quickly.

Silence.

Deep in the pit a hiss spurted; heat touched her face. She leaned over, feeling down with her fingers, the oddly smooth sides, the ridges and furrows and small lichens. Then, afraid of scorpions, she jerked her hand back. There was danger here. Gods asked too much of you, brought you down. In all the poems, the epics, the ones the gods chose were doomed. "Can you hear me?" she whispered.

Yes. The new Archon. He is here. I am here.

Where? She was desperate. "Be quick!"

A god is not used to being ordered. There is a market, a small dusty square, a house with too many children. A boy. He is ten years old. He is very thirsty.

"It could be anywhere!"

There is a word, and the word is the place. The word is Alectro.

"It's a village," she said. "But I don't know how far. Out in the desert. South of the Port."

I am here. I exist. Fetch me, Mirany.

She felt giddy. For a second her whole being seemed to fall toward the pit; it yawned, a black mouth, breath rising from it, and then her hands caught at the quartz-edged rocks and she hung there, gasping.

She had to pull back; she scrambled up and managed a few steps before her legs went weak and she sank down on hands and knees, breathing deep, smelling the warm evening scents of the jasmine and bruised sandalwood.

Miles away and long ago, the gongs had rung. Now there was silence.

Mirany staggered up. No time to think; they'd be passing on their way to the City and she couldn't be found here. Hermia mustn't know.

She ran quickly back up the coiled path; it seemed to kink suddenly and she almost fell out between the stones of the doorway, and they were coming through the twilight, Hermia's litter being carried, and someone else's—Rhetia's, with luck—but the rest of the Nine walked, masked. As she stepped back into the bushes she counted them, and yes, there were Nine.

Breathless, Mirany stared.

Chryse was at the back, she wore the mask of the Taster-for-the-God, and beside her a girl walked in the Bearer's mask, the gold-and-flame-red one that Mirany should wear. What was going on?

Had she been replaced already?

As she crouched deep in the myrtle bushes the armed

escort passed her first. Argelin was, as usual, on horseback, and the animal's hooves raised small clouds of dust on the road, so close to her that she almost coughed, and had to cover her nose and mouth with both hands, her eyes streaming. Looked up at through the haze and clatter and the afterglow of the sunset, the general seemed a towering man, gleaming with bronze, his broad face with its almost oriental cheekbones glancing back, the dust settling on the razored perfection of his beard.

From the saddlestrap, the empty eyes of his helmet looked at her.

He was ruthless, everyone knew that. And she was a fool to have done things so recklessly, because he must know about Oblek by now.

They passed her, the swaying litters, the quietly talking girls. Just before they turned down the steep ramp of the hill, there was a pause; one of the litters had to be adjusted.

From the scented leaves Mirany whispered, "Chryse."

The mask of the Taster turned to her, blue slashed with silver. For a panicky second the thought came to her that it wasn't Chryse under there at all but someone else; then the answer came, breathless and relieved.

"Mirany? Where are you?"

"Here." She rustled the branch.

Instantly Chryse dropped back, caught hold of the girl beside her, and pulled her off the road. "Quick," she hissed.

The Bearer pulled off her mask and to her amazement Mirany saw she was one of the slaves that worked as an embroideress, a cheeky girl called Berenice. The slave grinned and slapped the mask into her hands; in seconds she had it on her face, the metal hot and smelling of garlic. She slid past the girl on to the road, but Berenice didn't move. Instead she held out her hand, insistent. Chryse dropped two silver coins on her palm. Then the girl turned and ran into the twilit olive groves.

Just in time. The litters were moving, nearing the Oracle. Mirany walked behind them, breathless, cold with sweat. No one seemed to have noticed; the other girls were a little ahead and the armed guard out of sight. After a while she muttered, "I can't believe you did that."

"Nor can I." Chryse's voice sounded a little smug.

Watching Hermia climb from her litter, Mirany rubbed her hands nervously. "What if she'd gone in there? To the Oracle!"

Chryse gave a small shrug. "I knew you'd come. You owe me the money. And next time I'm late I expect you to cover for me."

Mirany stared at her, amazed. *I may not be here that long*, she thought.

At night the City of the Dead burned. It was a labyrinth of flames, leaping in braziers, on walls, in brackets, reflected in bronze and copper and gold. Darkness made no difference to the dead, or the thousands that served them, and the hurried fuss of the preparations for the Archon's funeral went on without interruption. With the sun gone, torches spat at the subterranean doors of every tomb and all along the wall, making the colossal statues up there crackle and seem to turn and move and converse. A beacon that would be tended for the whole nine days roared without ceasing on the platform of the stepped pyramid, and in great iron baskets, looped with copper serpents, flames played their scarlet glare on the brass doors of the houses of mourning.

The nine houses were arranged around the base of the pyramid, three on each of three sides, huge, white marble buildings, pillared and collonaded. Except at the time of an Archon's death, they were kept locked, but now the first two were open, and the doors of the third had been propped wide to welcome the body that had once held the god.

He was carried with reverence from the House of Music, already in his painted wooden inner coffin, and the exhausted musicians that had played there all day followed to the very shadow of the third house. As soon as the coffin crossed that threshold, every instrument stopped in midnote.

Weary and hungry, the musicians trooped away, past Mirany, girls with flutes, men with zithers, great brass horns, even a tiny boy with a shrill whistle.

Their part was over.

The third house was the House of Opening.

Lifted out, placed on a great stone slab in the center, the Archon lay. Coming in, Mirany looked at him once, then away. The golden mask was on his face, and in the fantastic light of the hundreds of flames, the eyeholes of it were the only dark things in the room. She looked at his plump, folded hands, thought of the way he had placed the left one so calmly in the bronze bowl.

I know where you are now, she told him. *I'll find you. I'll get you back here, but I'll need you to help me.*

The embalmers entered. Three men, in long white robes they would later remove, their faces and arms covered with strange scorpion designs, painted on the skin.

Their instruments lay in neat rows on a wooden table; jagged, sharp things, long probes and knives and sinister hooked filaments of wire. Incense and herbs smoked in bowls, the aromas of aniseed and cypress and sandalwood mingling and rising, and behind it, already, the stench of decay.

Hermia looked round. The Nine gathered, took hands around the Archon. In the shadows the embalmers waited.

"Our brother is dead," she said. "We mourn him."

"We mourn him."

"Our eyes which were bright, are dark. Our thoughts which were swift, are heavy. But the god, the Bright One, lives forever. His shadow is darkness. When the blue sky above and the brown earth beneath were created, he was there. When the Woman of Water came from the sky, he was there."

Mirany, caught by a movement, let her eyes flicker.

Argelin was leaning just outside the door. His smile was sidelong, the flames making small patterns of light on his smooth skin. He glanced at her; rigid, she looked away, hot in the beautiful metal face that covered her own.

"And ever he will be," the Nine murmured quietly.

Hermia turned. In her normal voice she said, "The Opening will begin now. The Washer-of-the-God will remain with the Archon tonight. Without eating or leaving until he leaves. Understand?"

Persis nodded confidently.

Hermia said, "Good," went to the door, and took off her mask, breathing in the cool night air. Behind her, like dark carrion on a corpse, the embalmers moved in.

"What now?" Argelin said, just loud enough for everyone to hear.

"Now I speak with the god alone, at the Oracle. He will tell me where to send the searchers for the nine candidates. Your men are ready to ride?"

The herbs scorched, their smoke stifling Mirany. She saw how Argelin nodded, his hand resting on the hilt of his sword. "The sooner we know the better," he said drily.

Hermia glanced down. "Leave it to me," she murmured, her voice soft, unrecognizable.

Argelin smiled at her, a careful smile.

Then, as Mirany shrank past him, he turned like a snake and caught her arm, so that she almost dropped the empty bronze bowl. "Lady, I want to speak with you."

"Me?" she breathed. "Why?"

"I think you can guess." The flames rippled his dark stare. "Will you receive me in the morning? After the Ritual?"

It was a polite request. It was also an order. She wished she had the nerve to fling his hand off and put him haughtily in his place. Instead she breathed, "Yes. Of course."

He lifted his hand, bowed slightly, and strode away. She stood still, her heart thudding.

Behind her in the smoky house, with infinite care and small ripping sounds that went right through her nerves and teeth and fingernails, she heard the body of the Archon being opened.

He Feels the Danger of the Dark Places

The message had been pushed inside the papers on his desk. It was elegantly written, the wedge-shaped letters flowing and sure, and it chilled him. He hadn't seen much of the Jackal's face but his voice had given him away. An aristocrat. Educated. The man's hands, too, had been manicured. Seth scowled. What sort of man would rob the dead without even needing the gold?

It said: AT THE HOUR OF SUNSET BE AT THE FOOT OF SOSTRIS UNDER THE WALL. HAVE WHAT WE NEED WITH YOU.

If anyone else had found it, it gave nothing away. He burned it quickly, thinking of Mirany, holding it in the flame till every trace was gone. Then he turned back to his desk and glanced up the long hall to see where the overseer was.

Nowhere. Which meant he'd probably slipped out to the illicit water supply he kept in the passages under the wallwalk. Seth grinned. He'd find it lower than he left it.

His hand slipped under the lists of the Archon's rice and grain and olives and the requisitions for the carved ivories and found the older, flaking papyrus that was hidden there. Taking one more wary look up the hall of scribes, he pulled it out.

The tomb of Sostris was ancient, and not many people would even have known where to look for its plans. He smiled to himself, that cocky smile he knew infuriated others. Well, he wasn't most people. He'd been fourth assistant archivist only a few months, but he'd made it his business to learn the contents of every shelf in the vast storeroom that ran under the length of the hall, down the circular stair in the corner. He'd spent hours there, taking notes and reading and prising open flaking scrolls no one had unrolled for decades; he'd rummaged through boxes of documents, browsing, absorbed, breathing in the must of decaying words, the deeds of dead Archons; had followed the tiniest and most airless of tunnels, his dusty fingers feeling the way along the walls. Knowledge was power, and it was power he searched for. If anything was lost, he'd be the one who could say where it was. He'd be indispensable. Soon he'd be first archivist. . . .

But there was no time for dreaming.

The drawings were in a bad state. They needed to be recopied, but he wouldn't give them to a scribe until after the theft. The word stung him. He shook his head, a small, fussy movement he often made to himself.

"Someone spelled your name wrong?"

Seth almost jumped; his hand slammed across the plans and he turned fast.

It was Kreon.

He wasn't even a scribe. He cleaned the place. He leaned on his straw broom and said, "Jumpy."

Seth scowled. "Get lost."

"I can't. Know the passages too well."

That was probably true. The rumor was that Kreon had been born in the City of the Dead and had never left it. Some of the mouthier scribes said he'd never seen the sun, and it had been too dark for his mother to tell who his father was. They took bets on how often he'd walk into things and they sent him on useless messages for papers that didn't exist. Kreon went if he felt like it. He limped and spoke to himself in corners and slept on a great heap of old parchment scraps in the portico. Seth was never sure if he was quite right in the head. Now he watched Seth sidelong, and Seth watched him. An albino. His skin was pale as milk, his eyes pink, his long hair stark white. It made him look old, though he wasn't.

Cautious, keeping his hand over the plan, Seth snapped, "You heard me. Go away. I'm working."

Kreon leaned closer. "They're opening him," he whispered.

It was hard to tell his age. His breath stank. His tunic was gray with dirt. He was thin and gangly, too tall, as if he'd grown in the dark.

"Who?"

"Him. Me. The Archon. Taking his insides out. His brain. What are they looking for? Is it the god? Are there tunnels inside men, where the god hides?"

Seth frowned. "Look . . ."

"I've tried that. But you can't see a god, can you? Though down in the passages, I've seen his shadow. Walking. Just around the corner stretching out in front of me, and when I stop, he stops."

The overseer was back. Seth shoved the plans under the papers with a curse and began to note the numbers of oranges to be stored in the tomb, swift black wedge-shaped letters stroking down the page.

"Get lost," he said again, quietly.

"How is your sister?"

Seth stared. "How did you know I have a sister?"

The cleaner swept a thoughtful scatter of dust. "Someone must have told me. She's been ill, and there's drought, out there, where the living are. What are you doing about it?"

Furious, Seth clutched the stylus tight. "My business." Catching the odd eyes on him he controlled his voice and said, "She's much better."

"You love her, then. You would do much for her."

"Yes. Now—"

"Get lost." Kreon nodded sagely. "Not easy for me. But for others in the darkness, only too easy." He moved away, a loping shuffle. After a second he turned back. "What's her name?"

"Telia." It came through gritted teeth, and he kept his head down, writing.

When he looked up, later, Kreon had moved away and the overseer was sitting in the high seat. Seth's stylus stopped, as a sudden thought shivered through him.

How had the Jackal known which was his desk?

How had they got the message in here?

Suddenly scared, he looked round at the hundred other men in the room, their bent backs, heard the eternal soft scratch of their busy pens. Was one of them in on the plan?

Surely not.

He got up quickly, took the file of foodstuffs for burial and stuffed the plans into it; then he walked without looking round between the rows of desks to the circular stair and went down it, the pen scratch growing fainter behind him, the air mustier and warmer as his feet pattered down the dim steep steps.

At the bottom the storeroom shelves stretched into darkness.

Seth walked down the long central aisle, the stones underfoot gritty with sand that seeped in everywhere, even here.

Right at the far end the light was dimmest. One small lamp guttered in a pool of oil, throwing a huge shadow of himself on the wall, a sinister companion. Picking the lamp up, he slipped between the tightly spaced rows of shelves, down to the end, turned right, then left, into the airless region that was the oldest part of all, rock hewn, where the moth-eaten plans of forgotten tombs crumbled in unreach-able compartments, roof high.

He had learned Sostris's tomb, had spent all night learn-ing it, testing himself. He knew the turns to take and the ways to open the secret doors, which were the false pas-sageways, which led to the antechamber, and the burial room, and the treasury. He'd read the reports dictated by a General Macri two hundred years ago, who'd been lost down there for a week. He'd taken special care to study the list of traps and pitfalls, worn and frayed though the papyrus was, and though he knew it was certain not all of them would even have been written down. The slaves who had made them would have been killed to keep the secret; their bones lay with Sostris's now, in the silence and the dust.

He held the lamp up, scanning the shelves. To rob a dead Archon was the ultimate treachery. It was a desecration of the dead, a betrayal of the City. Above all, it was an appalling risk.

What if he pulled out? He already knew the answer to that. Even if he went to the overseer now, his career would be over. No more water for Telia and Pa. And he'd be found in an alley one morning with his throat cut. He was too far in to back out. Besides, unless he was caught, no one would know anything about it.

No one alive, that was.

It took a while to locate the dingy narrow pigeonhole where the folded plans had been. He pushed them back, carefully, right inside, so no one would see they had been disturbed, but they crumpled and snagged; with a hiss of annoyance he pulled them back out and plunged his arm deep into the slot, impatiently feeling the cold accumulated drifts of sand and fragmented fibers for the obstacle. His fingertips touched something hard and small.

It stung him.

With a screech of terror he whipped his hand out, the scorpion clinging to him; he flung it down and as it rattled he stamped on it hard, and again, the small armored body cracking under his boot.

God, he thought. God! He was finished. He was punished. *By Sostris. It had to be Sostris.*

Shut up. Stay calm. Think.

A bead of blood oozed from his index finger. The puncture was tiny. No swelling yet. He felt sick, hot, feverish. Poison worked fast. Too fast to do anything about.

He crumpled to his knees, shivering, looking desperately to find the creature in the swinging lamp shadows. If it was one of the little black ones, he needn't bother to get up again.

His fingers touched the hard curved body and jerked away. Oil drops spattering the straw, he saw what it was.

Not black. Red. Its eye glinted oddly.

Pain forgotten, he stared at it in amazement.

The scorpion was made of some hard, precious stone. Delicately cut in fine ruby facets, it reflected the light, minute rainbows glowing deep in its tiny body, its curved tail a miracle of the jeweler's art. Small gold eyes looked up at him, darkening as he reached down and picked it up, the sharp pin bent where he'd stepped on it.

A fastening pin. A brooch.

Very precious, very holy.

A treasure beyond anything he could earn in months.

At first, relief swamped him into weakness, and then just as quickly, he felt wonder and a sharp greed. His fingers closed on the brooch, his own blood dulling the ruby glow. He wiped it clean thoughtfully.

What was it doing here? It certainly hadn't been there when he'd taken the plans out. A wild notion that the overseer knew he'd had them and had placed this to test his honesty flitted through his mind but it was laughable and he knew it. Maybe it had been there. Maybe he'd missed it, like everyone else. Maybe for centuries.

He had no idea how he could sell it safely.

A mosquito whined in his ear. He glanced up the dim crack of space between the shelves, utterly black except where the last flickers of the lamp threw shadows of himself, shifty restless movements on the heaped shelves of scrolls. Then he pulled out the pouch he wore round his neck and dropped the brooch in. It clinked against the few coins.

Hurriedly, scorched with a sudden guilt, he snatched up the lamp and almost ran through the tangled junctions of the shelves to the central aisle. Just as he got there the lamp finally dimmed, guttering to a blue sputter, then going out, but he tossed it down and stalked, slightly breathless, up the great spine of the storeroom, back into the light, up the curving stair.

Halfway he stopped, stiff with surprise.

Kreon leaned against a hidden shelf in the hall, broom in hand.

He waved slyly.

"I'm getting lost," he said.

"Do come in," Mirany whispered.

She was so petrified her lips felt dry and her stomach was a tight pain. Argelin gave a half nod of mock reverence and walked past her and looked around. She had placed two chairs on the marble floor of the reception room, taking ages to get them just right. Now she went and sat on one, but to her dismay he did not take the other. Instead he put his hands on the back of it and leaned over.

"Would you mind explaining to me," he said softly, "exactly what you want with the musician Oblek?"

Despite herself, she licked her lips. His politeness terrified her; it was a silky, careless threat. All night she had lain awake planning and plotting what to say, how to do this. If she failed now, she and Oblek and the scribe were all finished. And she would have failed the Archon.

So she smiled sweetly. "I'm so, so sorry about that! I had no idea I was making such trouble for you. Such a nuisance of myself!"

He looked at her a long moment. Then he came round the chair and sat down. It felt like a small victory. Gravely he said, "You knew he was to die with the rest."

"Oh no! I had no idea! Absolutely none! I was morti-fied when I found out. I said to Chryse that if I had, it would never have occurred to me—"

"To break him out of prison?"

She giggled. He wore black gloves with tiny metal studs over the back; as he peeled one off she saw his hands were smooth and sunburnt, oddly hairless. "I know! It sounds so bold!"

"It was bold, lady. I find it amazingly so. And your reason?"

"Well, I told you. Didn't I? Oh, it was just that he used to work for my family. Years ago, I was only a baby. On Mylos. So I thought, when the Archon died, well, if he wanted a new job, my father would love to see him. I mean he was a bit of a drinker, between you and me, but played such lovely things."

Was she overdoing it? She looked modestly down at the rings on her fingers, felt Chryse's face powder heat her cheeks. It was caked on clumsily. He'd notice that. He noticed everything.

Argelin nodded. His smooth face showed nothing. "I see. My optio—who by the way is now on half pay for a few weeks—swore that you were very persuasive."

She simpered, and even managed to lean forward. "General Argelin, I'm so sorry for the poor man. Won't you let him off this once? I'm sure he's a very good guard. I just wanted my own way." She gave a small pout. "It's what comes of being one of the Nine. But if you really think . . . I suppose half pay is not too terrible? . . . "

"Where is he? This Oblek."

Her eyes widened. "On board ship, of course. I gave him money for the passage yesterday."

"I've had inquiries made at the only three ships leaving for Mylos, lady. He doesn't seem to have taken up your offer." There was a trace of sarcasm now.

Mirany managed not to bite her lip and instead looked scandalized. With studied dignity she pulled the expensive shawl over her shoulders and said timidly, "You don't think he's drunk that money away, do you?"

Argelin's smile was calm. "I really don't know what to think."

Did he believe her? It all depended on how much had been legible in the fragments of the note, and who had read it. Cursing herself for not burning it properly, Mirany gave him an arch look through her kohl-blackened lashes. "I promise I won't do anything like it again. I'm so embarrassed!" She moved forward, just a little. "And, General, if he's got himself drunk, do go and find him. Take him back to be put in the tomb. Though surely one silly little man won't be missed."

His eyes considered her. "As Bearer, lady, you should know more than anyone that the god must have his due. When the Archon dies his household dies with him. All of them. And I understand this man has always been a troublemaker."

Pale, she put her fingers nervously to her cheek. "Yes," she whispered. "I see."

Abruptly he stood. "But as you say, if he's drunk in some alehouse, my men will find him. Thank you for your time, Lady Mirany."

Awkward, she tried to rise gracefully, the shawl slipping off her shoulders. She clutched at it. At the door he turned. "In future," he said quietly, "I suggest you attend to your own duties and leave my men to theirs. It will prevent this sort of . . . inconvenience."

"Oh yes," she stammered. "Yes, I'm so sorry. What a fool you must think me."

He was silent a moment, watching her face. Then he said, "No. I don't think you are, I assure you."

Long after the door had closed behind him she stood staring at it, every inch of her cold. Then, wearily, she sat.

Had she convinced him? Did he think she was just some spoiled, thoughtless, giggling girl, too dull to be taken seriously? Desperately she wanted him to think it. But it was too hard to tell. His last remark had been chilling, strangely amused.

She made herself get up, walk about, start to wipe the muck off her face. One thing was sure. They had to get Oblek out of the Port.

Tonight.

HE STANDS BETWEEN THE JACKAL AND ITS PREY

"No chance." Oblek spat out the rind of the lemon. "I told you, I've got plans of my own."

Mirany sat down, breathless. "There are soldiers out looking for you! On all the ships!"

A cup of water was placed on the table before her; she looked up in surprise at Seth's father.

"For me? Are you sure?"

"Drink it, lady. We've got . . . enough."

It was cool and delicious. As she gulped it down Seth's father said sourly, "You! You should listen to the girl. If Argelin's out to find you—"

"Stuff Argelin. I don't run."

"No. You just clog up my house and eat me out of it."

He went to the door with a glance at Mirany, who caught his arm. "Did you send for Seth?"

"He's a scribe, lady; he works all hours. But yes, I sent."

He laughed oddly. "He'll come, if he thinks it'll profit him."

When he had gone, Oblek put his feet on the table and leaned back, staring at her, chewing more of the acid rind slowly. "Still alive, then," he said.

"Still." She was scared of him, his size, his violence.

He nodded. "I'm not ungrateful. But I'm not leaving."

"Not even to find the new Archon?"

His eyes widened slightly, but before he could say anything the curtain moved and Seth walked in, looking calm and slightly pleased with himself. Mirany was so glad to see him it surprised her.

"What's happened?" he asked quickly.

"Argelin. He's looking for Oblek."

"We already knew that." He was sitting, pouring water. His self-possession annoyed her; ignoring Oblek's snort she said firmly, "And I know where the new Archon will be found."

Oblek's feet came off the table. He sat up fast. "How?"

Turning the ring on her finger, she said. "The god spoke to me."

It was so quiet. They were indoors, and even the street sounds were muted. But the silence was deeper than that. She looked up at them. "It's true. I was at the Oracle. I heard his voice just like I hear your voices. Only, inside my head."

"What did he say?" Oblek asked, intent. And suddenly she saw that neither of them were as astounded by this as she was. After all, she was one of the Nine, a priestess of the

Oracle; perhaps they supposed the god talked to her all the time. She wanted to shout at them, *Didn't you hear? He's real. He spoke to me!* but instead she folded her fingers and said quietly, "That the new Archon is a ten-year-old boy. He lives in a small house with many other children, somewhere near the market, in Alectro. We have to find him and get him here for the Choosing. You have to."

For a moment Oblek's small eyes held hers. Then he stood up and paced, a caged, lumbering shape, barefoot, his tunic filthy. "Say we do. Say we find him, bring him here, present him as a candidate. Is Argelin going to let him win? Use your head, girl. A child is easy to kill."

"Not if we keep him safe."

"None of us is safe. Even you."

She knew that. But she said quietly, "The god won't hurt me."

The big man had his back to them. When he spoke, his voice was hoarse.

"I loved that old man."

"So you've told us," Seth said dryly.

Oblek swung round, fury darkening his face. "Shut your mouth, ink slave. You've never loved anyone, from what I can see. Your sister's sick and you never come near her."

Slowly Seth stood.

"Please," Mirany muttered. "There's no time for this."

Neither of them looked at her; anxiously she moved between them and faced Oblek. "Leave the Port tonight. I'll pay for food, whatever you need. Find the boy and bring him to the Island. You have to do it. For the Archon's sake."

Over her head he glared at Seth. But it was her he answered.

"On one condition."

Her heart thumped. "What?"

He looked down at her, sucked his teeth, and then went back to the canvas chair. As he lowered himself into it, it creaked. His voice was harsh. "Argelin. He's the problem. Any new Archon will be in his power, just like the old man was. Argelin's the god here; he's the Oracle. It was his idea for the old man to be sacrificed, to be replaced. He keeps the taxes high and the poor thirsty, he controls the army, packs the council with his followers." He watched them both. "Let me tell you what the god has said to me, lady, because musicians, too, hear him. He says, *Give me Argelin. Destroy my enemy.* In my ears, since the old man died, I have heard that song. Those notes."

Somewhere outside a hand cart was rumbled by, the man pushing it whistling. Telia's voice sang a high tuneless croon from the courtyard.

"What do you mean?" Mirany whispered.

"You know what I mean."

Seth shook his head, incredulous. "You'd kill him?"

"Not me. The god." Oblek jerked an accusing finger. "The god she carries in the brazen bowl."

They were both silent with the horror and fascination of it. Mirany felt a chill go through her.

"No," she breathed.

"Not our choice." The musician smiled, a lopsided leer. "I will strike, and if the god wants him he takes him." He sat back. "I'll get this boy for you. But in return, lady, we deal with Argelin, the three of us in the god's conspiracy. I owe the old man. You owe the Oracle. You know this is what we have to do."

"What about me?" Seth clunked the cup down, agitated. His face had gone pale; he breathed quickly. "I'm not in this. It's madness! It's got nothing to do with me!"

Oblek scowled. An ugly line creased his forehead. "You are now. Because if you talk, I swear I'll call down every curse I know on you. Musicians know a few. The dead will walk out of your nightmares, and will follow you down the corridors of the City till they find you and suck the lifeblood out of you. Besides, what the god wants, the god gets. Even a smug little beggar like you."

Mirany turned away from them, bewildered. She felt as if she had blundered somehow through some smother of cobweb into another existence, could hardly remember how simple life had been only days ago, when she hadn't known any of this, her only worries whether her tunics were clean, if she'd have to talk to any strangers that day, or what catty remark Rhetia might make. When had the world become so strange, so full of danger? To assassinate Argelin! It seemed something from a legend. And yet she had heard the god's voice, the Oracle had spoken, and its words had been soft and sad and clear, as if the statue in the Temple had spoken. As if the sand of the desert had whispered.

"Listen," she said, and to her surprise it came out clear and firm, and they both stared at her.

"The boy comes first. Oblek, you must go tonight, and Seth will go with you."

"I don't want him!"

And at the same time, "No chance," from Seth.

She stepped close. "You will go. Both of you."

Seth wanted to laugh, to scoff. But her eyes were dark and the look in them was a shock to him. She meant it. Yesterday she'd been scared, a shy stammering girl who could rarely manage to look at him, but something had happened. Had changed. She was one of the Nine. And suddenly each of them knew it.

"I've got someone to see," he muttered, stubborn.

"When?"

"Sunset."

"Then leave straight after." Not waiting for any objection, she turned on Oblek. "Don't let me down."

"I'm doing it for the old man, lady, not for you." Oblek, at least, was unchanged. He came after her smelling of sweat and stale wine, and as he bent toward Mirany she stepped back from the heat and threat that was in him. But all he did was ask quietly, "I've lost track. What house has he reached? What will they do to him tonight?"

There it was, the weakness in his bluster. She felt it like a draft through a crack in a great wall.

The fourth. "The Enfolding," she whispered.

He nodded, grim. After a while he said, "So big a

funeral, so many mourners. All that ritual and song, the masks, the complicated words. And in all the world, I'm the only one who loved him."

The foot of Sostris was enormous.

Wedged into the crack between the biggest toe and the next, Seth crouched and listened to the sand making small rustling noises in the night. Above and behind him the toppled statue rose to vast heights, a black basalt torso without head or arms, its upper half wearing away with the abrasion of the wind, the centuries' work of sand grains, heat of days and iciness of nights. Not far away a great nose and one eye lay half-buried, the nostril a den for lizards.

Against the sky the wall of the City rose; he could see the seated Archons and the bats that flitted round them, and over their shoulders the scattered brilliance of the stars, burning with dim colors. He pulled his coat round him, weary and thirsty.

Oblek was crazy. If this was true, if they were planning an assassination, he wanted no part of it. What profit was there in it for him? Unless . . . a new Archon would need people he could trust . . . some really high administration post . . .

They were here.

The knowledge shocked him, though he'd been watching, intent.

Two shadows came round the great toe and became men, one on each side of him.

Seth stood. "About time." He was scared. His voice came out too loud.

The Fox was wrapped up against the cold. He put a bangled hand out and slammed Seth back against the stone toes. "You sound surprised, pretty boy."

"You've got the plans?" The Jackal's voice was as calm as it had been in the opium den.

Taking a breath, Seth said, "Yes."

"I don't see them."

"I've memorized them."

There was a moment of silence, so intense it hurt. Then the small man grabbed him hard. "Let me cut his tongue out, lord."

The Jackal didn't move. In the starlight his strange eyes were uncanny; they watched Seth with a cold, steady scrutiny. Mildly he said, "If I did we would have silenced our guide into the tomb."

"Look." Seth pulled away. "I can't get the plans out of the building. It would take weeks to copy them in secret. So I've learned them. I've been trained to do that, and I have a sort of . . . gift for it. Memorizing things. Lists."

The Fox spat on the sand in disgust.

"There was no other way." He was talking too quickly, gabbling. He made himself slow, spread his hands, tried to sound reassuring. "It's not a trick, or a double cross. You think I'd try that with you! I promise you, this way is better. And there's nothing to incriminate any of us."

The Jackal folded his arms. His silence was terrifying.

"And it makes no difference in the end," Seth gabbled. "We still—"

"It makes all the difference." In the desert wind the man's fair hair drifted, a ghostly movement. "It means you will have to come down into the tomb with us. As you no doubt intended all along."

He gave the slightest nod; Seth heard a knife unsheath.

"You don't trust me . . . . I know that. But—"

"Your *father and sister* received the water?"

It was no courteous inquiry. He nodded miserably, watching their faces. It hadn't taken them long to find that out.

"Then our side of the bargain," the Jackal said dangerously, "is being honored."

"So will mine be. I swear to you." They were going to kill him. He'd gone too far. He'd be found lying here in the morning, his blood congealed in the sand, the vultures picking at him.

He tried to step back. Sostris blocked him.

The Jackal's voice was dry and light. "Perhaps it would be best to conclude our agreement here and now."

"*No!* No. Please. Trust me." Sweat was in his eyes; his shoulders ached with tension. "Look, I have to go away for a few days . . . my work . . . arrangements for the new Archon. I'll be back by the seventh day. We'll go in then. Any time. Whenever you want."

He felt giddy, as if his life was weightless, a delicate thing, a feather. The Jackal's almond-shaped eyes considered his fate. In the silence the desert crawled and rustled.

Around his neck the purse hung heavy. He had a sudden impulse to snatch it and spill out the scorpion at their feet to prove to them he had secrets they could never dream of, but even before he could move a hand, the Jackal, as if he had come to some decision, said quietly. "So be it."

"Lord?" The Fox scowled. "You're trusting him?"

The tall tomb thief watched Seth calmly. "He irritates you, Fox? You must learn to control that."

The small man glared at Seth. "Too full of himself."

"Nevertheless, he's clever. And this time, has convinced me. But we go in on the eighth day, the Day of the Shadow. Everyone will be in silence, locked in their houses. The Port will be empty and the City dark and still. No one would fear such an intrusion, on such a night. And you"—he reached out and touched Seth's tunic lightly—"will guide us. I'll waste no breath on threats. Should this be a trap, a betrayal in any way, you know my revenge will follow you, wherever you go, however many years may pass. Your imagination will eat you alive, your own fears; and finally, scribe, I'll find you."

He glanced at the other man, a sidelong jerk of the head.

And they were gone.

Alone in the shadows, sweating, Seth released a long, shuddering breath.

His hands were clenched; he made himself open them, his fingers a raw pain, inky and rigid.

Tiny crescent nail marks cut into his palms.

• ◆ •

At the same time, through the eye holes of the gold-and-flame-red mask, Mirany watched the Enfolding. Now the Archon was only the shell of himself. Within his bones and skin was nothing but a packing of natron and resin, wads of cloth and clay, rammed sawdust. Supported under neck and back and ankles, he was wound around with finest fabric, the hands of the Enfolders, all women in blue tunics, softly moving in a deft, complex dance around shoulders and arms, chest and stomach. Beads and amulets and tiny scorpions of jade were threaded into his hair, his crossed arms, the layers of tight cloth. They would spend all night lifting him into the coffins, nine of them, one within another, of paper and lapis and bronze and painted wood, of ebony and alabaster and precious sliced jade and finely engraved silver. Finally the gold casing, the final lid, would be lowered, and he would truly have become a new creature, glittering, splendid, hard, a god with golden hands and turquoise eyes, his old existence so far down under the layers it was lost.

Where was he now, Mirany wondered. Where were his dreams, his likes and dislikes, all the myriad hurried thoughts of his life? Were they with the god? Or were they somehow transferred to this boy at Alectro, buried, half-sensed?

As she stood, she held the brazen bowl by the rim, its emptiness reflecting Hermia watching her carefully.

The bowl had been empty for three days now.

Wherever the god was, he wasn't here.

THE FOURTH HOUSE
OF THE ENFOLDING

There can be no darkness without light. Once I fought a great battle with my own shadow, an epic fight, over continents and oceans. He ran, and I pursued him, and still we chase each other across the sky. I love him, and I fear him.

Night wins, then day wins.

Yesterday I was beaten by a different strength. Dimly, I felt the blows, and was bruised. I cried, and my tears were wet, and amazed me, and I cupped them in small fingers and stared at them, tasted them in the dirty cracks of skin.

They taste of the sea.

As the Rain Queen warned me.

I have asked her to find me. For I am empty inside. Someone has buried me deep in layers of skin and bone and muscle. Someone has come and stolen all my dreams.

The Desert Enfolds Them

"I'm sure he said this way." Seth rubbed sweat from his eyes and stared in exasperation at the broken landscape. The path had divided again, or maybe it was just a sheep trail wandering off. In the terrible heat the land shimmered, a quivering mirage of low foothills studded with scrubby olives and aromatic thorn bushes humming with bees. One track wound down to the left, the other up into the hills. That had to be the one; the goatherd they had awakened hours ago had warned them it was narrow.

He turned. "Will you keep up!"

Oblek was far back, leaning on the big rocks. The musician was just slipping something into the bag slung over his chest, a furtive movement. Seth set his teeth. He knew what it was. How Oblek had got hold of it he had no idea; Pa had bought the food and drink, and he, Seth, had made sure there was no wine.

The musician stumbled up.

"Watch your tongue, ink boy." Oblek's words were already slurred.

Seth slid down quickly. "Give me that."

"What?"

"The drink."

Oblek gave a leery grin. "Get your own."

Seth was furious, and hot, and weary. Short of a fight there was nothing he could do and Oblek knew it. The man was big, and reckless. Besides, scribes didn't fight. The trouble was that Alectro might still be hours away and, even if they were on the right track, the musician would be drunk before they got there. And he was sure there was something wrong with the sky.

"Calm down," Oblek slurred. "I think better like this."

Seth turned and stalked on, grimly, into the invisible veils of heat. Oblek clattered along behind. "Sure about this track?"

"It goes up, doesn't it? We have to cross these hills. I thought you said you'd been to Alectro."

"Been everywhere. Played everywhere. They all get to look the same. That was years ago, when I was good, when I was the best." His voice was suddenly maudlin, which Seth detested.

He nodded, preoccupied, "Pity you didn't stay there."

Yellow. The sky was slowly turning a sickly yellow.

Oblek ignored the jibe. He plodded on, head down, lost in a bitter self-pity. "In all the Two Lands I could go anywhere and be welcomed with open arms, any lord's house, any temple. God, but I was good! Songs came to me out of the air; I could pluck them out of nowhere. Women, money, I had it all. And I was young then. . . ."

"A long time ago that must have been."

Oblek raised bleary eyes. The comment seemed to puzzle him; Seth could almost see the moment it registered into hurt, and anger. "Oh, you can mock. A pretty, spineless, mother's boy, you. Green as grass. Need the corners knocking off, son, and by god, I'd do it myself if it wasn't so blasted hot." He looked up. "What do you know about music, eh? About the power and the fire of it, about inspiration? When the god takes hold of you and you can't breathe with the joy of it? Nothing. That girl, that mousy little thing, she knows." He stood still, fumbling again for the flask. "Could see it in her eyes."

Sour, Seth strode on. "I'll never sink as low as you," he muttered savagely.

Oblek drank. "That's what you think." His voice was raw.

Sand spattered over them. Seth looked up, alarmed. To his horror he saw that the sky was low, hanging above him, as if the sand had swirled up in great clouds, smothering the sun.

He stopped, aghast. That's exactly what it was.

A sandstorm.

Oblek had noticed. When Seth turned, the big man was staring at the sky.

"Run!" he said quietly. "We need to move."

But they had barely climbed past the next turn of the track before the world changed, and the sky crashed down.

There was a hiss of warning, a hot blast of air, and then the storm slammed against them, a stinging, stifling body blow of confusion and dust, clogging eyes and nostrils. Unable to see or breathe or smell or hear, for an instant Seth fell on hands and knees. Gasping for air, he coughed and retched; dragging a scarf out of his pack he tied it rapidly round his face, scrambled up, and turned.

Oblek had vanished; he was alone in a whistling, burning furnace, scorching in it, arms over his head, terrified. Then a great clump of it darkened and thumped against him, and the musician was there, yelling, "That cleft, see it? Up there!"

There had been a cleft, but Seth barely knew which direction he was facing anymore. He staggered for two steps against the raging wind, then Oblek's grip hauled him back, turning him and shoving him behind. "Follow me!" the big man thundered.

They climbed. That was all he knew. All he could see was the dark lump that was the back of Oblek, and the pebbles and scree the big man's feet dislodged, making him slip and stumble. The world was a roaring furnace, a howling of unbelievable noise, and through it came a wheezing chuckle that scared him all the more, until he realized it was Oblek laughing. Seth scowled, furious. No drunk would laugh at him. Though he knew the scream of the storm was turning him sick with fear, making him imagine only too clearly the precipice they would come to without knowing and step off, the long tumbling crash into blackness.

Keep calm! He'd seen sandstorms before. But that had always been from the City, safe in the deep security of the walls and passageways. Even in the Port, there were streets to grope along, walls and houses to recognize. Out here there was nothing. He felt as if he had been swept right off the world, into a maelstrom of heat and scorching sand, into a deep hole, down and down.

As if the god had taken all the world away.

Then Oblek dragged him, yelling. "In here!"

Darkness. A cliff wall, something high and solid. As they staggered under it the storm flung a final stinging face-ful of sand into Seth's eyes; then, miraculously, he could breathe. Air opened around him.

"We'll sit it out in here." Oblek's voice was oddly echoey; wiping his stinging eyes, Seth found himself in a deep overhang, its small cracks and crevices crammed with the fat leaves of aloes.

He crouched, breathless. He was gray with sand. It was in his clothes, his shoes, his mouth, his ears. As he pulled the scarf off it fell in showers; rubbing his face, he felt its dryness in the cracks and wrinkles of his skin. If Oblek was anything to go by, he was caked and crusted with it; as he scratched his hair, gritty crystals cracked under his finger-nails.

Oblek eased himself into a corner and sat, breathing

deep, gazing out at the roaring, hissing inferno. Then he held out the flask. "Drink. You should."

Despite himself, Seth took it and drank. The wine warmed him. He handed it back. "How long will we be stuck here?"

"You're the educated one. Aren't there records? Statistics of storms? Complex observations going back centuries?" Oblek took a drink, grinning.

There probably were, Seth thought sourly. "We just wait, then."

"Nothing else to do. Except eat."

There were olives and cheese and bread. Oblek chewed noisily; gusts of sand blew in and coated the food; Seth picked it away in irritation. After a while what he was thinking came out in words. "How do we recognize him? This boy, I mean. Alectro will be full of little boys. And how do we get his parents to let him come?"

"Just tell them." Oblek swallowed a mouthful of cheese. "They'll be honored. Fools."

"It might not be that easy."

"Trust the god, ink boy. Besides, I have a plan. How much money is left?"

Seth fished the purse from under his coat and opened it, peering in. "Sixty . . . seventy . . . "

Oblek's great hand came and grabbed it; before Seth could move, the contents were tipped out carelessly in the sand. "Think I'm going to steal it? We may need to grease a few palms."

Oblek stopped.

His fingers pushed coins aside, lifted the red scorpion from the grit.

For a long, astonished moment he looked at it. Then at Seth.

"Well. Maybe I've underestimated you, pen pusher."

Seth was furious, but he made himself keep calm. "I found that," he said quietly.

"Sure. And I'm a dancing girl from Spalis."

"It's true." Seth wanted to snatch it back, but Oblek's broad fingers held it tight.

"Where?"

"Down in the hall of records. It had been forgotten. Probably for years."

"So you took it."

Seth was silent.

"Were you going to sell it? How?"

"I know people."

Oblek's small eyes were watching him intently. "Do you, now. Like who? What sort of scams are you running, *scribe*?"

"Give it to me," Seth snapped, furious.

"This is from the god."

"I told you, I found it. . . . "

"He sent it, haven't you realized that?" Oblek's voice was tight with sudden obsession; he turned the scorpion greedily. "Listen, ink boy, the god sends his signs for a reason and this little beauty is clearly—" He jerked, hissed, flung it away. Then he jumped to his feet. "It's alive!"

Seth stared. "What?"

"It moved! In my fingers. *It crawled.*"

In the roar of the storm the scorpion lay among rubble. Sand blew over its rigid ruby body. Seth bent carefully. Then he picked it up.

Its small eyes watched him.

Quickly he flipped it into the purse and scooped the hot coins in on top, jerking the cord tight. As he looked up, the musician whispered, "That thing is holy. You should have told the girl about it. It may change everything."

The storm was dying. They both heard how its roar had weakened, turned to gusts, the spatter of sand less fierce. Seth shrugged. "I'll tell her when we get back."

Oblek came close. "What other little secrets have you got? Plans to betray us to Argelin—"

"Of course not!"

"Good." The big man looked tense, his eyes bleak. "If I thought that, I'd see you pegged out in the desert myself." His firm fingers grabbed Seth's tunic, hauled him close. "Maybe I should leave you here. Where no one will find you."

Seth's hand moved to his knife. "If you think you can," he whispered.

And then, over the musician's shoulder, he saw the woman. With a hiss of fear he pushed Oblek back; the big man turned and stared.

This was no cliff, no rock overhang. Above them the

storm opened, shriveled, fell back, and they saw they were sheltering in the ruins of a vast temple, its great columns so hacked and eroded by the sand they seemed as pitted as rock. The desert had devoured the roof and floor, it had scoured the marble and clogged the portico. Succulents grew in the doorways; faces of the god and the Rainwoman and whoever the temple had been raised by peered through spiny growth and gnarled stems of vines that split eye from eye and mouth from nostril.

The Rainwoman. That's who the woman must be.

Beautiful, treacherous, she smiled at them from the painted wall, the mask on her face a shimmer of gold, her tunic blue and rippling as if it ran with damp, and it did, because Seth pushed past the musician and climbed up and felt it, the cold, clammy pigment soiling his spread palm.

And under her arms, which spread wide and glinted with quartz, were two doorways, and through them Seth saw a scatter of huts built in the broken outbuildings, and as the storm swept back a few scraggy hens wandered out, a door banged, a baby cried. Out of the yellow swirls of sand a village was blown, a filthy stink of hovels, a fly-infested market square, a choked well.

He felt Oblek's bulk close behind him. "Where are we?" he whispered.

The musician spat on the sand. "Alectro."

Seth's heart sank. *"This?"*

Oblek laughed sourly. "No one said it was a palace."

◆ ◆ ◆

But as they scrambled down the scoured track into the set-
tlement, Seth thought that even Oblek looked uneasy.
Alectro had clearly suffered more from the drought than
anywhere else they'd been. Doors opened and through the
cracks veiled women watched them pass. A few men came
out, openly hostile, holding scythes and knives. There were
children, too, half-starved, ragged little things. Unsmiling.
Their eyes quick and sly.

"Remember." Oblek's voice was low and urgent. "Stick
to the plan. And watch my back."

Seth shrugged. The plan was Oblek's, formed as soon as
they'd seen the state of the village. Arguing had been useless, though it sounded crazy to him.

By the time they'd reached the market, a group of men
were waiting for them, and as Oblek raised his hand and
said, "The god's hand on you," only a few of them mumbled anything in reply.

Seth stayed back. These were starving people. He could
see it in their eyes, in the shifty, considering glances at his
clothes, the packs of food and water.

Maybe Oblek's way was the right way after all.

The head man was thin and wiry and small. He wore a
tunic that might once have been red and he said sourly,
"What do you want, strangers?"

Oblek spread his hands. "To trade."

"We have no money to buy and nothing to sell.
Especially water."

That would be it.

Water would be like gold here, deep in the desert. Drought was drying the village out. A lot of the houses looked empty. Seth wondered how many people had died.

"We have our own water." Oblek hesitated, then pulled his knife out, threw it down and stepped over it. Seth had to admire the man's nerve. But then Oblek looked as filthy and dangerous as the rest of them. "I'm sure you have other things to interest us."

The headman shook his head. "Nothing. No food, no cattle, no salt. Move on, fat man. There's nothing here for you."

Oblek leered. Then he winked. "I'm sure you have children," he said softly.

It was a moment of pure danger.

Seth was sweating; he leaned down and grasped the hilt of his knife.

For what seemed an age the villagers looked back, impassive.

Then the headman smiled, a sour smile, and nodded.

"Of course we do."

Oblek folded his arms and rasped a thumb down his stubbly chin. "Children," he mused. "They eat too much, are always thirsty. They cry at night. But in the Port, in the palaces, the citadels, on slaveships, they need children. Children are easy to train. Children are cheap labor."

The headman looked at Seth, then around at the other men. One nodded; another looked uneasy, then shrugged.

As if something had been decided, the headman turned

and walked up to Oblek, picked up the knife and handed it to him.

"Maybe we can do business, trader," he said.

They wasted no time.

The children were brought quickly and lined up against a wall in the hot sun. Most were sullen, too cowed by thirst or sores or hunger to care. A few women sobbed and cursed, but the men just took the children out of their arms and dumped them with the rest.

Seth glanced round, licking his dry lips. What in the god's name was he doing here? His desk in the Office of Plans suddenly seemed like paradise, like the garden of the Rain Queen, far and fair and unattainable. He might never see it again.

Oblek almost seemed to be enjoying himself. He inspected the children sourly, tipping up their faces, opening their mouths and looking in, feeling the pitifully thin arms.

"No girls," he growled, after a few minutes musing, and with a curt wave the headman dismissed them. Most of the older ones looked desperately relieved, Seth thought.

There were about fifteen boys. Two were too young; the rest could have been anywhere between seven and seventeen, they were so stunted and starved.

Not only that, they all looked similar, dark eyed, dark haired, as if the villagers were all related to each other, as they almost certainly were. One boy wept, another talked to himself, gabbling over and over. They all had sores on their faces. They all looked filthy.

Oblek stroked his chin. Then he came over to Seth and said quietly, "Well?"

"How on earth do I know?" Seth watched the villagers. "This is crazy. We can't buy them all anyway. If the god brought us here, he'll have to show us which he is."

"All right, bright boy. How?"

Seth licked his lips. Then he said, "Maybe if we explain—"

"That we're looking for the new Archon? Certainly. Then the price would go up thirtyfold. Or they'd take the boy straight to Argelin themselves. You know what would happen then. If that's your only plan—"

"No." Seth stepped past him. "It isn't."

He walked along the row looking at the frightened faces. A small boy at the end looked back almost cheekily. Was this the one?

Suddenly he had an idea. He pulled his left hand into the sleeve of his coat and felt the hard knob of the scorpion, pinned there for safety. Tugging it off, he held it tight in his fist.

Tell me which is you. Sting the knowledge into me. Tell me. Quickly.

He walked back down the line. The boys, bewildered, looked at the sand, looked at their mothers, cried. Impatient, the headman said, "You can have a special price for the lot. Name it."

Nothing. No stab of certainty.

He wasn't here.

Turning quickly, Seth snapped, "Are these all? Are there any others?"

"None."

"Are you certain?"

"None worth selling."

But the man's voice was subdued; another of the villagers said sourly, "Your own stepson, Karim, he should be with them."

Oblek gave Seth a glance. "Bring him out."

The headman shrugged. "The boy's weak in the head. Useless. A dreamer."

Oblek's voice was a growl. "Then you won't mind making money out of him, will you?"

For a moment Karim stood still; then he walked over to a small hut nearby and yanked the door open hard; Seth saw it had been roughly fastened with a loop of rope.

"Out," the headman snapped.

The doorway was dark. Something moved in its shadow.

A boy. Thin, tearstained. He was dark haired, and though his face was cut and bruised, they could see his astonishing beauty; he walked toward them slowly, his arms hugged tight around his body, shivering.

After three steps he stumbled, crumpling with a hiss of pain. Seth moved, but Oblek was faster. The big man grabbed the boy and lifted him up, a frail burden. The boy's dark eyes looked at him, close, and he whispered something, a murmur of reproach.

"You've been so long finding me, Oblek. So long."

The musician's face was set and white. *"Archon,"* he hissed.

They Negotiate the Price That Must Be Paid

She had heard it at the dawn Ritual. It had not come from the statue of the young god; his lips were marble and they hadn't moved, and his grave smile hadn't turned toward her. But from somewhere he had said, *You're so long finding me.*

It had been soft, weary, a tired child's complaint.

Mirany had licked her lips, gone rigid, half glanced at Hermia. But the Speaker made no sign that she had heard.

Now, halfway down the loggia on the way to her afternoon bathe, the voice whispered again. She stopped, the clean white robe over one arm.

Mirany.

All down the spotless corridor the poised beautiful faces of long-dead Speakers gazed out to sea. In the heat the marble under her bare feet was cool and smooth.

"I'm here," she whispered.

Don't be afraid of me. I won't hurt you.

"I know that. You said." Her voice was tense; she turned, alert. The corridor was empty, all its doors closed.

I'm looking for the rain, but I'm not sure where they keep it. A god should know, shouldn't he? Do you know, Mirany?

She shook her head. The tunic stuck to her back. "Listen. Have they found you? They started out last night. . . . "

They?

"The musician . . . "

Oblek!

Nothing else. Just that name, like a whisper of recognition. *Oblek.*

A door opened. Rhetia came out and stared; instantly Mirany walked on, hurrying out into the courtyard, between the olive trees, down the steps to the sheltered pool with its glinting, clean salt water that twenty serving women emptied and refilled daily, toiling with buckets down the cliff path. Now the petals of white hibiscus floated in a scented clotted mat on the surface. She took her tunic off and slipped into the warm water, swimming out easily into the center. Turning, she watched Chryse and Ixaca and the others coming out of the Lower House, pushing and arguing about something, giggling, Rhetia glaring at the pool coldly through the pots of pink flowers. She felt the familiar dread creeping over her, even here, of having to speak to them, of having to be awkward little Mirany. Because deep inside, now, there was someone else.

And she realized with a shiver that she had not had to go to the Oracle to hear him. This was the Oracle. She was the Oracle.

Chryse ran and plunged in with a great splash and a shriek; the whole mass of water rocked and swelled and slapped up over the paving in a wave of spatter. Mirany backed lazily. In the blue sky the sun was an unbearable furnace. She thought of Seth and Oblek in the desert, and dipped her face guiltily under the water, coming up with petals plastered to her hair. The musician was wild, unpredictable, his plan for assassinating Argelin a terrifying vengeance. And Seth. Could they trust him? She frowned. What was it that made her think they couldn't?

Chryse swam close. "Be careful," she whispered.

"What?"

The fair girl slicked her wet hair back. For a moment she looked solemn. "They're up to something. Rhetia was talking to Hermia for ages. Then after, I saw Argelin going in and he was sitting with her on the balcony. They were laughing, and sitting far too close."

Mirany lay back and floated, arms wide, feet splashing. "We all know she's mad about him. What's it got to do with me?"

"Because you're the Bearer."

Chryse turned a somersault and came up in a stream of petals. Eyes closed, she whispered, "It's changed you. And I know you're up to something, Mirany, something secret. Maybe the others don't realize, but I do. And Hermia, she knows, too. She watches you, I've seen her, at the Ritual, at meals. This afternoon, when we were at the theater, she wasn't watching the play. Behind that fan, she was looking at you."

Mirany swallowed a salty mouthful and coughed. "It was a boring play," she said quietly.

Chryse glared at her, resentful. "What's got into you! I'm just trying to warn you—"

"I know. And thanks. But listen, Chryse, nothing's happening. It's just Rhetia being spiteful. You know what she's like."

Chryse looked hurt. In the sunlit splashes and slaps of the water, she was silent. Until she said, "I always thought we were friends, Mirany." Then she swam away.

Seth's hands clenched; he caught hold of his astonishment as if it was a real thing, whispered, "Keep your voice down. Get him out of here."

He turned, said loudly, "Put him with the others," and walked briskly over to the group of men.

He had to keep their attention and his own composure so he snapped out a ridiculous price.

"Seventy staters. For the lot."

"One hundred and fifty."

Seth laughed, mirthless.

The headman leered, showing a broken tooth. He gestured to one of the dark doorways. "I suggest we go out of the heat, master. And negotiate."

Seth glanced over at Oblek. The musician had turned, his face cleared of that lapse into recognition. Now he looked dangerous, lowering. "Very well," Seth said, knowing the whole village could hear. "My . . . partner will get the children ready to go."

"Go? Not tonight, master." The headman spread his arms. "That would insult us. Darkness is coming and you must eat and sleep as our guests. Tomorrow you'll have the cool of dawn to travel in."

It was the last thing Seth wanted. All his instincts screamed at him to get out now. Travelers disappeared all the time with their money, and if these men were ready to sell their children they could do anything. But Oblek had already grunted "Good idea" and turned back to the boy, hauling him toward the others. Seething, with a shrug that even he knew looked arrogant, Seth stalked past the men and ducked under the low lintel of the doorway. How had he got into this? How had that timid little girl got him into it?

The house was bare. Beaten earth floor, worn rugs, a sleeping area screened off. The heat was as bad as outside and the mosquitoes worse. Flies buzzed over something in a dark corner.

With a sigh Seth flicked dust off a low bench and sat down. The village men sat opposite, facing him in a row. Well, he knew how to bargain. As long as they believed him.

After a lot of haggling and conferring and shaking of heads and contemptuous laughs, the price was agreed at one hundred staters for all the children, which was probably what the men had had in mind from the start. The headman spat in his hand and Seth shook it. Then a woman brought in cups and a small green jug, hastily, as if she'd been waiting and listening. She poured out a hot, muddy concoction, barely a splash in the bottom of each cup, and her eyes met Seth's briefly.

She looked devastated. He lowered his eyes quickly. She must be the boy's mother.

"A good bargain." One of the men held out his cup.

Seth smiled, nodded. "For all of us."

They drank. It tasted like mud, too, he thought.

When Oblek came in, dragging the pack, Seth moved up and the big man sat, waving his cup to be filled and downing the contents in one preoccupied mouthful. There was no way they could talk alone, so they sat there all evening and listened to the interminable gossip of the villagers, their complaints, stories, inquiries about the cargoes and opium dens of the Port. When the food finally came, plonked down in chipped bowls, it was pitifully little, and Seth could only pick at the spiced meat, wondering what animal it was and how long it had been dead. Even whether it was poisoned. Oblek gulped everything, quickly and carelessly, talking with his mouth full, reckless with a secret triumph that Seth was sure everyone could sense. When the musician pulled the bottle out and passed it round, the men laughed, and slapped him on the back. Talk went noisy, animated. When the drink came to him, Seth sniffed the neck of it. Not wine. Stronger. Some distilled spirit. That was all they needed.

But after a while he realized Oblek was barely wetting his lips, while the village men roared and argued and passed the bottle and brought out some of their own until one fell asleep against his neighbor, drunk with the unaccustomed fire of the liquor. Perhaps the musician had it right after all. Because now Oblek stood, crumbs and sand still falling off him, and crossed to the woman collecting dishes, and said something to her, a quiet inquiry. She nodded, went out.

The headman watched, his narrow face flushed. "How much for her, trader?" he asked slyly. "If you're interested . . . "

"I wouldn't dream of insulting you," Oblek said sourly.

When the woman came back, she carried a wooden lyre. She handed it to him and he took it. Then he came over and sat by Seth, and began to tune the strings.

"Can you play that thing?" The headman's fingers waggled for the drink. He watched Oblek over the tipped bottle.

"I learned once." Notes rose and fell as the strings were tightened and slackened. "Needs oiling," Oblek muttered. Then, without another word, he began to play.

It was a revelation to Seth. Because the dirty, loud, vengeful man with his rolls of fat and small shrewd eyes was an artist. His fingers plucked ripples of notes, rhythmically stroking them into a tune, into music, a sound that seemed to come out and curl round them, and at once the miserable hut was a dark, lamplit haven, the men's faces softened to shadows in the flickering of the one lamp. Night had come, sudden as always, and had transformed things. The god's magic had fallen over them.

The music was so intricate it slowed their talk and then stopped it. In a weary silence they listened, as if all the energy of the day drained out of them, and Seth, tired from the unaccustomed journey, almost drowsed, only coming slowly to realize that Oblek was singing.

His voice was deep, slightly hoarse, a voice that mingled with the smoke from the cooking fires outside, and the song he sang was in praise of the Rain Queen, of her garden far to the west, where fountains rise and pools are deep and clear, and green trees and flowers spring from the saturated soil. The music moved over and under the words, became drips and splashes and rivulets; for a sleepy moment Seth felt the whole building dissolve into water, he could taste it on his dry lips, it trickled from leaves and pooled and dripped down the steps like the soft fabric of a dress, a gown of moisture, a coolness that passed in the air.

And then someone moved against him and he jolted awake, and the villagers were going, saying quiet good-nights, one supported by a friend, staggering against the doorpost.

When they were alone, Oblek leaned the lyre against the bench and looked shrewdly at Seth. "How much?"

"A hundred. We can do it, thanks to Mirany's gold. Let the rest of the children go tomorrow, a few miles out. Or let them escape." He wandered over to the mattresses and pulled the dirty sheets off, inspecting them. "God! Lice."

Oblek said nothing.

Seth yawned. "Still, I'm worn out. It's been a long day."

He heaved the straw pallet over, smoothed a cloak of his own on it, lay down and closed his eyes.

"It's not over yet." Oblek's voice was mild and amused, as if the music had soothed something in him. "Because, if I'm any judge, as soon as the moon sets, a few of our friends here will be paying us another little visit. Only this time there'll be no carousing. This time they'll just cut our throats."

In the moonlight the steps of the Oracle were shadows, gritty with blown sand. The torch Hermia carried sent shadows over the platform, catching the edge of the brazen bowl, filling it with movement flickers, shifting shapes. Mirany walked over to it, and crouched.

Behind her, she felt the Speaker, tall, the torch raised, sensed her smile behind the mask. "Is the god to be with us tonight?" Even her voice was light and cold.

Mirany swallowed. She put both arms around the bowl and lifted it, feeling again the weight, the awkwardness of it. Through the eye slits she watched its coiled, slithering contents with rigid dread.

"He is with us," she whispered.

I Know Those That Are My Own

Seth sat up slowly. "What?"

"You heard. These people may be desperate but they won't be selling their children to anyone."

"They bargained."

"To keep us here till dark. To string us along." Oblek sucked a tooth. "It obviously worked with you. I must say I'm surprised. Thought you were too slick to be taken in by a bunch of villagers."

Seth swung off the bed. He tried not to sound as shaken as he felt. "We're leaving then."

"We get the boy and go. He's locked up in that hovel we saw earlier. Looks like the stepfather beats him. I couldn't talk to him with the others there." He bent over to tie his sandals, which were already tight, then paused, still. "He knew me. You heard that."

Seth shrugged, pulling his shoes on. "What did you expect?"

"Not this." Oblek's small eyes looked across the room at nothing. "He was old. Older than me."

"And now he's not." Seth snatched up the bags, crammed a blanket in, the precious water, the remains of the food. "Will you hurry! We'll grab him and then get out. Come on!"

The musician grinned acidly. "And you were so worn out."

There was no one outside. The dilapidated village was utterly silent under the low moon, except for a dry wind that banged a door and the rats, rustling in the pile of stinking straw by the track. Flattened in the shadows of the wall, Seth let his eyes adjust to the dark, made out the outlines of flat houses, and on the crag behind, the broken temple, its fine stones tumbled down the hill, stacked up at the bottom inexpertly in walls and clumsy animal shelters.

Over the dark mouth of the well a bat flitted to and fro.

"You cross first." Oblek's bulk was close, sweat smelling. His breath smelled of spirits. "If anyone's on the watch, I'll see them come after you."

Seth rubbed his face. He wanted to say, "No, you go," but even as the words were formed he silenced them. If any of the villagers had to be knifed, he'd rather Oblek did it. He was a scribe. He left the dirty work to others.

Before the musician could say anything else, he slipped away, running bent, keeping in shadow, though between the houses the long white slants of moonlight were alleyways of light that picked him out mercilessly as he raced across them, and beyond the village the desert was bare and ghostly.

Breathless, he paused under a shuttered window. Someone was talking inside the hut; he breathed hard, trying to hear, but his heart thudded so loud it seemed to jump in his chest and he struggled up and ran on, behind one hut, past the well, around the rim of the deserted market.

At the hovel he crouched, gasping.

The village was a patchwork of black and white. Dust gusted against its shuttered doors.

Seth reached up and unfastened the rough rope. The door opened; he slipped inside.

"Are you here?" he whispered.

Something rustled.

"Yes."

The space was black and stuffy. He felt straw prickle his legs. A flea bit him and he swore. Then his hands touched the boy's head; he groped down his shoulder to his hands and took a knife out and cut the bonds. "Don't be afraid. Oblek's outside. We're taking you away, out of here. You know Oblek, don't you?"

The boy didn't answer at once. Then his voice was quiet. "I remember his music. There were empty rooms and there was his music. I think it was in a dream."

Seth hauled him up. "Yes. Well listen, don't make—"

The door creaked.

He whipped round instantly, knife out.

A shadow moved in the doorway. Then it came in. Too small. Too quick.

"I've got a weapon," Seth hissed, circling, "and I'll use it."

But behind him the boy caught his arm. "Don't. It's my mother."

He could see her now, a frail, terrified face, hands clutching some miserable crust, a tiny flask of water. "What do you want?" she breathed. "You're taking him!"

"No. Listen . . . "

She stepped back. He knew she was going to scream. The drawing in of her breath was like a despair, like a horror; he couldn't move, knew he was lost.

Until a fat hand came from behind her and clamped down over her face.

"Not a good idea, lady." Oblek maneuvered her as he kicked the door shut. "Do you want her to know what's happening?"

"No," Seth muttered, but the question hadn't been for him.

The boy pushed past him and said, "Of course I want her to. I'll tell her."

Released, the woman sobbed, a breath of terror. "Alexos."

"No. I've told you. That's not my name anymore. My name is a secret now." His voice was almost harsh but he put his arms round her and in the dimness Seth saw him smile. "It's all right. I have to go with them; I warned you this would happen, didn't I?"

The woman clung to him; she turned on Seth, her face set. "Strangers, listen to me. My son is mad. He was always a strange one, a dreamer. His father used to beat him for it, now his stepfather does. His work is never done, he lets the goats roam, all he does is lie on his back and sing and let his mind wander. He has nightmares; when he was young, how many nights I spent hugging him, rocking away his terrors."

The boy listened, still faintly smiling. As if he listened to a small child's nonsense.

"Woman!" Oblek growled.

"But now it's worse. This last week, his mind has gone. Sometimes he doesn't know me, pretends I'm a stranger to him. He talks of deep passageways, and the places under the City, and sings to the Rain Queen, over and over. He's crazy! What use is he to you? Leave him, leave him here where I can look after him. What profit will you get from a crazy boy? Who will buy him? He'll end up begging in the sun, living with the dogs and jackals, having stones thrown at him, cursed, wretched." She grabbed Oblek's sleeve. "Have mercy, trader."

"That's enough." The big man stepped back, shaken.

In the shadows the boy watched, his dark thin shape as tall as Seth, his bruised face sharp. Then he whispered, "Tell her, Oblek."

Oblek glanced at the door. "The boy is the new Archon." His voice was low, a breath. "We are . . . searchers, sent out by Argelin. The whole slaver business was just a cover. We don't want the other children, just the Archon. He must come, and quickly, before the men get up enough courage to come slinking after our money. Now!"

He reached out a hand but the boy didn't move. He watched the woman, and she stared at him through the dimness.

"The Archon! But he's Alexos! My son! I've wiped his nose, slapped him for naughtiness. How can he be the Archon?"

Alexos nodded calmly. "That's all true. But inside me, so deep inside, I feel the god. Like a river. Like a song. Like a coiled snake." He smiled, and his fingers felt for hers and closed over hers, and he gripped her tight. "I've always known he was here, but in these last few days, he's come alive, moving up through the watercourses and channels and veins in the rock, out to the sun, and on, and on, until it burns me, through the darkness, between the stars! And my shadow and I have fought and will follow each other forever, and the Rainwoman watches, and the rain never comes!"

For a moment she looked at him. Then she took her hands away and stepped back. "You're mistaken, strangers," she said dully. "My son is deranged."

"There's no time to argue." Oblek grabbed the boy. "Are you ready?"

"Yes."

"Then we head for the coast and find a boat." He pushed the boy to the door, then turned, and said

brusquely, "He'll be well cared for. The Archon has everything he wants. When things are settled, we'll send for you;
you'll have a palace of your own. Handmaidens, jewels,
whatever you want. You won't be able to talk to him. But
you'll see him."

Outside something shuffled. Seth opened the door
quickly, looked at the silent houses. Then he said, "I think
someone was listening."

"Then we go." Oblek pushed past him; briefly, in the
doorway, the boy turned and looked at the woman sadly,
dark under the stars. "Be at peace, Mother," he whispered.
"Remember me."

Seth said awkwardly, "We'll take care of him. Don't tell
anyone. Just say we took him. Please."

Tears were running down her cheeks.

For a moment he thought she would spit at him, reach
out to scratch his face. But she just turned away.

He ducked through the door, into shadows. In his ear
Oblek whispered, "We'll head south. They won't expect it.
Then we work our way over the hills and down through the
Glass Valley to Prescia and get a boat to the Port. A day and
a night."

Without waiting for an answer he ran, pushing the boy
ahead of him. Seth scowled, strapped the pack on, and raced
after them.

Night lizards scuttled from under his feet.

Behind, in the village, a dog began to bark.

◆ ◆ ◆

She had got this far. To the house itself, the fourth house, and the snake in the brazen bowl had not uncoiled, not even moved, except for the odd white unslitting of its eye to look at her once, when she'd stumbled.

Now she knew she was too tired to hold the bowl anymore, could never make it back. Sweat stuck her clothes to her, ran down inside the intolerable heat of the mask, made the smooth bronze a slippery horror. And she was becoming sure this was not the god.

He had not spoken to her.

He appeared in many forms, all the scuttling, slithering life of the desert, but the snake was different. It didn't feel right.

"They're up to something," Chryse had said, and she sucked her dry lips and struggled to hold the heavy container, and through the eye slits of the mask sensed Hermia's tension in the way she spoke the words of the Telling of the Way.

Because this was the House of the Guidance, and all down its walls was writing, every inch covered with bright pictures, lists, instructions, the secret spells that would lead the soul of the Archon deep into the Underworld, through the black halls, into the light, along the silver road that ran between galaxies, to the garden of the Rain Queen. And with a clang the heavy lid of the Archon's gilded mask was lowered onto his face, and exhausted slaves unfastened the ropes and stood back, and pushed the vast wooden crane outside, and the Nine came and gathered around the gleaming, polished gold inner sarcophagus.

The face smiled up at them, beautiful, at peace. It looked nothing like the Archon, Mirany thought.

Then, as if the snake heard the thought, it began to uncoil.

She drew her breath in, a shudder of fear, and Chryse next to her turned slightly and gasped behind her mask, and Hermia stopped speaking in midprayer.

The snake slithered and poured, it rose and swayed and slid its smooth slinky muscles up the brazen bowl, over the rim, on to her hand, her arm, toward her face.

Mirany was rigid. To breathe would be fatal.

How heavy it was. The small scales were firm and cool, their greenish shimmer a strangeness in the dim flicker of the tapers and oil lamps.

Its head drew back, and with a tiny hiss its forked tongue vibrated.

Fangs gleamed, pinpricked with venom.

No one moved. Even Hermia's hands, spread in prayer, were frozen. The slaves stared in horror; the soldiers at the door sweated in silence.

Is it you? Mirany screamed in her mind. *Is it you? Tell me!*

The snake moved with slow, sensual laziness around her shoulders. It was so heavy and thick it felt like a great rope, and through her thin tunic she felt the scales flow and ripple, smelled the faintest musky smell of it. She dared not move her head. She couldn't see it now, through the eye slits. What was it doing?

Then he said, *This is not me.*

"What?"

This snake, Mirany, is not me. It's dangerous. It has been drugged, and is now waking. They have put it here to kill you, because you know about their treachery. Do you trust me?

"Yes." Perhaps she said it aloud. Chryse gave a whimper; the snake hissed and rose and Mirany saw its head, whipping in, darting at the mask that covered her face.

Then carry the bowl to the tripod and leave it there.

"If I move . . . "

I will not let you be harmed. Trust me.

It was madness. It was just a voice in her head. There was no god. She was talking to herself.

She moved, one foot, gently.

"Stand still, Mirany!" It was Chryse, a wail of terror.

And oddly, it put courage into her, and she stepped forward, and took another step, toward the tripod that waited in a dim corner, the snake swaying around her, slithering fast down her shoulders, looping over her arms. It coiled down her dress, round her waist, its thin head zigzagging in, and she closed her eyes and gasped as, thump, its gaping fangs clattered against the smooth gold and scarlet of the mask. Venom splattered. Chryse screeched. Mirany heard the hiss of the snake's frustration, its whipping round for another attack; she ran, tripped, reached the tripod, raised her arms and dumped the heavy bowl on top, wriggling out from the snake's frantic smooth uncurling, its slither back down her arms, and she shuddered and squirmed, and it turned and looped in one great coil to the floor and wrapped round her foot.

And bit her.

Alexos stopped. Breathless, he fell into the cold gritty sand; Oblek hauled him up pitilessly. "Come on!"

The moon had set. The night was a semicircle of darkness scattered with stars. Jackals whined up in the hills.

"I shouldn't have gone." The boy was in pain, doubled over. His fingers clutched the sand; as Oblek lifted him it trailed out of his palm like dust.

"She'll be fine. I'll carry you."

"She'll die. When they find out I'm not there, she'll die."

"It's too late for that." Seth had scrambled to the top of the next dune and was looking back. Small lights fluttered and bobbed, a line of them, from the direction of the village, far behind. "They've already found out."

The pain was a fire; it shot into her ankle. She gave a gasp and crumpled onto her knees, slumping against the tripod, sending the whole thing crashing. Hands grabbed her shoulders; voices shouted, strange, echoing voices, and the painted figures on the wall had come down and were bending over her, calling desperate instructions into her ear, telling her the way, the way down, the way to the coolness and the rain.

Her mask was tugged off; gasping for air, she saw the

snake slide into a corner; it rippled down a hole there and was gone, deep into the underground, where the Oracle was, where the darkness and silence were, the road to the garden of the Rain Queen.

Leaving her body to topple forward, Mirany got up and went after it.

THE FIFTH HOUSE
OF THE GUIDANCE OF THE WAY

Let me tell you what happened. He was always my opposite. Where I was light, he was darkness. When I sang, he watched in silence. When I walked the desert and delighted in the scurrying things, the heat, the blue and yellow, he slid into the holes of the earth and went deep, into volcanoes, into redness.

He is my brother, my twin, my reflection.

The world is ours, but at first we could not share it between us. We fought. Do you know what it is to fight with your very self, left to right, fingertip to fingertip?

The earth convulsed with our struggle.

But after centuries, after eons, we heard someone laughing, and the sound was like droplets, so that, exhausted, we turned and looked at her.

She was sitting on the ground and her dress flowed; fishes lived in it, and eels and weed.

And I said—or was it he that said it—"Who are you, goddess?"

And she answered, "What you fight over."

DOES THE DESERT DREAM OF RAIN?

The scree slope was treacherous. Seth clattered down it, sliding, slipping, filthy, his boots full of sand. Below him Oblek was a bulky darkness, and the boy, who'd got down and was further ahead, was barely visible, a source of small scuffles and a cascade of pebbles.

Near the bottom Seth was so tired his foot went from under him; he slithered the last few yards, arms flailing wildly, crashing up against Oblek, whose firm grip was waiting for him.

They breathed, bent over, Seth crouched on his heels.

All around them the hills were still.

Except for the dogs barking.

The villagers were close. They knew the ground, and they had the dogs. Seth scowled. "Why are they coming? I wouldn't have thought your stepfather cared about losing you."

"Profit," Oblek said sourly.

"But if he thinks we're official searchers . . . "

"He doesn't. Argelin's men wouldn't be creeping around like this. They'd be armed, and would have ridden in with half a dozen scribes and a few rich robes to dress the boy in. There'd have been gifts all round for the father, the father's father, and every other relative that crawled out of the woodwork. If we'd had more time we might have set that up." He turned and started walking, wading through the drifts of accumulated sand. "He wants to take the boy to Argelin himself. Maybe he's thinking there's something in it after all."

Seth looked at Alexos. Silent, the boy walked, head down. He looked frail and weary and distracted, as if none of this was of any importance. "Did he treat you very badly?"

Alexos shrugged. He gave Seth a dark, unsettling look. "Yes. But a god should know pain. How else can he feel for his people?"

Chilled, Seth glanced at Oblek, who wheezed out a laugh. "That's telling you, ink boy. The old man would have said something similar, and then smiled at me like a baby. Archon, it's good to have you back."

Alexos said, "And you, too, Oblek. I dreamed of you." He stopped, looking up at the landscape ahead of them. "Once, too, I think I dreamed of this place."

It was the Valley of Glass.

Seth had never been here, but he'd heard of it, and the

stories hadn't been pleasant. He could see why.

Before them the track led into a splintered highland. If it was rock, it looked like some sort of basalt, black, shiny, and faceted, catching the starlight with faint gleams. Perhaps centuries ago a volcano had spewed it out, and it had hardened, or some fearful heat had vitrified the whole mass into this nightmare of spikes and shards and viciously sharp edges. Seth drew his thumb along one, and swore as the flesh was sliced and blood dripped instantly.

On each side of the track pinnacles rose in bizarre towers and twisted spiral formations, as if they had melted and reformed. The valley glimmered; reflections of themselves moved as they walked cautiously into it, deformed images and half-seen movements, as if other watchers traveled with them. A whole crowd, glimpsed, imagined, silent.

Oblek was hurrying. "This would be a good place to stop them."

"How?"

"Bring a few rocks down. At a narrow place in the track. Or perhaps work on their superstitions with this." He folded a corner of the pack down and showed the wooden lyre.

Seth stared. "You stole it!"

The big man grinned. "I'm a musician, and touched by the god." His voice echoed oddly in the rocks above them. "All instruments are mine, if I can play them. That's the law."

They scrambled up. At a twist in the track, Seth saw the sky was paler here, a faint purple; at first he thought it was dawn coming, but it was too early for that. Then he realized the valley itself gave off some ghostly luminosity; the farther they climbed into it, the more easily he could see his companions, their skin an unearthly paleness, their eyes dark shadows.

Not far back, the howling of the dogs split and magnified. The villagers had reached the valley mouth.

"Move!" Oblek whispered.

They ran. Glassy rock closed around them, over them. They ran inside a honeycomb of openings in the fused basalt, took the first opening, then the next, trying to keep south. Above them, blurred and seamed by the glass roof, the stars were smears and glitters.

Paws clattered. Dogs were howling, yelping. Men yelled in anger.

"They won't come in!" Seth's voice astonished himself; it whispered and hissed and rebounded all around them.

"The dogs are scared."

"My stepfather will come." Alexos was white with weariness. "He won't lose the fortune he could make."

Seth laughed, mirthless. "Did we tell you Argelin won't want you? That he'll have his own candidate?"

The boy shrugged. "I am the Archon. What Argelin does is not important."

"And if I have anything to do with it, he won't be alive long enough," Oblek muttered. Catching the boy, he pushed him up the stairs of slippery rock that had suddenly blocked their path. Behind, the racing feet of the pursuers

were so close they must only be round the last bend; hauling himself up, Seth knew they couldn't outrun them.
Oblek knew it, too. "Here!"

The top stair, strangely fissured, led to an opening that
seemed to have been blown, like a great airhole in the
molten mass, hardened into a black bubble.

Inside, the cave was inky, its floor piled high with small
round pebbles of glass.

And it was a dead end.

"Now what!"

"Keep your nerve." Oblek waded chest high into the
mound of glass drops, and gathered a handful thoughtfully.
They clattered and slid, thousands of them, rattling.

"Right. We push this lot onto them."

"That won't stop them!"

"So what's your better idea, pen pusher?"

Seth had none. Except to give back the boy.

"At least we might block the steps. Gain some time.
Ready? Archon, are you ready?" Oblek was already bent,
arms wide, shoving the slithering pebbles. But Alexos took
no notice. Instead he crouched, and hugged his arms round
his body.

"The Rain Queen," he whispered.

"What?" Furious, Seth stood over him. "Come on!"

"She's here. She's come."

The boy was crazy. They were all crazy, even being in
this mess. He was trapped in a bubble with a fat fanatic and
a god. Even the Jackal would be preferable to this. Savagely

he hissed, "Get up!" and grabbed the boy's thin tunic.

The boy looked sidelong, shivering. His eyes shocked Seth. They were narrow and calculating as a snake's. When he spoke, his speech was a hiss of venom. **"Don't touch me."**

Seth jerked his fingers off fast. They were wet, icy cold.

And all around him the glass pebbles had begun to melt.

"Where is this?"

Your garden.

She smiled. "It's very beautiful."

It was. A great field of green, misty at the edges. Trees met overhead, enormous trees such as she had never imagined, heavy with leaves, cool with shadow. And water, in fountains, ran splashing down smooth rock faces, trickling through ferns and mossed stones and over the algaed faces of fauns and nymphs carved in twisting dance under the rainbows of waterfalls.

Everything dripped and trickled. Petals dropped into cool wells. Bright unknown birds flitted and rustled and sang odd, sweet notes of song.

The garden of the Rain Queen.

"Does this mean I'm dead?" She looked around, saw she was sitting on a cool stone step. Beside her a blue bowl held six ripe oranges. Their color astonished her. She took one and began to peel it, digging her nails into the thick pith, tearing it back, the juice running down her fingers. The smell was intense, mouthwatering.

Do you feel dead?

"No. But there was a snake." Her fingers paused, then she tugged the orange apart fiercely, and sucked it. "I'm so thirsty! And hot."

Mirany. We need your help. Will you take the water in your hands and pour it on the step?

She laughed, the sweet juice running down her cheeks. "To make rain? Is that how it's done?"

Please. Be quick. I do not want to go back to Karim.

The name meant nothing to her, but she put the orange pith to float in the small stream and watched it bob away under the low green shade. Then she cupped water in her hands and drank, and filled them again. And again.

Hurry.

"Like this?"

She opened her fingers. The water splashed onto the step, soaked up dust, trickled, ran.

It was water. Real water.

Seth stared, backed away. "God," he hissed, his voice hoarse. "Look!"

Oblek swung round.

The sea of glass pebbles surged and shimmered. They clicked against each other, became each other, were a glistening mass, flowed round Seth's waist, foaming, a sudden weight of water that poured roaring over the lip of the stairs in a phosphorescent cascade. Oblek grabbed the wall, staggered, then yelled with triumph. "Archon!" he breathed. "What have you done!"

Emerald, energizing water. It thundered and crashed, and from below the men screamed and were hurled back and washed away, and Seth hung on to Alexos, dragging him against the smooth cave wall, staring wildly round, blinded by spray, deafened by the echoes. Where was it coming from?

How could this happen?

Alexos clung tight. He looked dazed. Behind and above him Seth saw light, not the eerie glimmer of the water on rock, but paler, a cold dawn light. Oblek had seen it, too; the musician forced his way back against the torrent, its thrust making him stagger, its foam creaming against his chest.

"Up! Up there!"

Yes, there was a way up, but she didn't want to take it. Lying here was calm, the grass under her body, the faint tickle of it against her heels.

Green shadows moved over her closed eyelids.

"Climb up!" Oblek was yelling over the roar of the waterfall. "There's a crack. We can get through."

"No," she said lazily. "Not yet."

We have to, Mirany. There have always been cracks and passages in the earth. Gods move along them, up from the Underworld, from the streams and the darkness.

"I'm not a god. I like it here."

The Oracle is a crack in the world.

"I know. But I just want to sleep."

And water, it rises, doesn't it, from deep wells? Do what he says, Mirany. Please.

So they climbed through the black shiny rock. Seth slipped and smacked his elbow and hissed a furious curse; above him the boy moved easily and happily, hauling himself up on thin arms as if the chimney of rock was a place to play in, and behind, Oblek wheezed and heaved his great bulk from foothold to foothold, squeezing through. Breathless, Seth thought about Pa and Telia and Mirany. God knows where they thought he was. And his job—would she make that all right, like she'd said? Maybe she wasn't such a mousy little thing after all. But he was finished with her after this.

Up and up. Through darkness until the rock began to pale, become transparent, as if the earth's skin was broken and letting them through, and hand pulled hand up, and she could see him now, just ahead, the young god from the temple, leaning down and saying, **Not much farther, Mirany. You'll see. We can get there.**

It really was dawn. It was a glow over the desert, and as Seth crawled out onto the massif the sun burst over the far horizon to welcome him, and Alexos was standing there, breathless, staring out at it with a grin on his face. Their long, spindly shadows stretched behind them, mingled over the rocks. And far on the horizon, the sea glimmered, dark as wine.

"Get me up, will you!" Oblek was almost exhausted. Together they dragged him out of the opening, a vast weight, and he collapsed on the top, splayed, coughing and gasping for breath.

Seth wiped sweat from his hair.

They were all soaked to the skin.

The hands were cool and touched her face with water, and she knew she was surfacing from the swimming pool, through the floating mat of petals, because the petals clung to her cheekbones, blurred her eyelids, even after she'd opened them, even after the sunlight had burst in on her through the window of the room.

Well done, Mirany, the voice said.

"It's me, Mirany. Can you hear me?"

And the sunlight was on Chryse's anxious face, and the water was in a jug by the bedside.

WHAT BETTER PLACE FOR A GOD TO HIDE?

Seth stood on the deck with the cloak wrapped loosely about him and scrutinized the Port. From this far out no one would recognize him, but the linen hood was over his head, and he leaned his chin on crossed arms, feeling the hot smooth wood scorch his skin.

The sea was deep, and blue, and dolphins swam in it, their fins scoring the water. To his right, rising steep and strange out of the waves was the Island, with its complex of white buildings, the tiled facade of the Temple, its brilliant flowers and the goats that climbed its slopes.

He had never been on the Island. Most men weren't allowed. He had no idea how to get onto it now.

Oblek was below, snoring. Since they'd bribed the merchant to take them on at Prescia he had slept, a snuffling, sweating bulk in a dim corner. The boy had sat on the deck for the whole journey; Seth looked at him now, sidelong.

His legs were over the side and he was watching the dolphins in a sort of fascinated joy. He hadn't eaten or spoken all afternoon.

Gloomily Seth watched the Port as they sailed in. The houses were stacked one above another, cascading down the perpendicular cliffs of the drowned volcano in a waterfall of white roofs and walls and arches and stairs; the steep streets zigzagging, the marble of the Archon's Palace high above on the lip of the desert, a blaze of sunlight.

It was very quiet. Even from here he could sense how the town sagged under the relentless heat, its awnings drooping, its walls and tiles too hot to touch, the fierce glare of reflected light dazzling the eyes. No one was about; walking on the cobbles would be painful, the heat burning through sandals. Even the cats had sought the shade, and the paint on the fishing boats scorched and blistered on the oily sea.

As the ship coasted in to moor and the crew ran down the sails, he smelled the eternal fish stench of the quays, and behind it, spices and the faint tang of rotting fruit. He looked carefully along the small knots of workers, keeping his head low. Fishermen, idlers, traders, the usual mix of foreigners and desertmen. Three, no, four of Argelin's soldiers, sitting in the shade with their feet up on a barrel. A dead dog in a corner.

The soldiers were the problem. This morning, as the ship had put out, he had been certain he'd seen Karim and the other villagers pushing their way furiously through the crowd on the beach at Prescia, though the ship had been too

far out to be sure, and when he'd asked Alexos, the boy had
shrugged and smiled and said nothing. What use was a god
who had no answers? If Karim had ridden hard from there
all day, he might have made it here overland before them,
and might even be on this quay. The sleepy afternoon might
be a trap. Or if he'd gone straight to Argelin . . .

Seth straightened. "Get Oblek," he called, and the boy
slithered up and ran below, the same secret smile on his face.
Should you order the Archon around? He had no idea, and
after that amazing flood in the dry cave, the boy terrified
him anyway. He just wanted to get him to Mirany and stay
out of it.

Besides, he had the Jackal to worry about.

Before the familiar dread of that betrayal could sink into
him, Oblek climbed up, his big hands heaving his bulk out
of the dark. Yawning, he looked along the quay. His eyes
were puffy, half-closed against the light. But Seth wasn't
fooled; by now he knew how shrewd the musician was.

"Four of Argelin's men."

"Think they're waiting for us?"

"Possibly." The musician scratched his sunburned face.
"No sign of Mirany."

"She'd hardly come here."

Oblek grunted, agreeing.

"And we're not taking *him* to Pa's place." Seth's voice
was quiet; as the ropes were tossed ashore the boat swung
in and grated against the stone steps. Oblek hung on,
unsteady.

"Where else—"

"No." Seth was firm. "I've had enough. He's yours now. You get him to the Island. You do what you want, but leave me out of it."

"Cocky little tyke, aren't you." Oblek sounded amused. "After all, I saved your skin back there. What if I tell the girl about that little gold brooch you're carrying round?" Suddenly he stiffened. "Look there."

The crew were off-loading the cargo, barrels of oil, their skin shining with sweat. Between them a thin man had slipped, shoved something into one of their hands and was gone again in seconds, into the shade of an alley. "That was your father."

Seth knew it. He glanced at the soldiers. None of them seemed to have noticed.

The sailor climbed the ramp wearily. "Message." He threw a longing glance at the nailed-up water barrel and trailed back down.

Oblek opened the paper. "Scribe scribble." He sounded disgusted, and handed it over.

Seth read quickly.

The house is being watched. Probably so am I. The girl will be waiting at the land end of the bridge one watch before sunset and you have to get the boy there. Take the fat man, too, because I don't want him here. And for the god's sake get yourself out of this mess. Telia is well.

◆   ◆   ◆

It wasn't signed, but he recognized the clumsy letters. Quickly he raised his eyes and scanned the shady entrances to the alleyways.

"Well?" Oblek hissed.

Seth smiled, relief from a forgotten worry warming him. "My sister is better."

"And?"

"Mirany will be at the bridge a watch before sunset."

"The bridge! How do we get there?"

Seth looked at Alexos, who was lying on his stomach dropping iridescent scales into the blue depths. "Ask the Archon. Maybe he can turn us all into fish."

The door closed. Mirany sat up in the bed instantly, though it made her dizzy again. "Quick, Chryse, listen! You have to do something for me."

It was the first time they had been alone. Either Rhetia or Callia or Ixaca had been here all morning, the tall girl frankly bored, the others sewing or chatting or trying out Mirany's few glass flasks of perfume till the room stank of scent.

Chryse looked startled. "Sit still. You're not supposed to get up until tonight."

"There's nothing wrong with me."

"And that's such a miracle, Mirany, do you know that! The god bit you."

"It wasn't the god." But her head ached, and she was sweating. She leaned back on the pillows and said carefully,

"I want you to do something for me. But it's a secret. You must promise . . . you must swear to me you'll never tell anyone, not even Hermia."

Chryse's blue eyes were wide. "I knew it," she said. "I knew you were up to something."

She came and sat on the bed eagerly. "What is it? It's a boy, isn't it? Oh, Mirany, I'd never have thought you—"

"Be quiet." She didn't have time for this. Already the afternoon was half-over, and Rhetia would be back at any second. "Put a cloak on and go to the land end of the bridge. Wait there, and make sure no one sees you. Two men will come, a young one and a fat, older one. They should have a boy with them—"

"Oh, *Mirany!*"

"A ten-year-old boy."

That silenced her. Her eyebrows shot up. "Ten!"

Mirany caught her hand. "Chryse, listen. Get this into your head. This is no love tryst. The boy is one of the candidates for the new Archon. In fact, I believe he is the Archon, the God-in-the-World. I really believe that."

The blond girl shook her head, bewildered. "But the candidates are being fetched by Argelin. Nine of them, with their parents and everything. To the general's house."

"Those that Argelin wants, yes. Look, I haven't got time to explain everything, but we think Argelin and Hermia are setting up a puppet Archon. Their own choice. They'll rule through him, and that can't be allowed to happen."

But Chryse was almost tearful now. "Don't be silly! Hermia speaks to the god—"

"No." She took a deep breath and said it. "She only pretends to. The god speaks to me, Chryse. To me."

The room was silent. Through the open windows the faintest of sea breezes drifted the gauzy hangings.

Chryse was staring at her, aghast.

Mirany said quickly, "I know, you think I'm delirious, but I'm not."

"How? How does he?"

It was a whisper of horror. Mirany felt Chryse's hand pull out of hers.

"I don't know how. In my head. Through the Oracle."

The fair girl sat on the bed. She seemed numb. Mirany said anxiously, "He's told me what to do. It's all right! We think—"

"Who's we?"

She hesitated. "Their names don't matter. If you don't know, you can't give them away."

It was a mistake. Chryse looked terrified. "Oh, Mirany, what are you mixed up in! It's a conspiracy, against the Temple!" She jumped up. "I won't get involved. I just won't."

Outside, in the loggia, low voices conversed, coming closer. Rhetia. And Hermia.

There was no time to be cautious.

Mirany knelt up and hissed in a low, hard voice, "Do this for me, Chryse, or I'll never speak to you again. I mean it. Fetch the boy onto the Island. Take him to the Temple. Hide him there."

"*The Temple!*"

"Yes! What better place for a god to hide?"

Chryse opened her mouth wide, but before she could gasp out anything, the door opened and Hermia swept in. She came straight up to the bed and said, "How are you feeling, Bearer?"

Mirany was still with tension. "Better. Thank you." She glanced across the room; Chryse was standing rigid, frozen with fear. For a second Mirany knew that she would blurt it all out, wail out that she couldn't do it, would never do it. Hermia said without turning, "You may go, Chryse. Rhetia and Callia will stay with her now."

There was an agonizing second of utter silence.

Then, without a word, Chryse went to the door. As she backed out she flashed one blank look at Mirany. The door clicked shut.

Slowly Mirany lay back on the pillows, making herself relax. Chryse would do it. She had to.

"You will be fit for the House of Gathered Goods?" Hermia asked coolly.

"Yes, of course."

"It was a strange thing that happened." Hermia went to the window and looked out at the blue sea. She was wearing a white dress that rippled, and the tall headdress of the Speaker; she looked austere and calm, and for a moment the whole notion of her being a traitor was utterly ridiculous.

Until she turned, and said sharply, "Why would the god give you this warning, Mirany? What have you done to offend him?"

Mirany felt her face redden. "I don't know," she whispered.

Hermia came and stood over the bed. "No? I have asked the Oracle. He has spoken to me. He is not pleased with you. He says you have a secret that you keep from him. Tell me what it is, Mirany. There should be nothing hidden from the god."

For a moment they were face-to-face.

Hermia sat down on the silk sheets. She smelled of lavender and lemons. Her fingers had sharp long nails; they reached out and picked up a small fruit knife from the table, turning it over.

Mirany inched back, into the pillows.

Quietly she said, "I have no secrets from the god, Speaker."

Hermia was still. She held the knife tight. She barely breathed.

And then the door opened and Rhetia came in and sat down, looking bored.

The Speaker stood quickly. "Who sent for you?"

Rhetia stared. "You did, Speaker. You told me . . . "

"It doesn't matter! Be silent!" She dropped the fruit knife onto the sheets, and turned abruptly to the door. "I'll pray for you, Mirany," she snapped. It was more like a threat.

When she had gone, Mirany sank back and closed her eyes in relief. She could hear Rhetia's needle and thread pulling angrily through the cloth, and beyond that, faint in the distance, a soft slap of waves at the foot of the cliff.

She was in such danger. Thinking of it brought a sharp pain to her side. But she'd get better, be there tonight, at the sixth house.

And yes, it was a miracle she was still alive.

You did that, she thought. *You saved me.* Then, urgently, *Where are you now?*

There was no answer.

He Was Playing at Being God

It had to be the Jackal's men who were watching Pa's. Surely Argelin couldn't have found out Seth had been at Alectro. Though the optio at the garrison had seen him clearly. A few inquiries . . . Creeping through the littered alley, hooded, with the begging bowl ready to thrust out at anyone who came close, Seth scratched his painted scabs and worried.

Oblek uttered an agonized groan. He had been doing that every few seconds, ringing the plague bell and groaning, and Seth was getting sick of it. "You're overacting," he snarled.

The musician shrugged, the soiled bandages round his face creasing. "I've played at the theater. I know how to overact."

They were halfway there. The steep streets of the Port were empty, the sun too hot. Only starving cats watched them, and Alexos had long since pulled off his tightly tied bandages and was walking behind, light and calm.

"Look at him!" Seth fumed. "Anyone might recognize him."

"He's filthy and bruised enough." Oblek came to a corner and peered round it; instantly he whipped back, and swore so viciously Seth went cold.

"What!"

"Soldiers. Grab him."

Seth ran, caught the boy and yanked him down against a wall. Oblek threw himself beside them; they covered faces, put the begging bowl down. "Curl up," Seth snapped. "As if you're asleep."

Alexos laughed, but he did it.

Flies buzzed in the heat. Mosquitoes bit Seth's arms. "Don't talk," he hissed, desperate, at Oblek. "It's you they're looking for."

The soldiers strode round the corner quickly, an escort, armed. Behind them a litter was swaying, carried by six men gleaming with sweat. The curtains were drawn back.

A boy sat inside. He was small, his face smooth and well fed. He wore a sumptuous robe of gold and red, which must have been nearly unbearable in the heat, Seth thought, but the boy seemed unconcerned. He lay swaying on fine silks, drinking from a cup. Beside him was a woman, her face veiled, and another, younger, with dark hair.

The boy caught Seth's eye, and sat up. "Stop!" he called.

"Oh god," Oblek breathed.

The slaves staggered to a halt.

"Lower the litter." The boy's voice was high and commanding, but before he could be obeyed, the guard captain had halted his men and come running back.

"Sir. You must not—"

"Don't tell me what to do. I am to be Archon, aren't I? I want to give these beggars a gift."

"It's not safe, sir. They have a disease."

The boy looked put out; his mother, if that was the veiled woman, said anxiously, "Tell the men to go on."

"No." The boy leaned out. "You! Come here! If I'm Archon, I won't catch anything, will I?"

Seth couldn't move. Beside him Oblek groaned. This time for real. Then Argelin came round the corner with a group of riders.

Instantly the musician stiffened. Seth felt fear shoot through him. "Don't do anything hasty," he whispered behind the wrappings. "Stay calm."

"What's happening?" Argelin sounded hot and weary. "Theo, get back in the litter."

"Uncle, I want to give these men a coin."

"Then throw it, and move on. They're poxed." He glared at the bearers. "Now! Before the candidate is infected and I have your hides!"

Beside Seth, someone moved. Before he could stop him, Alexos had jumped up; already he was at the litter, looking up at the boy with his strange smile. "Are you really to be Archon?" he asked.

The boy took a coin from his mother and threw it, self-important. "Yes. This is to buy water."

The silver rang and rolled on the cobbles to Oblek's feet. The big man's fingers grabbed it.

For a moment Seth feared he would hurl it back, then they both froze as Alexos said gravely, "Being a god hurts. Did you know that? They'll think you know the answers. They will expect you to bring rain. All the silver drops. Will you make them fall like that coin from the sky?"

The boy stared at him, blank, a little afraid. Seth scrambled up, limped forward, but the boy wailed "Uncle!" and Argelin was there, and with a vicious slash of his riding whip he knocked Alexos flying, back into Seth; they both fell, a crumple of pain.

"Move on," the general growled.

Jerkily, quickly, the litter swayed off.

The general called one of the guard back. "Get this rabble out of the Port! The desert gate."

"Right, sir. Move, you."

Alexos was bleeding. He touched the red flow with his fingers, looking at it in awe. With a mutter of wrath Oblek mopped it, examined the wound carefully, and swore.

"He dies for this, for sure."

"Shut up." Picking himself up, Seth watched the guard. He was young, and now that the general was gone, a little nervous. He had a parade spear; he held it out, prodded Seth's back, and said, "Don't you come any closer, any of you scabheads. Start walking. Well ahead."

In one way, it was a godsend. No one looked at them or talked to them; they were marched, limping and sore and silent, straight up to the desert gate; the gate was opened and they were thrust out onto the road.

"And don't come back," the guard said, nodding for the bars to fall.

Outside it was hotter than ever. The desert shimmered; a billion cicadas rasped in its wave of heat. Seth sipped some precious water, then Oblek took a great swig and passed it to Alexos. "Drink, Archon. We'll soon have you safe."

The road to the bridge was empty of travelers or pilgrims. They tramped its length and once they reached the cliff edge, collapsed into the furzy bushes that lined the track, desperate for shade. With the last of the water Oblek bathed the long cut on the boy's face, and muttered, "You shouldn't have spoken to him, old friend."

"I had to, Oblek. It was all a game to him. He was playing at being god."

"Not for long."

"That sort of game never finishes. Inside him, it will go on."

"Whatever you say, Archon. But you should lie down now and rest, eh? We'll see you safe. You're with me now."

Alexos smiled, wan. "I'm glad you came for me, Oblek." He turned. "And you, Seth."

Seth shrugged. "When you're Archon you can pay me back."

The boy nodded, and lay down. His eyes closed.

Quietly, so that Oblek could not hear, he whispered, "There's a jackal near. I can smell him."

Rigid, Seth stared at him. Then he stood and looked round slowly. The scrubland stretched, empty, to the walls of the Port. Across the desert the City of the Dead glowered, a darkness in the draining light, and behind it the sun was sinking into the Mountains of the Moon, the mysterious high range that marked the edge of the world, ominous, jagged peaks that no one had ever crossed. Out at sea, the Island, close and pale, glimmered in the twilit haze that seemed to rise from its fragrant gardens.

"Sit down." Oblek leaned back with a sigh and unwound the filthy bandages. "She's late. Are you sure she said—"

"I'm sure."

"Think we've been followed?"

"No." He sat slowly. Had the boy meant a real jackal? Or did he know, as the god must know, about Sostris's tomb?

Alexos already seemed asleep, curled on the stony track. Oblek looked at him fondly. "Wait till he's Archon. There'll be some changes."

"Will it rain?" Seth's throat was raw.

"What?"

"Will it rain? Because the last one couldn't do that."

"He *is* the last one." The musician propped himself up on one arm. "And yes, there will be rain, and enough for everyone to eat, and lower taxes. And a new general."

"You, I suppose?" Seth turned to face him. "Are you really so stupid that you think you can assassinate Argelin and take his place? You'll get us all killed, Mirany, me, Pa, him."

Oblek was watching him closely. Finally he said, "I am that stupid. So are you, pretty boy. Because for Alexos to be Archon means Argelin has to die. There is no other way, and we're already bound to the god's service. You think you can back out now, sneak back to being a scribe, bury your head in dust and documents? Well, you can't. Because sometime, somehow, the god spoke your name. You took a step too far and here you are. None of us can ever go back. Even if we wanted to."

Despite the heat Seth was chilled. He was sweating and tormented with thirst, and ants were crawling up his back. He scrambled up. "I could go right now."

Oblek gave a sidelong smirk. "You couldn't."

"Watch me."

"He won't let you. Not till this is finished."

Seth wiped his dry mouth. "I'm going home. And you'll never see me again."

But before he could breathe, before he could turn, Alexos sat up and whispered, "Someone's coming!"

Seth whirled, saw a flicker of pale linen on the bridge.

He rang the plague bell quickly, and stepped back off the road, covering his face. "Give food, lady, water," he muttered. "For the god's sake."

The girl stopped, breathless, and her mantle slipped.

She was small and blond and very pretty. She wasn't Mirany.

She looked at them and the boy. Then she whispered, "Is that *him*?"

Alexos did something very strange. He walked up to her and took her hand. Then he kissed it gravely. It was the act of a grown man. "I am the Archon," he said.

The girl looked flustered, terrified. She knelt briefly and went red, then scrambled up and said in a sort of wail of fear, "I have to take him to the Temple."

"Where's Mirany?" Oblek growled.

"In bed. She was bitten by the god. The snake."

"Who are you?"

"Chryse. I'm Taster-for-the-God. Now listen—"

"How do we know that?" Seth said quietly. The Nine wore masks. He had never seen any of them uncovered except Mirany.

The girl all but stamped her foot. "Because I am! I say I am! I have to take him to the Temple, and we have to hurry. Before Hermia finds out!"

She was plainly terrified. Seth threw a glance at Oblek but the big man had his hands around the boy's shoulders, and pushed him forward. "Now's your chance then," he growled at Seth. "Get back to your job in the City. Abandon all of us."

"It might be a trap." He felt torn. He wanted to get out of all of this, and yet he was surprised how anxious for them he felt. Alexos shook his head gravely.

"Don't worry, Seth."

"No, don't." Oblek looked at the girl. "He'll be all right. Because I'm going with him."

She was white with fear. "You can't!" she hissed. "It's the Temple! Only the Nine and the god enter it! Anyone else they catch will be tortured to death."

Carelessly Oblek pulled the bandages off and scratched his sweaty head. "What do you say, Archon?"

Alexos put his hand up to the big man. His dark eyes watched Chryse. "I'd love you to come and see my house, Oblek," he said proudly.

The sixth house was enormous, and already full. Around the Archon's vast coffin they had piled his furniture, each piece specially made, gilded and carved, tables and stools and an elegant bed. Linens were heaped in stacks, lamps and statues and chests of clothes and money. A great fan of ostrich feathers was propped against one wall; below it the distorted shadows of huge jars of oils and perfumes and unguents darkened a damask hanging of monkeys in a green forest. Polished to bronze brilliance, a propped mirror showed Mirany a dim slanted reflection of her own face.

The ritual was over, and the sixth of the Nine, Ixaca, had to spend the night here. She was looking around in apprehension. Servants and tomb workers moved silently in the shadows, fetching more and more pots and vases and food vessels.

"You'll be safe. There are guards outside," Mirany said.

She wondered why; no one would dare to come here. Even tomb robbers were not that reckless.

"I know." Calmly Ixaca lit the last of the lamps and stood back. Shadows flickered among the heaped artifacts. Gold and bronze gleamed softly. "Thanks for staying, Mirany, but I'm sure I'll be fine. It's just like a vigil in the Temple, after all. I'm not afraid of the Archon."

Maybe not now, Mirany thought. She wasn't looking forward to her own turn at this. But she nodded, said, "See you tomorrow," and slipped out.

The City of the Dead was a black labyrinth around her. As she walked between the guards they stiffened slightly; then she was crossing the vast windy spaces before the ziggurat; it rose high into the sky, the smoke from its beacon drifting across the stars.

The night was hot, even now. She hadn't stayed for Ixaca's sake. There had been no way of talking to Chryse during the ceremony; when she had tried to edge close, Rhetia had been there, and only once had she caught a glance from Chryse's blue eyes, looking frightened in the narrow slits of the blue-and-silver mask.

But she had to find out if the boy had been brought to the Temple. That meant going there, now everyone else had gone.

"Mirany!"

The voice was quiet and stopped her instantly. For a moment she thought it was the god. Then she glanced around.

He was waiting in the shadows of one of the gateways; she ran across the moonstriped emptiness of the plaza and slid in beside him.

"Seth! Did you find him?"

"We found him."

He looked very tired, she thought. "What happened?"

"It was a nightmare. The boy—Alexos—his stepfather followed us. I think we lost him at the Port, but he'll certainly go to Argelin. Your friend came and took the boy and Oblek to the Temple."

"*Oblek!*" She was aghast. "I didn't mean Oblek to go!"

"Well, he won't leave him. Says it's the Archon . . . it's scary, Mirany, how they knew each other! It scares me. And the boy created water; he made water out of stones!"

Something triggered in her memory; she tried to catch it, but it slid down a tunnel in her mind like a snake. "Stones?"

"Yes. The girl said that you were bitten by a snake."

Mirany went red. "I'm fine. Sometimes a bit dizzy, but fine."

Seth wasn't listening. He stood away from her and she could see he was working himself up to something. The moon caught the darkness of his hair, the glint of some purse string round his neck.

"Mirany, listen to me. I don't want any more part in this. I've done what you asked, brought you the boy. Now I'm finished. I won't betray you, I won't say a word. But you can't ask me to get mixed up with it anymore. Oblek, he's dangerous. Fanatical. He might do anything! And I've got Pa and Telia to think about."

Mirany looked past him to the flames of the ziggurat. The disappointment she felt was a shock; it felt like fear. She murmured, "If you feel like that . . . "

"Take this." He was holding something out; as he pushed it into her hand she saw it was wrapped in linen, a small, hard thing. "Call it an offering for the god. I came across it."

"We'll miss you." Without his help, what would they do, she thought.

He shrugged, that arrogant, annoying way he had. "Good luck with everything. I hope things . . . work out."

"Work out."

"Well, you know . . . "

"That I don't die, you mean. That Oblek doesn't die."

Seth scowled. "Yes."

"That Argelin doesn't have us all killed, and then take over. That he doesn't tyranize the people any more than he needs to."

"Look, you have to understand."

"Oh, I *understand*." Her bitterness amazed him; it seemed to blaze out of her. "You're just like all the rest. If you get enough to eat and drink you're happy. If you can bribe and threaten and blackmail your way up to be first archivist, you're happy. And everyone else can rot!"

He stepped back, cold with controlled anger. "I didn't say that. But since you obviously think it—"

"I do. And we can manage without you." She had pulled the thin mantle so tight round her shoulders it almost tore. "The god doesn't need a conceited little scribe. Oblek was right."

She turned, but he caught her arm and pulled her back. "What do you know about work? When have you ever had to worry about getting enough to eat, saving and scrimping enough to pay for water? All my life we've been as poor as dirt, Mirany. To get them food, water, you have no idea what depths I've had to sink to! Look at you! Rich and spoiled and thinking you can hear the god! We can all hear the god, Mirany; it doesn't take an Oracle!"

"Let me go!"

He did; she jerked away furiously.

"And don't tell me your family didn't bribe you into the Nine." He smiled scornfully. "They'd never have accepted you otherwise."

The moon slanted between them, a silver streak. Mirany's hands were clenched on the tiny gift. For a moment he thought she would throw it in his face, then she turned, and ran, over the slabs of the courtyard, toward the shadowy gate.

Silent, bitter with shame and anger, he watched her go.

THE SIXTH HOUSE
OF THE GATHERED GOODS

I have cried and laughed and now I have bled. This has all happened before, many times, but each time it seems new. As if I have indeed grown young, become innocent.

Last night I lay in the desert, and it was my body. Hot and fevered it lay under the stars. Beyond the Mountains of the Moon, around the curve of the earth, my shadow stretched, and within me scratched and crawled small living things.

I was sand and rock. My innards were crusted with gems. My heart was molten.

Then this was a dream, and lice in my clothes.

To Tell a Secret Is to Drop a Stone in the Pool

She hadn't been able to sleep. At first she had been too angry, lying awake arguing furiously with the ceiling, and then when that had faded out of her, it had been too hot, the gauzy draperies in her room not stirred by the slightest breeze. Even the sea had sounded weary, breaking in exhaustion on the rocks below. Finally she had got up and sat on the windowsill, drinking water, and had remembered the small linen parcel and opened it.

The scorpion brooch looked up at her with its jeweled eyes. Amazed, she fingered it. Surely it was hers, the one she had given the god! There was the slight dent in the tail, though now the pin was bent. She had stared at it in terror. She had given it to the god, so how had Seth come by it? Had the boy given it to him? Because the boy was the god?

Shock wore down into wonder, into resentment. She had climbed back into bed and curled up. Whatever it meant, he was gone. They'd never see him again.

Now, in the drowsy familiarity of the dawn Ritual, she watched the god being dressed, and brooded on the food laid at his feet, the precious water that the parched children of the Port would have fought over, the fruits and bread and sweetmeats. He smiled at her, over their heads.

"Are you really here?" she asked him.

She prayed he was. There had been no chance to talk to Chryse, though the blond girl had managed a breathless giggle of excitement on the way in, so meaningful and hastily smothered that the rest of the girls had stared. Outside the masked circle of the Nine, the building was dark. Sunlight slanted in behind through the open door, a long slit, but it barely pierced the silent crowd of pillars, a confusion of darknesses, their plinths and cornices, corners and alcoves and empty adjoining rooms dim and cob-webbed, softened with sand that had slid in overnight and made the floor gritty.

Hermia spoke the prayers remotely, with her usual grace. When she had finished, she gave one masked glance at Mirany, and turned, leading the procession out, the hems of their robes sweeping small ripples of sand into waves on the paving, like meanders on a beach. Mirany waited behind. She took off the heavy mask with relief, then crossed to the side of the statue and lit a small lamp, filling it slowly with the pungent sacred oils, stirring them, mak-ing the flame carefully from the tiny tinderbox left there.

No one came back to look for her. Breakfast was being

served in the Lower House, oranges and passion fruits and soft warm bread. Outside the cicadas scraped their hot chorus; a few seabirds called, far up over the cliffs. Very faintly, from the Port, came the horn to signal the opening of the gates.

The Temple was utterly silent. Mirany arranged the lamp, walked to the open doorway, looked out, and then tried to drag the great bronze door shut, but it had not been closed for decades, and the growl and hoarse scrape of it in the rutted paving would have brought all the Island servants racing.

She sighed, and walked back inside, her footsteps soft on the stones. Then she said quietly, "So where are you?"

There was silence, and she was suddenly afraid that Chryse had failed after all. Then a shadow disengaged itself from a pillar and became a fat, shaven-haired man, stubbled and weary.

"Oblek!" She crossed to him quickly. "Is he here? Did you find him?"

"We found him." The musician smiled his leering smile. "He's behind you."

She turned quickly.

He was tall for his age, and his hair was black. His face, though bruised and dirty, was the face of the statue; she looked up at it, startled, as if to make sure it was still there, had not come to life, but it smiled at her gravely, just as he did.

"Hello, Mirany," he whispered.

For a second she had no idea what to do. She should

kneel, but that seemed strange, and anyway he had caught both of her hands and had swung her arms wide and was looking at her.

"You're just like I thought you would be! In my dreams I saw you, and in the garden. Remember the garden? Where the water ran and rippled?"

Confused, a little afraid, she nodded.

"And me? Am I like you thought?"

She gave a quick glance at Oblek. "Yes. You . . . you are."

"That's all right then." Shy, oddly satisfied, he dropped her fingers and turned to the god's offerings, spread out on the small gilt tables. Horrified, she saw how he broke open the white bread and ate it, and handed some to Oblek.

The big man's hand took it, but even he licked his lips with a sort of fear. "Archon . . . "

"My son, I am the god on earth. This is my feast. And I don't want my friends to be hungry." A strange voice. It echoed oddly in the hundred pillars of the hall, and the flames of the lamp flickered, and the words seemed immensely old and distant.

But only a boy poured water from the jug, carefully, spilling a little so that it fell in round dusty drops on the pavement.

He drank thirstily. Then he said. "My mother called me Alexos. That will do till I am Archon."

Mirany turned quickly to Oblek. "They'll notice the food is gone."

"Say the god ate it," he said, shrugging.

She wanted to scream. Instead she made a great effort to be calm and said, "Move deeper into the hall. Keep silent, and don't let him go outside. No one will come here until the Ritual tomorrow, but I'll be back tonight, to check you're all right."

He nodded sourly. Alexos had poured some of the water into the lustral basin, and was washing his face with it. Sand and dirt were scrubbed off. His hair flattened and gleamed under the splashing cascades. He laughed softly.

Oblek drew her aside. "Leave him to me. Tomorrow is the House of Red Flowers, right?"

Unhappy, she nodded.

He laughed, a short harsh sound. "Good thing I haven't been caught, or my throat would be cut then with the rest of them. Will the boy be safe here until the ninth house?"

"He ought to be. But, Oblek"—she stepped closer to him—"you'll stay with him, won't you? You *can't* leave the Temple. If they found you anywhere on the Island . . . "

"Don't fret yourself, lady." He leaned his great hand against a pillar and looked down at her, chewing the bread. "Oblek has a shrewd head. I'm not as sunstruck as you might think."

For a moment then, for the first time since she had met him, she felt as if all his bluster and rudeness was some deliberate act, some hiding of himself. As if underneath there was another man, only discovered half-drunk, late at night, playing softly on the lute.

He laughed, and swallowed, and turned away.

At the doorway she looked back, but the pillared hall was a blackness crowded with shadows, the star of the lamp deep inside it.

The heat and glare of the morning was fierce; it seemed something solid that she had to struggle through toward the Upper House, a shimmer in the courtyards and terraced gardens. Chryse was there, with some of the others, giggly and chatting, but the steward, Koret, was with them, supervising the sampling of great amphorae of scented oils sent up from some merchant as an offering. Mirany dodged away behind the hibiscus bushes before they saw her. She didn't want to hear Chryse's breathless gush of excitement anyway. Telling Chryse had put the whole plan in danger. She didn't trust Oblek, he was consumed with his plan for revenge. And the boy was . . . what?

The god.

She scowled. Seth was the only one with any sense. But Seth had walked out on them. Seth had made his feelings quite clear. She whipped a branch savagely out of her way, and ducked under an arch into the loggia of the Upper House.

And stopped instantly.

Argelin was there. He had his back to her, and he was talking to someone.

She jerked down. A heavy creeper of gloriously scarlet flowers smothered the face of the building; in its open blossoms an army of bees hummed and droned with relentless industry. Mirany edged closer, deep into the leaves, on hands and knees. The soil was baked hard, and hot.

Argelin was sitting on a bench in the shade, his armor unlaced, a cup in his hand. He said, "I assure you, my men have searched. The musician may really have taken ship and escaped. If the girl was responsible, I think you, lady mine, should deal with her, though from what I gather that's been tried already?" He smiled his sleek smile, and drank.

Hermia's voice was quietly rueful, and it came from the white marble balcony that jutted out over the sea. "She was lucky. Next time, she won't be."

"I thought you chose her because she was a little mouse."

"I did."

Mirany gave herself a small spiteful scowl.

"I may have misjudged her. This conspiracy is worse than we thought." The Speaker rose; she came and sat on the low warm stones at Argelin's feet, leaning back. Her hands were deep in the leaves, only inches from Mirany. Bees hummed between them.

"In what way?"

"There's a plot to place a boy on the Archon's throne."

Mirany went cold to her bones. But Argelin chuckled over his cup. "I know there is, lady. Our plot."

"Not ours. Another. That girl is part of it. One of the Nine is . . . shall we say, extremely loyal to me, and has told me all about it. I know a boy has been brought from Alectro—"

"Alectro?" Argelin stared. "We've had a report of some trouble there. Tiresome crowd of villagers outside my office all night, demanding to see someone. Abduction. Two men."

She nodded. "One is the musician."

"What?" He watched her, intent. "How do you know?"

"I know many things. I even know where the boy is hidden." She smiled archly. "Do you want me to tell you where?"

Mirany couldn't breathe. She thought she would choke, that the pains in her chest would make her gasp.

Argelin was sitting up now. Deliberately he put the cup down on a marble table. It made a tiny click. "Yes. Tell me."

Hermia pushed herself nearer. She reached up and took his hand, smoothing it with her own.

"Do you love me, Argelin?"

Grimly impatient, he muttered, "You know I do. But what—"

"I wonder." Hermia's gaze was a cool scrutiny; she watched him intently and her reddened lips did not smile. "If I was not the Speaker, would you still love me then? If Chryse was Speaker, or Rhetia, would it be her you loved?" Her grip was tight on his. "Are you making use of me, my general? Or are you telling me the truth?"

He was silent; for a second Mirany thought he would stand and fling her off. But he bent forward and caught her hands and kissed them, never taking his eyes off her face.

"You know that I love you. The power we have is equal,

General and Speaker. Neither of us could do this without the other. We are linked together, Hermia, in conspiracy, in success or failure, in death, and the land beyond death." His voice was low, his face intent.

She watched him, considering.

Mirany began, hurriedly, carefully, to inch back.

Ants were crawling over her hands.

"I suppose I believe you." The Speaker's words were a murmur.

"So tell me about this boy. Why choose him? Who is he?"

Hermia pulled away. She looked disturbed. "That's what I want to know." She was silent a moment, as if she feared his controlled anger would scorch her. Then she whispered, "I'm afraid . . . "

"There's no need."

"Afraid he might be the real Archon."

Argelin stared. Mirany froze. And then he burst out in a snort of contempt that astonished her. "The real Archon! The Archon is dead. We made sure of that. The god can enter the body of any boy we choose! The god isn't interested in who it is, anyone will do. But for us, Hermia, for us, it has to be a boy we can control. And you are the Speaker; you will know what the god wants, because the gift you have is special, is sacred. No one else can hear his words as you can hear them!" He grabbed her hands, tight. "You are not betraying the god. You are choosing the fittest vessel for him."

Her smile was unhappy. "Yes. I suppose . . . "

"Then where is this brat from Alectro?"

Hermia pulled out of his grip as if it hurt her. But she said, "He's here."

"Here?"

The ants were biting. Small red-hot pepper-points of pain. Mirany scarcely felt them. Bees rose above her, their hum loud. She heard " . . . the Temple . . . " and then " . . . death for the sacrilege alone."

She was out of the bushes.

Breathless, sweating, she ran. Through the gardens, almost knocking down one of the serving girls, out of the courtyard and across the open space to the Temple, high on its platform. Racing up the steps, she heard, behind in the house, a shout, and plunged into the inky forest of pillars.

"Oblek! *Oblek, it's me! For the god's sake, where are you!*"

Her scream had him out in seconds; unable to stop, she crashed into him.

"What? What!"

"They're coming! They know!" She pushed past him into the dark. "Where's the Archon?"

"Here, Mirany."

He was clean. And he had taken the white tunic off the statue and was wearing it, and the fine silver circlet of the god. She stared at him and he said, "Are they really coming already?"

"Yes!"

Oblek drew his knife. "Then Argelin dies here."

"Shut up. *Shut up*! Let me think!"

A man shouting, giving orders. A horn, blaring down on the bridge. She grabbed Alexos by the hand. "Come on."

Through the hypostyle hall they raced, shadows in the forest of pillars, threading the faded mythologies of the serpent and scorpion. At the back, behind the statue itself, was a small doorway, leading to a storeroom with steps in the corner, leading up.

"The roof?" Oblek gasped.

"We can get out. There's an outside staircase."

Racing up, she flung herself against the door; it was old and warped and never used, and wouldn't move until Oblek shoved her aside and barged it with his shoulder, and it cracked and burst wide, almost flinging him out into emptiness.

They were in the blue of the sky. Behind them the Temple parapet rose, a triangular façade; but the roof was flat and they ran across it, through years of accumulated birds' nests and fishbones.

"How?" Oblek gasped. "How could they know! That girl! It must . . . have been."

"If it was," Mirany hissed, "I'll strangle her myself."

At the back the Temple faced rock; the steps were ancient and crumbled. Alexos ran down and jumped. Oblek followed, falling heavily, then picking himself up to catch Mirany. "We've got to get off the Island!"

"No! This is the only place you'll be able to stay hidden." She pulled him behind a rock where Alexos crouched looking up at them calmly.

"Yes, but where?"

"Below. Down the cliff."

"God's eyes, girl, how do I get down a cliff?"

Mirany rubbed her face. "Through my window," she said quietly.

The Upper House was silent. They crept their way to it through the back courtyard, but all their precautions were hardly needed. The noise told them where everyone was, at the Temple, or at the bridge watching the squad of armed men marching hastily across.

Even so, they flitted down the bright sunlit terraces like ghosts, pale and terrified, and Mirany was consumed by terror that one of the doors would open, that Chryse would step out and scream, that Hermia would be waiting for her in her room, sitting in the chair with a smile of quiet contempt.

But her room was empty.

Hauling the bed out, Mirany jumped up on it and leaned over the sill. The cliff dropped steeply, the tiny goat path wandering away over a giddy outcrop of rock, losing itself in the gnarled olive trees.

"There!"

Oblek had squeezed up beside her. He swore briefly and then hauled his great bulk up onto the sill and swung himself over, dropping down so that only his fingers clung on, and then those were gone. A thud. Bushes rustled and scraped. He muttered, "Archon."

Alexos sat on the window ledge and looked back.

"Come with us, Mirany. If they know about me, they know about you."

"Yes." Undecided, she looked at him.

"You'll be in danger."

"I'm one of the Nine. I can't be replaced until I die, and I can't be touched by fire or sword or water. Only the god can . . ."

"There are always accidents," he said sadly. "A fall. A disappearance."

"No." She fought for breath to think. "No. I'll stay. I have to stay. This is my place. I can't let them drive me out, because I'm the Bearer, and I have to be there, at the ninth house."

"For the god's sake, come on!" Oblek roared.

Mirany pushed Alexos. "Jump. Hide on the cliff. I'll drop food from this window tonight, if I can."

He squirmed round, slid his legs over. Watching her, his smile was grave, his hair under the silver circlet dark. He did not speak.

But in her head, the voice said, *I will find us the rain, Mirany. I promise.*

He jumped just in time. Footsteps were pattering up the terrace, fast, light steps, and she shoved the bed back and spun around, and the door was hurled wide and Chryse ran in.

Her hair was loose and she was gasping for breath. "Mirany! They know! They're at . . ."

Mirany took two steps and grabbed her; shoved her

hard against the wall. "You betrayed me to Hermia!"

"No!" It was a squeal of terror; Chryse was almost sobbing. "Oh I didn't, Mirany, I wouldn't! You're my friend. I'd never . . ."

"Then who did you tell?"

"No one . . ."

"Liar!" Mirany released her and stepped back. She was furious, anger beating like a sharp pain behind one temple. "Liar, Chryse! Who did you tell?"

Chryse's shoulders rose and fell in a great sigh. A tear ran down her cheek and she wiped it away. Finally she looked up. Her face was white and stricken and Mirany knew the answer before she even whispered it.

"Rhetia. I told Rhetia."

What Is Death but the Most Scarlet of Flowers?

A shadow fell on the desk. It darkened the papers and the gleam in the black ink pot went out.

Hastily Seth grabbed his stylus and looked up.

But it wasn't the overseer. It was Kreon.

He was leaning on the broom handle and watching, his colorless eyes fixed on Seth's fist.

"Daydreaming," he whispered.

Seth felt hot. His desk was a mess, inventories uncopied, plans askew. He couldn't concentrate, kept thinking of Mirany's anger, of the boy, of Oblek's threats. Would he really try to assassinate Argelin? And then tomorrow night, he, Seth, would break into a tomb. "Some of us have a lot on our minds," he whispered dully.

"I know." The albino leaned over and swept a flicker of dust from the desk. His hands were thin, and pale as milk. Then he said, "What you found is mine."

"Found? I haven't found anything."

"The boy. The scorpion."

Seth's fingers were tight on the stylus. He put it down, dismayed to see how his fingers shook. He licked dry lips, wishing he had some water. "I don't know what you're talking about. Leave me alone."

Kreon ignored that. He squatted, leaning on the handle of the brush, knees up. His eyes were a faint pink, all wrong. "The scorpion is mine. It was an offering to the god; you stole it. All of it is mine."

"All of what?"

"The hidden jewels. The treasures of the Archons, far below. In the tunnels, the secret passageways."

Seth watched him, curious. "You mean the tombs, don't you. They say you sleep down there somewhere, that you've got some sort of den. That you've never been outside. Is that right?"

Kreon shrugged, knotting his spindly fingers round the broom. "What's to see outside? Empty sea, empty sky, empty sand." He looked at Seth calmly. "Down below the sun doesn't burn you, the wind doesn't scorch. There are no days and nights, no colors in the dark. No pigment."

He tapped Seth's pots of green and blue and gold inks with a scornful finger. "I have no use for colors. My brother, now, he enjoys them." Suddenly, with a quick, decisive movement, he stood up and said, "What have you done with the scorpion?"

His voice echoed down the hall. Seth glanced hastily round. "Keep it down! They'll hear!"

"Men don't hear, or see. All that sun blinds them." He brought the bottle of gold ink close to his weak eyes; the gleam of it shone on his white skin, a reflected aura. Then his eyes slid to Seth. "Once gold bites you, you are infected."

Seth was tired and suddenly angry. "I've given it as an offering. Did you think I'd keep it?"

Kreon considered him. "Yes," he said quietly.

"Well, you're wrong. Did you put it there? Have you been robbing the tombs?"

The thin shape bent with sudden, astonishing speed. *"I am not a jackal,"* he hissed, *"nor am I a fox."*

In the silence the whisper of a thousand styli cut hiero-glyphs of terror into Seth.

"What?" He felt numb. His heart thudded.

"Only this." Kreon leaned close, his milk-white hair long and tangled. "There is the god, and there's the shadow of the god. The shadow lives in dark places, in the depths. It watches. It sees. It guards the souls of the dead. Do you think you can threaten them without it knowing?"

He dropped the bottle and it fell on the desk with a crack. A few scribes turned to look. Seth slapped his hand on it instantly.

Kreon smiled. "Remember," he whispered.

Then he was gone up the long aisle, sweeping a small cloud of dust that made the men cough and swear at him and hastily cover their drying inks.

Seth sat in utter disbelief. How could he know? How? There was no way on earth. Unless . . . He huddled on the stool, knees up, struck by a thought. The Jackal. Professional tomb thieves must have some inside help. Maybe the albino was in on the plan. Maybe it was Kreon who had left the message on his desk.

And yet if so, why would the crazy fool warn him off? Unless he was running the same sort of operation, and didn't want competition.

For a moment Seth felt lost and bewildered and utterly sorry for himself. His whole life was a total mess. He was doing this for Pa and Telia, and there was no one he could explain that to. Pa wouldn't understand. Would be furious in fact. And now Mirany . . . there was no way she would ever speak to him again, except as some groveling little clerk, some pen pusher. Though he'd been right to back out, he thought defiantly; they were all mad, the plan was pathetic and without him to sort it out for them they were even less likely to survive, but . . . He bit the end of his stylus, brooding.

Maybe he could have pretended. Maybe—and the thought made him sit up—maybe he could go to Argelin now, and warn him. Stop it all.

But that was a black thought. So deep and terrible that he wouldn't let himself finish it. Alexos and Oblek would be killed, and Mirany . . . well, they couldn't hurt Mirany. Or could they?

Suddenly he stood, grabbed a file, and strode down the ranks of desks and up the steps to the gallery that ran all around under the roof of the hall. In the first alcove was a rack with the fat, tasseled rolls of the Precepts of the Temple stuffed into its pigeonholes, scholars' tags hanging from marked passages.

He pulled out a few, found the laws governing the conduct of the Nine, and unrolled it quickly.

"Seth!" The overseer's head came up the stairs. "Are you ready?"

"Just a minute. Checking something."

His inky finger moved quickly down the list. The words, when he found them, were small, a postscript, crammed into a margin, and as he read them he realized he had known them anyway, known exactly what they said.

> *The Nine may not be harmed. Their lives lie in the hands of the god. But should there be proven treachery, should one of them betray the Temple, her fate is this:*
> *To be buried alive, without air, without water, in the tomb of the Archon. Thus will the hands of men be clean, and the god unsullied.*

"Seth!"

He let the scroll go. It closed up with a slap.

And he had left her with a musician who might do anything and a boy who thought he was god.

"I had to tell her!"

Chryse sat on the bed and clutched her hands together in her lap. "I couldn't stop thinking about it all, Mirany, it was so . . . scary! Last night, she was in my room and she said what was I so secretive about, and I said I wasn't, and she went all haughty and said if I didn't trust her she didn't care and then I just felt as if I was bursting. . . . "

"But you knew she was trouble! Chryse, you're hopeless!" Mirany could have shaken her, could have slapped her. Instead she turned away and paced anxiously; at the door she went out and looked up the terrace. The Upper House was oddly quiet.

"They'll kill that boy." Chryse was white; her eyes stricken.

"They won't. He's not there anymore."

The face that turned to Mirany was such a caricature of amazement that she almost laughed. Instead she made herself sit down and pick up a scroll from the table.

"But how?"

"Listen." Mirany's voice was firm. "Stay calm. The Temple is empty, I promise you that. No one's there. They've got no proof of any of this."

"But Rhetia knows! She knows I'm part of it!"

"You'll have to say you made it up." Trying to look unconcerned, Mirany unrolled the book and found her place.

Chryse was speechless.

A door was flung open, far off. Voices echoed.

"I can't! Oh, how could you get me into this, Mirany!"

"I'm sorry. I couldn't think of anything else." Mirany settled the scroll on its stand. "Pick up that sewing. Quick! This is going to be the best performance of your life, Chryse. You owe me that."

But when the door opened, it was only Hermia who came in.

She looked at them both. "What a peaceful scene."

Her voice was so choked with anger that it sounded raw. Mirany made herself look up from her reading. "Speaker? Is something going on?"

Hermia stood tall, her hair immaculately controlled in its tiny curls, her strong angular face hard. "Don't insult me," she hissed, "by any pretense. What have you done with that boy?"

Mirany tried not to bite her lip. She forced herself to meet the dark, furious eyes.

"What boy?"

Her voice was so collected it impressed even her.

Hermia slammed the door so that Chryse jumped. "One word," she hissed, "one word from me—"

"Would do nothing." Mirany clenched her shaking hands. "I'm one of the Nine now. Not even Argelin can harm me, because if he tried, the god would punish him with plague and the bronze birds would rampage through his dreams, and he knows that."

She stepped forward. Something was happening inside her. It felt like something breaking. It felt like rain in her face. It said,

"Hermia."

The Speaker stared. "What did you say?"

"Hermia, listen to me. Do you hear me? Can you hear my voice?"

Chryse was standing. "Mirany, I don't think you should . . . "

But the words came out like a deluge, like a cloudburst. *"I try to talk to you but you shut your ears to me. I call out from the Oracle and you don't answer, no one has answered for such a long time! Being a god is lonely, Hermia. Buried so deep and so dark, with such a long way to climb and scramble up to the light. You failed me. I wanted you, and where were you? I don't know where to go to find you, and my shadow waits for me at the entrance to the garden. Are you hiding the rain, Hermia? Is it because of you the world has dried up?"*

Hermia had stepped back.

Fear had entered her. Her face seemed to have narrowed, she breathed in, a deep shuddering breath.

In the painful stillness Chryse was crying softly. Mirany became aware of that all at once, and the sound of the sea, and the cry of the birds, as if they had come back from some utterly remote distance, and brought her with them.

Hermia backed. Without a word she opened the door, her hands groping behind her. Then, halfway out, she turned her head and the vicious look on her face turned Mirany cold.

"We are enemies. Beware, Mirany. Have the slaves taste everything you eat and drink. Because I won't stop now until I destroy you. In any way I can." She tried to smile. The failure appalled them all.

When she had gone, Mirany sank into the chair and

couldn't stop shaking. Chryse plumped down next to her. "What have you done?" she wailed. "What did you say all that for!"

Mirany licked her lips. She felt sick and terrified and utterly worn out. "I suppose it's no use telling you it wasn't me," she muttered.

Tools to Use and Throw Away

All afternoon the heat worsened. The cicadas rasped themselves into silence, and a stultifying hush descended on the Island. The air became an ominous burning weight. No one went outside. In their rooms the Nine slept or read, or had the slaves fan them with great ostrich feather fans, but nothing could keep out the humidity that made every movement a sweaty effort, every thought wearisome.

It must be worse in the Port, Mirany thought.

She sat on the windowsill, knees up, listening. In Pa's house it would be stifling, and in all those close stinking streets even the rats would be dying with their tongues out.

"Will it ever rain?" she asked silently.

No voice answered.

Perhaps he didn't know the answer.

She had a small flask of water and some fruit; to get anything else she would have had to go over to the kitchens, and she knew they were watching her. Koret was out in the courtyard, sitting in the shade, writing the accounts. She had opened her door and looked down at him, and he had glanced up. A steady stare.

So they thought they had her trapped in here. Mousy little Mirany.

She slipped her sandals on, slid the water and fruit into a shoulder bag, then wriggled over the sill and dropped.

The soil was dry and powdery; to keep her balance she had to grab the branches of the thin trees, and after only a few steps saw how Oblek had slithered here, making a great gash in the slope. Terrifyingly far beneath was the glitter of blue sea.

Hand by hand, she eased herself down. The sun was a weight on her bare arms. She had no idea how far Oblek would have gone, but the trail of snapped branches was fairly easy to follow, though the goat path was so narrow her feet could not fit in it side by side.

Soon it wound out of cover, and she crouched with a shiver of fear, finding herself on a thin ledge of rock that jutted well out over the sea, birds wheeling below her. Breathless, she hissed, "Oblek!"

A gull screamed in and swooped away, the bird's great yellow beak wide. She ducked, with a stifled scream, pebbles scattering over the lip of the path and rattling down the cliff. Glancing up, she saw the tiled roofs of the precinct high above, its terraces and white walls shimmering. If anyone was looking out they would surely see her.

The path zigzagged. Around rocks and leaning boulders, down into scrambling dips and up again through scratchy furze and tangled olive stumps. Patches of dried dung black and hard as leather stank in the heat; flies and biting insects rose round her in clouds at every step.

How far could they have gone?

She crawled under an outcrop of rock, caught a glimpse of color, turned, slipped. For a giddy instant she seemed to hang over an emptiness of stone and crashing waves. Then Alexos said, "I've got you."

His hand was cool on her burning arm.

He dragged her back; she held on to him, breathing hard.

Oblek was asleep under the rock hang, propped up and snoring. Beside him an empty wine flagon lay tilted.

"Where did he get that?" she asked, aghast.

"He brought it from the Temple." Alexos helped her up the slippery scree; together they crouched in the narrow band of shade. "What's happening, Mirany?"

Mirany looked at him. "Argelin's men searched the entire precinct, and Hermia herself searched the Temple, and the Oracle. The Island is sealed off. Soldiers have been posted on both ends of the bridge, and at the entrances to the Upper and Lower Houses—for our protection, of course."

"Of course."

"And they've taken Chryse off somewhere to be questioned. I don't know what she'll tell them."

"And you?"

She shrugged. "They think I'm in my room. It's a stand-off. They can't do anything without proof." She wriggled round and turned to him. "Why did you make me say those things to Hermia?"

"Me?"

"The god. That's you, isn't it?" When he looked away, she said quietly, "It's strange. I thought if she could hear the god she'd be on our side, but it just seemed to make everything worse."

Alexos watched her with dark eyes. "She may think she does hear him. She must tell Argelin so."

Startled, she said, "Yes! But perhaps if he knew the god really spoke to me . . . "

The boy had arranged a pile of stones in a circle. Nine small stones. "Be careful, Mirany," he whispered. "They've tried once to hurt you."

"The god promised me. He said he wouldn't let me be hurt."

Alexos dropped a pebble in the circle's heart. "Yes. *But what if the gods tell lies?*"

Behind them, Oblek stirred. He rolled over and groped for the flask. Mirany kicked it away, but only a drip slid out.

"Oblek!"

He sat up, looked at her through small bloodshot eyes, rasping the stubble on his face. "God, I'm hungry. What have you brought?"

She handed over the fruit and water.

For a moment she watched him drink, his throat working. Then she said, "I need to know what you're going to do."

He lowered the flask and put the stopper in deliberately. Out at sea one small craft was tacking in, its sails collapsing as the wind died.

"What you don't know can't hurt you—"

"If you try this and fail, then the plan is finished." She squirmed round to look at him, then caught his filthy, sunburned arm. "You're endangering all of us. Don't do it, Oblek! Make it your revenge to get Alexos to the Choosing; the god will do the rest. Forget Argelin!"

He laughed sourly. "I told you, the god wants me to kill Argelin. The god put it in my mind. Maybe I'm the arm of the god, me and you, too. His tools. To use and then throw away, if he wants. To sharpen or to break."

Chilled, she took her hand away, then looked at Alexos. "What do you think?"

The boy was peeling an orange, carefully, sniffing the pungent scent as if it was totally new.

When he looked up, he seemed delighted. "It doesn't matter, Mirany. I don't mind."

They were both too strange for her, beyond her. She felt a sort of dread as she looked at them, because their utter unknowableness was a terrible thing, a gulf that could never be bridged. If only Seth was here. Seth was normal.

The bell rang, once, high up in the house.

She looked up in panic. "That's for the procession. I

have to go. Don't try to get off the Island, Oblek, please!" She dropped on her knees and made him look at her. "Promise me! I'm begging you."

Gruff, a little embarrassed, he heaved himself up then, a heavy, unsteady man, sweat on his face and the burned skin of his bare head, and he pulled her to her feet with his firm hand.

"The Bearer-of-the-God doesn't beg. Certainly not from me. But I won't fail us, Mirany," he said earnestly, his voice thick. "I will kill Argelin. We'll get off the Island. I can swim; the boy can cling to me. I'll be hidden in the crowd at the seventh house. Be ready. Because if the god wants us to win, he'll have to do something after that. Something wonderful."

And he looked down at the boy laying the orange segments in patterns on the dusty stone.

In the dusk Seth ran across the plaza. Twilight was gathering, a brief mothy time. Far to the west the sun was setting behind the mountains, in steamy, sizzling veils of haze. The beacon on the ziggurat crackled and spat, sparks rising in a sudden puff of air, collapsing with a crisp rustle of ashes.

The evening burned. It smelt of flames and charred wood. Up from the Port the smoke of cooking fires drifted, and the horns on the gates of the City had a brazen, searing sound, as if their metal was warped and the lips of their watchmen parched.

He was late, and he shouldn't be here anyway. But if

Oblek struck it would be tonight, at the seventh house, when the Archon's servants tasted the red flowers and went with him into the dark. It would never work. Oblek would never have planned it properly. He, Seth, would have.

Dodging round the base of the ziggurat he put his head down and walked purposefully toward the blazing doorway of the house. Above him on the walls, the sentinels watched, and the stone Archons stared out across the desert at the last rim of the sun closing up like an eye.

Until suddenly, it was dark.

That was when the whisper came, a sly word.

"Scribe."

A tall man, wrapped in a cloak. Probably a pilgrim. Seth slowed, turned, and the man moved his hood aside.

The Jackal's eyes were sharp and amused.

Seth froze. "What are you—"

"Doing here? Where else does a tomb dog lurk, but in the City of the Dead?" He smiled. "Do you think I have never hunted here before? This place is riddled with secrets, scribe."

Seth looked round quickly. "I don't want to be seen with you."

"No one sees. I wanted you to know that the final arrangements are made. We meet at the doorway to the second level at the mausoleum of Hamox, sunset, this time tomorrow. Bring nothing; we'll have everything we need. Understand?"

Rigid, Seth nodded.

"And if you're not there," the Jackal said pleasantly, "we will come looking for you."

"I'll be there."

"Quite. And you will lead. In every passageway you will go first. Thus we will be sure where the traps are."

Seth cursed. He turned away, then spun back to argue. But the shadows were empty.

The seventh house was painted red and gold. It was open, its flaring lights streaming out into the dark. The heat inside was almost unbearable; behind her mask Mirany breathed shallowly, feeling light-headed with tension, wanting to cry out with it. And it wasn't just the heat. On each of the copper tripods herbs and strange narcotics were burning, secret recipes of the herbalists, the silent men in orange robes who tended each one, spooning on the mixtures of incense that released the dreamy, fragrant smoke.

Masked, waiting, the Nine sat in a circle on painted stools, the empty bronze bowl at Mirany's feet. Her eyes watched the crowd, searching every face anxiously.

In the center of the ring, in the very center of the house, lay the Archon's huge gold coffin, and around it, empty yet, the striped daybeds, their gilded wood gleaming darkly, their precious zebra skins piled high and soft.

Mirany moved her eyes stealthily behind the narrow slits.

As usual, hundreds were pouring in through the vast doorway. Scribes, workers of the City, veiled women. From one of them a wail of mourning rose up, high and sobbing, quickly silenced.

She couldn't see Oblek. Hands clenched, she prayed.

"Don't let him come. *Don't let him.*"

Horns sounded. With a rustle of silk, Hermia stood, and all the Nine rose with her, and from her place at the Speaker's side, Mirany saw them: Rhetia, tall and proud, Chryse's gold hair, Callia, Gaia, Ixaca. But whether it was the heady spiced air that she couldn't breathe, or the fear that was like a pain in her side, something had made a change in them, a shimmer, a desert mirage that hung in the chamber, so that the white-gowned girls in their golden, plumed masks were suddenly strangers to her, a ring of bizarre, terrible metal faces, each with a soft smile that would never know pity.

She wore that smile, too. If she had a mirror, she wouldn't even recognize herself.

And then with a crawling tingle that crept up her arms, she saw that the cats were slinking in, the sacred black cats that infested the City; they lay flat under the chairs and coffin, sprawled in the heat; stalked through the crowd, tails high. People backed, whispering. In the hot, smoky chamber their eyes were small mirrors of green and amber.

At the door the people were shoved back. Argelin strode in, his bronze armor burnished, and behind him a phalanx of soldiers escorted the first hundred personal servants of the Archon.

Serving women, a cook, garden boys, scribes, the steward, the physician, the astronomer, the vine grower, the barber. Five huge slaves who would have carried the Archon's litter. Slim girls who would have danced for him. Sixteen hefty bodyguards. A scarred, limping creature with a monkey in his arms. Forty musicians, with their harps and lyres and small brass bells and a drum.

One by one they walked in, some weeping, some supporting each other, one or two looking blankly round at the ring of masks and the crackling flames. They would have been drugged, Mirany knew. The herbalists guided them to the couches, and laid them down, murmuring, reassuring. The stable boy held the monkey tight; it lay half-asleep on his chest, a small brown creature that must have been the Archon's favorite, because his other hounds and birds and pets and exotic beasts already lay embalmed in the House of Gathered Goods.

The soldiers clashed in salute.

Hermia held out her hands, and the Nine did the same, linking fingers. Mirany's hands were hot; the Speaker's fingers felt cool, they held her own tight. From the silence a flute began to play, solitary and strange, and the Nine moved slowly, in the formal, ornate steps of the dance of death.

She had learned it, and practiced it often. It had seemed fun, one more of the pointless things they taught you. Now it was real, a movement of menace, and as she circled in the pattern of steps, Mirany felt the breathless terror inside her rise like a pain, and the hiss and spit of the torches, the acrid

smoke, the half-glimpsed faces turned around her like
images in a dream, the soft drums that had come from
nowhere beating and beating like her heart, a tense vibration that seemed to set the very air trembling. They would
die, these people. They would go to the Archon, but the
Archon was alive, was here! And for one brief, fierce second, yes, she wanted to scream for Oblek to come, to finish it all, to slash open the stifling murk of the house. And
she lifted her eyes, and through the slits of the mask, she
saw him.

He was wrapped in a gray cloak, and had edged behind
the guards. As she turned, Chryse hid him, then Rhetia;
when she found him again he had worked around to
Argelin's shoulder.

She flashed a glance at the general; he was watching
Hermia, intent, at ease, arms folded.

"What do I do?" she breathed. *What do I do?* And then,
fiercely, *Do you want this to happen? If not, stop it now!*

The answer was an odd, chattering sound. The monkey
had woken. It raised its head and looked up sleepily, straight
at Oblek, no, beyond him, behind him. It gave a joyful
shriek, jumped out of the boy's grip and scuttled between
the robes and feet threading the dance, leaping with a squeal
of joy into the arms of Alexos as he pushed out and caught
it and flung it up in delight.

"Eno!"

Every cat in the chamber spat and arched.

The music faltered. Argelin spun.

Chest to chest with Oblek he stopped, eyes wide in sudden alarm. But the musician grinned.

His great fist shot out and caught the general's throat. From under his cloak he thrust the knife in, hard.

THE SEVENTH HOUSE
OF THE RED FLOWERS

My brother looks like me, but a reflection in a dim mirror.

When I look into water, I see him. Pale, attenuated. With no color in him.

A god can't be expected to love every aspect of the world, can he? Death, darkness, the crevasse in the rock where the scorpion crawls, these I leave to him.

I have found out that I like to laugh. At a cat chasing its tail, at the brightness of gold. At men's foolishness.

Even though I love them. Even though they will one day break my heart.

A God Is Not Responsible
for His Worshippers

Chaos erupted.

Mirany froze in the dance; Hermia's grip held her tight, jerking her round so that they were face-to-face. The Speaker dragged off her mask.

"Argelin!" she screamed.

The general was down. The crowd had surged in; his bodyguards were fighting to get to him, the chamber was a mass of panic, and squirming round. Mirany struggled to get away, glimpsing Oblek's bulk shouldering ruthlessly through the throng. Someone was yelling orders; they would close the doors and trap everyone inside, and where was Alexos?

Get out, she thought fiercely, and then she yelled it, a screech of warning. "Get outside! Quickly!"

In the smoke and shadows the soldiers were brutally forcing the crowd back, beating anyone who wouldn't move, and as if her cry had been meant for everyone, panic spread. Someone shouted, "Murder! The general's been murdered!" and the doors were suddenly crammed with fleeing people, and she knew no one could shut them.

Then she saw Seth!

He was a shadow in the corner. He had found Alexos; the boy was hugging the monkey, back against one wall, crouched, oblivious of everything. Seth grabbed him and pulled him to the doors.

Mirany's mask was torn off; Hermia hurled it down and dragged her, struggling, to the knot of men round the general. "Hold her!"

A soldier grabbed Mirany's arms. Hermia crouched, breathless. "Is he dead?" Even her voice seemed white with terror.

"No." The chief herbalist glanced up. "The breastplate turned the knife to the side."

And then Argelin's voice, a cracked breathless gasp, "Close those doors! Find the musician! Find him!"

Mirany moved. She twisted free, burst back toward the Archon's coffin, into the shattered ring of the Nine. Some had taken their masks off; Chryse was staring at her in utter dismay.

"Mirany."

"Shut up!"

The Archon's servants still sat there in silent stupor. She leaped up onto one of the zebra skin couches and yelled as loudly as her voice could bear. "Listen! Listen to me!"

The hubbub ebbed a fraction.

"Argelin is a traitor!" She screamed it into the sea of faces. "He and the Speaker are plotting against the god! They'll choose the new Archon, they'll control him! The new Archon will not be the right one!"

"Silence her!" The roar was Argelin's; he was heaving himself up, his men a close phalanx round him, pushing toward her, and she took a deep breath and managed, "I know this is true! The god has spoken to me!" before hands grabbed her and hauled her down, thrust her onto the couch, a circle of spear points bristling round her face.

She looked up, defiant. "You can't touch me."

Argelin bent slowly. His smooth face stared into hers, white with pain, a fine sweat soaking his hair. "By the god, lady, I'll cut your throat myself if you say another word."

In the sudden silence his soldiers looked at each other, appalled. Hermia, at his side, said, "Lord General."

His eyes were black with fury. He looked away from Mirany with a great effort, his arms tight around the torn, unbuckled tunic, and she saw the blood there, and his drawn-in breath of pain. Hermia caught his arm and turned. "You!" Her voice was clear and imperative. "Get the general out to safety. Four guards to take the Lady Mirany to the Island. Chryse, Rhetia, go with her. She's not to be left alone at any time. Any time! Understand?"

White-faced, Chryse nodded.

"Where is the assassin?"

The optio came and saluted, hot. "He's managed to get

out of the house, holiness, but he won't get far. I've got men out and the gates of the City are always guarded. Reinforcements are on their way."

Hermia's face was sharp with anger. "The City is a maze! He could be anywhere!"

"He doesn't know its ins and outs, lady. He was a musician; he would never have come here."

Reluctant, she nodded. "And the boy?"

"With him, perhaps. No one saw how they escaped."

Seeing Mirany was listening, Hermia turned. "Take her now." Then, bitterly, she swung back and said, "I swear to you, Mirany, you'll wish you'd never been born after this!" For a moment Mirany thought the Speaker would slap her; instead Hermia drew herself up and said to the optio, "Get the City plans. I'll organize the search myself."

Behind her, Argelin was supported by his men. As Mirany was led out she looked back once, and saw the two of them standing close, the Speaker's arms round him, her head on his chest. Over Hermia's shoulder he watched Mirany go.

Then she was outside.

The plaza had been cleared. Soldiers were everywhere, hundreds marching in. Fires were being hastily lit. Mirany glanced round. Where was Seth? Were they even together? If Seth had Alexos he would hide him somewhere in the City, wouldn't he, or would he hand him over? And where was Oblek, so easy to recognize, so reckless? Did he think he had killed the general? Or was he raging somewhere, sick with anger at having failed?

Hurriedly, the main gates were opened; the optio ushered Mirany and the others through, the guards behind them watching every shadow, spear points bright. In the flicker of torches a closed litter was waiting. The optio tugged the curtains wide. "You in here, lady. I'll travel with you."

Mirany flicked a silent appeal at Chryse who said, "I'll go with her."

"With respect, lady, it's more than my life's worth if she gets away from you. Follow in the second, please."

Mirany climbed in, sliding away from him over the red satin cushions. He perched opposite, yelling at his men from the window. The litter rose, unsteadily, then evenly, and she felt them move, the familiar swaying progress down toward the bridge.

She was clenched tight; her whole body was rigid, full of pain, and slowly, she made herself relax, ungripped her fists, sank back in the hot darkness, curling into a ball, pulling her linen mantle over her face.

Embarrassed, the soldier kept his face toward the window.

They had failed. The others would be caught, and killed. And she, tonight, would suffer the punishment of a traitor to the god. She would be walled up alive in the tomb of the Archon. And nothing anyone could do would save her.

Shuddering, in a sweat of fear, the huge aftershock

washed over her, and she let it, seeing again, stupidly, the monkey leaping, the jerk of Oblek's knife, his fierce joy. And then, like a flicker of dulled pleasure, that glimpse of Seth in the shadows.

But if they caught him he would die, too.

And then she really did cry, hands over her face, shaken with sobbing gasps, while the optio stared impassively out at the night.

"Left. *Left!*" Seth shoved Alexos through the door and pulled it shut behind them, slamming the bolts across, top and bottom. In the sudden blackness Oblek's breathing was labored, a huge wheezy gasping that filled the spaces of the passageway.

The big man slumped back against the wall. "Rest . . . have to get my breath . . . "

"If you do," Seth snarled, "none of us will breathe again. Listen!"

Doors slamming. The pounding of boots on the flagged floors of the counting hall, scrape of tables, frantic flinging aside of scales and weights. "They're up there. When they find the door's locked, they'll come another way; there are plenty." Seth glared at the big man through the darkness. "Why in the god's name didn't you use your stupid head! You should have prepared more! Found supporters, planted them in the crowd. Got somebody powerful in the army on your side; there'd be plenty happy to take over as general. Above all, planned an escape!"

The dim bulk that was Oblek lifted its head. When he spoke, his voice was a raw whisper. "You think you're so clever. You didn't even have the guts . . . "

"I got you out and don't forget that!" Seth was shaking with rage. "And him! You were so scared for your own skin, you abandoned your precious Archon without a second thought!"

"I swear I—"

"Save it! What about Mirany! How did you think she'd escape?" He was so sick with despair he slammed a palm against the stone wall. Alexos looked up, frowning. "Don't, Seth. You're scaring Eno."

The monkey was still in his arms. He seemed not to be worried about anything else.

With a groan Seth straightened up and stalked on, not caring if they followed or not. He should never, never have got back into this. He felt as if he was drowning in a sea of sand; however much he struggled he sank deeper and deeper, and now he couldn't breathe or see any way out. He stopped, and swung round. "We've got to get to her. Get her away."

Oblek clutched his side. "You're the one with the brains." The big man propped himself on one arm; he was bleeding from the brawl with the watchman in the plaza. "But we haven't got ourselves out yet."

As if in answer, a door clanged ahead of them. Seth swore, turned right into the corridor that led down to the manuscript painters' rooms and raced down it. At the bottom he groped for the steps that were there and found them, oily with something that dripped from the roof.

Alexos, behind him, said, "Where do they go?"

"There's a room down here where all the old parchment pieces get burned. A big furnace. Maybe if we crawl in there . . . "

He was deep in the darkness, the steps treacherous. Above he heard Oblek's snarl. "Maybe they'll light it with us inside. Save them a lot of bother."

They reached the bottom. The darkness smelled of stale smoke and ash.

The monkey chattered, a tiny sound. Seth muttered, "Keep him still!" but Alexos stopped right behind his shoulder. Then he whispered, "It's a warning. Someone's in here."

The chamber was damp and cool. High above them the vaulted roof rose, and a network of clay pipes, tangled in ducts and chimneys.

Water dripped.

Seth waited. Then he said, "Who's here?"

His voice echoed, whispering back from distant drafty spaces.

In the silence after it, he heard Oblek close up behind, a sweaty bulk. With a snicker the musician's knife came out of its sheath.

"Leave that where it is, master," a voice said calmly, just to their left. "That has done enough damage, I think."

Alexos took a sudden breath and stepped back. He

looked terrified, as if he wanted to turn and flee. Oblek grabbed him. "Who are you?"

But Seth already knew.

Lying on her bed, she wiped her eyes.

"Where were you? Where are you now? Don't you *know* what happened, what Oblek tried to do? If you didn't want that, why not stop him?"

A god is not responsible for his worshippers.

The answer came so clearly she gasped. Gaia, standing at the window, looked round. Mirany shut her eyes quickly and lay still.

"Are they safe? Did they get away?"

Somewhere dark. Somewhere underground. There are soldiers all around.

"Is Seth with you?"

Mirany, I'm afraid. I have a shadow here. Gods shouldn't have shadows, should they?

The door opened and Rhetia came in. She gave a quick jerk of the head and Gaia went out with relief, her tunic sweeping the floor. At the door they talked quietly. Mirany knew they were looking at her. Keeping her eyes closed and her breathing soft, she said, "You have to help us. We did this for you, because you told me to, and now everything's gone wrong. You have got to help us."

She found herself saying it carefully, as if he was a child. As if he was only Alexos, and not a god at all. Perhaps he was. She no longer had any idea what to think.

There was no answer. She lay there, waiting, but nothing came, and Rhetia wandered in and sat on the window edge, looking down at the blue endless expanse of the sea.

Mirany licked dry lips.

She slid her hand under the thin sheets, up onto the table, and found the slim fruit knife.

Carefully her fingers closed over it.

SHE COMES TO HEAR HER FATE

Kreon stood up slowly, unfolding himself like a pale spider. A head taller than all of them, he looked them over, his strangely colorless eyes fixing on Alexos.

"Is it you, brother?" he muttered. "Really you?"

Alexos had the monkey on his back; it pulled his hair with its tiny hands. "I'm the Archon," he said simply.

"And more than that."

Alexos looked frightened. "Do I know you?"

Kreon smiled his crooked smile. But a rattle made him look up; in the chamber above, the door was being jarred open, loudly.

"We need help," Seth said quickly.

It was a jagged moment. The albino only had to shout, call out. But instead he nodded and turned quickly. "This way. Hurry."

They ran through the vaulted hall, raising invisible

clouds of ash, coughing as they breathed it, to the final furnace chamber, a vast brick construction, broken and useless.
Kreon clambered over slithering tiles into its ruin; at the
very back was what seemed like a solid wall, but he touched
something on it and a door hinged back, and they saw the
wood was painted to look like bricks.

"Inside."

One by one, they climbed through, Seth first and Alexos
close behind. In the total darkness the monkey's small body
scrambled against their legs. Once Oblek was in, Kreon
closed the door and locked it; then he squeezed to the front
and said, "This is my kingdom, scribe. Swear you'll tell no
one what you see here. All of you."

"I swear," Seth hissed impatiently, listening to the noises
above.

"Fat man."

Oblek sighed. Seth had the feeling he was too tired to
argue. "Yes. Yes. On the Oracle."

"Me too," Alexos said, but Kreon shook his head. "Gods
don't swear, little brother. Remember that."

He turned and strode on, and they followed him more
carefully, their hands feeling the crumbling brick sides of the
passageway. Seth kicked a stone aside and tried to work out
where he was. Heading east, maybe under the scribal buildings themselves, or the huge barrack blocks where the slaves
lived in squalor. Deep, two levels down at least.

It was silent, except for their scrapes and scuffles. The
passageways divided; in the dimness he saw more than one

turning, and wondered if these were the beginnings even of the tombs, and then noticed the ground was sloping steeply. Kreon moved easily, feeling familiar corners by touch, never tripping, head bent where the passages were low. Who needs sight in the dark, Seth thought, and for a moment was almost lighthearted, till the thought of Mirany came crashing back at him, and then the Jackal, and finally, like a stab of pain, his father, looking out of the door down the narrow street, wondering why his son never came home.

He shook it away. Mirany was most important. They had to rescue her.

Kreon led them to the right, and then under a low archway, so low they had to crawl, and Oblek grunted that he was stuck, and had to be hauled through. Some culvert, maybe. Standing up, Seth felt something wet on his hands. Water?

After two more turnings and a flight of forty stairs down, Kreon came to a stop and turned.

"This is it."

He reached down, picked up a small lamp and lit it, a blue flame that sparked and steadied and showed the outline of his oddly white skin. Behind him they saw a door.

It was enormous, reaching high into the shadows, made of some coppery metal. Panels of peeling painted scenes covered it; in the lamplight Seth caught the flickers of faces and lost gods, landscapes of stories everyone but the poets had forgotten, episodes of fighting and love from mythologies before time.

He reached up to touch them, but the albino elbowed him aside, produced a small key from a string around his neck, and held it up for them to see. With a lopsided leer of a grin he turned and fit it into the keyhole, and turned it easily.

Then, with an effort, he pushed the heavy door wide.

"My kingdom," he said.

This time, Mirany slept. All night. It made her feel much better. She couldn't leave her room, though, even to bathe, and the Nine took turns to stay with her. Late in the afternoon she drank cool water from the crystal cup, tasting the faint tang of lemon. Over the brim she watched Rhetia.

The tall girl lounged on the windowsill, her knees tucked up. She was frowning, her dark hair coming loose, a careless tangle round her face. Beyond the Island the sky was utterly blue, a hot emptiness.

Sensing Mirany's stare, she glanced over. "You must be insane," she muttered.

Mirany finished the water before she answered. Then she put the cup down and refilled it, deliberately slowly, trying to think of some plan, anything. To get out of the house. That had to be first.

"Why?" she asked.

Rhetia swiveled. "To be part of a plot to kill the general!"

"That wasn't my doing."

"And all that stuff about Hermia!" Rhetia's laugh was

scornful. "All right, so she's not the greatest Speaker the Island's ever had, and if you ask me, her judgment is hopeless at times, but for you to think you could ever take her place! . . . " She looked across, a level stare. "I would never have thought you'd have had the guts, for one thing."

Mirany shrugged, feeling the stiffness of the small knife hidden inside her dress. "I suppose the plan is that when I'm gone, you'll be Bearer."

The tall girl surveyed the windless sea. "I'm sure I will," she said loftily. Then she looked back. "Though I don't know what you mean by plan."

"Liar." Ignoring the amazed hauteur, Mirany got up and crossed to the window. "You know exactly what I mean. You've been working as Hermia's little spy right from the start. You were the one who came in here and found the scraps of the note the Archon wrote to me, and you took them straight to her. You were the one who tipped her off about Oblek and Alexos hiding in the Temple! If she asked you to jump off the cliff, you'd do it for her."

Rhetia's stare was icy. She stood, and came over. Then she slapped Mirany's face hard. Astounded, Mirany staggered back, hand to her hot cheek.

"That'll do for a start," Rhetia scorched. "I'm nobody's spy, least of all Hermia's. I don't go scrabbling round on the floor for people's letters and I wouldn't lower myself to carry tales, even about you. So you can just tell me where you got that idea from!"

Mirany breathed deep. She was so surprised, she couldn't

speak for a moment. And what shocked her most was that Rhetia's utter scorn was real. Completely real.

Bewildered, she sank onto the bed. "It had to be you. There were only a few people who knew about the Temple. Seth—"

"Isn't that that scribe you went off with?"

"Yes. And Chryse, of course. I had to tell her because . . . " She stopped, uneasy. "And then she blurted it all out to you, and—"

Rhetia laughed. "That little air brain! You don't seriously think I'd be seen dead talking to her, do you?"

"You mean you didn't? . . . "

"I wouldn't waste my time."

For a long moment then, they looked at each other. Until Mirany said, very faintly, "I can't believe . . . *Chryse!* She wouldn't know how . . . she wouldn't have the intelligence. She's just giggly and silly and—"

"Maybe not so silly." Rhetia came and sat by her. "I can't believe she told you it was me! The cheek of the girl!"

Mirany was too devastated to speak. Chryse was her friend, her only friend in this place. Surely she could never play such a double game. But she had said that she'd told Rhetia, and now Rhetia denied it, and Mirany realized with a strange sinking feeling that if she had to believe either one of them, it would be this tall, proud girl that she didn't quite like. And that must mean . . .

"Are you sure—" she began, but Rhetia interrupted.

"She's always been in with Hermia."

"Has she?"

"Even before you came. Some of us notice what's in front of our noses."

Mirany was stunned. "So you know about Argelin and Hermia then? If you're that clever, you know what they're planning. . . . "

Rhetia shrugged. "Maybe." She was looking hard into her hands, opening them and closing them absently. Then she turned. "Mirany, that stuff about them plotting against the Oracle . . . "

"All that was true."

"That the god speaks to you? I don't believe it."

"He does." Mirany wanted to jump up, or yell, but with Rhetia you had to be calm, be restrained. So she took a deep breath and said solemnly, "The boy we found is the real Archon. The God-in-the-World. A great injustice is being done, and once I'm out of the way, there'll be nothing to stop them. Unless you take over."

"Me!" Rhetia laughed coldly. "Forget it. I'm going to be Bearer."

It was hopeless. Though there was something, some note in that laughter that rang false. She sat up and said, "Rhetia, take me to the Oracle."

"There's no way—"

"Get me to the Oracle. And I'll prove what I say."

Before Rhetia could answer or even look round, the door opened and Hermia strode in.

They stood quickly.

She was masked, wearing the full regalia of the Speaker, and only through the eye slits could Mirany catch a gleam of her eyes. Behind her the rest of the Nine followed, and each wore the mask of their office.

"Rhetia." Hermia held out the Cupbearer's mask. Rhetia hesitated only a second. Then she pulled it on quickly and took her place in the semicircle. All around Mirany they stood, the golden, smiling faces, and the one that was Chryse's was as golden and smiling as the rest. Mirany stared at her, a charged, angry stare.

"I trusted you," she hissed. "I thought you were my friend!"

Chryse's voice was muffled, smug. "Oh, be sensible, Mirany. I have to think of what's right."

"What's right for who?"

"Enough!" The Speaker raised a hand, then turned it over in the ritual gesture of despair. "The ring is broken. The court of the Nine has gathered, and has passed sentence, and it is for you to know your fate."

She knew it anyway. Everyone knew it. So she made herself stand very straight, lifting her chin. The thought of her father, sitting in his room on Mylos reading her last letter with pride nearly made her gasp, but she pressed her lips together tightly.

"You are guilty of treason against the Oracle. At sunset tonight you will be taken from this place and buried alive in the eternal tomb of the Archon. Without air, without water, you will suffer the slow death the god wills. After death your soul will wander the desert in endless pain, burned by the sun, scorched by the wind. You will never find rest. You will never drink in the garden of the Rain Queen, and your family will erase your name from their hearts."

Far out in the hot afternoon, a gull screamed.

The eight metal faces smiled, without pity.

When they had gone, Mirany sat on the bed. Her hands and arms were soaked with sweat; her legs shaky.

Silent, she watched Rhetia take her mask off and stand in awkward silence just inside the door. When the tall girl spoke, her voice was almost angry, as if at some weakness she despised.

"I'll take you to the Oracle," she snapped. "But this proof, Mirany, had better be good."

The Kingdom of Copies

The chamber was vast.

On each side of them it faded away into shadows, and Seth could see by the wall near the door that it was solid rock, a natural cavern, seamed with gleaming quartz. The crystals sprouted out of the walls, rose pink and white, sharp edged, faceted. The cave glittered.

And it was furnished like a palace.

Kreon loped forward, lighting another lamp, and then another, stars of yellow flame, winding his awkward way through couches and beds and chairs and tables, gilt-edged, painted, wonderful. "Do you like them?" he said. "My creations?"

Alexos let the monkey go, and it chattered and screeched, leaping down and swinging itself over to a bowl of oranges. "Yes," he said simply. "They're very clever."

Oblek collapsed wearily on a couch. "God, I could sleep

for a week. Are we safe here? Where did you steal it all from, anyway?"

"He didn't steal it." Alexos picked up one of the oranges and threw it to Seth. "Don't you see? He made it."

Seth caught the fruit and gasped. It was light, hollow. It was an orange made from papyrus, wetted and soaked and pulped and molded. It was a fake.

And suddenly he realized that all of the furnishings were made from paper, from the billions of scraps and notes and files and reports the scribes threw out and worked over and crumpled every day, dumped in the great circular bins for burning. Looking closer, he saw the tables were painted with stolen odds and ends of color from the workshops, that the pictures on them were crude copies of the tomb painters' arts, that the hieroglyphs and ornate, complex letters meant nothing and were full of mistakes, that the gilt was the wateriest of smears. Picking up a small scroll stand, he saw the letters of the original papyrus showing through the paint, a ghostly genealogy.

Kreon finished lighting the lamps in a circular holder and propped himself on a big chair with the winged back of a vulture. "All mine," he said with a quiet pride, waving his arm. "All copies. Shadows of the real. The furniture of every Archon, every piece that goes into the tombs, of soothsayers and priests and overseers and generals—I copy it. I make myself rich from small disregarded scraps."

"It's incredible." Seth wandered through the careful

arrangements of stools and fans and statues of cats and horses; he ducked under a vast standing image of some soldier, rigidly upright with a great black staff, staring across a nonexistent vista.

Alexos was exploring, too, his voice coming muffled and fascinated from the darkness. "There are vases here, and pots and dishes, all of paper. And look, Seth, come and see this!"

Seth edged his way through a dusty aisle of tall storklike birds.

The Archon stood at the foot of a great step in the cave floor; above him was an ornate screen, painted gold, its warm glow flickering in the torchlight. A fire burned behind it, a comfortable, crackling fire, and over it a spit. In the air the smell of meat lingered.

Seth swallowed. Suddenly he realized he was starving. He turned, but Oblek was already there; pushing him aside, the big man groped for the entrance and had swung through and was searching among the pots and pans even before Kreon came loping up. The albino laughed. "Fat man, you needn't worry. I don't have guests often; I surely won't starve them."

They ate thin strips of mutton, and fruit, and there were some small and rather wizened yams that Kreon cut with a rusty knife and divided with scrupulous fairness, but it wasn't that much, and even after they had eaten everything Seth was still hungry. Thirsty, too.

Alexos fell asleep, and Kreon brought an old coat and tucked it round him. Oblek lay back and put his feet up. "God, I'm tired. What hour is it?"

Seth had no idea. "Past midnight."

"Nearly dawn." The albino crouched by the fire, his long white hair stark. "But this is my land, where there's no day. Sleep. You'll be safe. I'll go up and see what's happening." He stood, looking down at them. "It was a foolish plan," he said quietly.

For a moment he sounded immensely old; his voice dissolving in echoes.

Then he went off into the shadows. They heard him unlocking a farther gate.

When he was gone Seth said wearily, "One of us should stay awake."

But Oblek was already snoring. Seth stared at him sourly. "It'll have to be me, then," he said aloud.

And closed his eyes.

When he opened them he could hear music. Nothing seemed to have changed, but he knew from his hunger and stiffness that hours must have passed. He sat up.

Oblek had found some instrument. It was wooden, with strings, but Seth had never seen anything like it. The big man was patiently tuning it, muttering and complaining, Alexos sitting cross-legged at his side, watching impatiently.

"Is it ready, Oblek?"

"Hold tight, Archon. Nearly."

He glanced at Seth, who picked over the remnants of the food. Then he began to play. The sound was amazing, echoing in the chambers of the cave. Seth was terrified that someone would hear—surely the tunnels must be full of searchers—but Alexos was entranced and even the monkey sat still. The song was a gentle one, almost a song to rock a child to sleep, and Oblek closed his eyes as he sang, his voice transformed. Seth watched, amazed. This was the man who had tried to murder Argelin in front of them all. How could people change so quickly?

The music ended. Alexos said, "Your voice is as pure as ever, Oblek."

"Thanks, old friend. My voice, but not the songs. The songs don't come anymore."

The boy looked at him with dark eyes. "When I'm Archon, we'll go on a quest. All of us. To find out where the songs come from. Would you like that, Oblek?"

Oblek glanced at him. For a moment he said nothing, then, quietly, "I'd like that, Archon."

They were both mad. Seth straightened. When he spoke, his voice sounded harsh. "Where's Kreon?"

"Not back." Oblek turned urgently. "You think he'll betray us?"

"I don't know. I should think not. But we can't stay down here."

"For a while we can. If they don't—"

Seth turned on him. "You're forgetting Mirany. Tonight she'll be walled up alive! We have to do something!"

Oblek sucked his hollow tooth. Finally he said, "Nothing to do. There'll be guards everywhere." His voice was sour and wretched and they knew he was right.

"We're going to try anyway!" Seth raged. "This is all your fault!"

Oblek said nothing, as if he agreed. Since the disaster at the House of the Red Flowers he had been quieter; now he seemed shrunken and strangely old. Alexos put a small arm round the folds of his neck. "It will be all right, Oblek," he whispered.

The big man looked at him. Finally he muttered, "If you say so, old friend."

Their voices echoed in the vast spaces of the cave, came back minutes later warped into strange deep growls. Seth turned, impatient. "Where is he?"

From the dark the monkey chittered, an excited, happy noise. Alexos jumped up. "Eno's got water."

Snatching a lamp, Seth moved toward the sound. Beyond the bizarre collection of furniture, the cavern was darker, the walls narrowing in. His own shadow crept up behind him, looming on jutting crags overhead, and a noise that he realized he had been hearing for a while, a murmur in the background, dissolved and fragmented into a familiar, precious trickling. After a few steps he came round a sudden outcrop of rock and stared in disbelief.

Water ran and dripped down the walls, leaving coatings of pale orange slime, smeared with the greenest of lichens. It plopped from the leaves of ferns, oozing into small rivulets that dripped and spattered into the pans and pots and amphorae Kreon had spread out to catch it. And all around, on moss and stone and rock shelves, hanging in the wet, glinting and twirling and shining and blazing in the light of the lamps, he saw gold.

Such gold!

Astounded, he tried to speak, but heard his voice fold up to a useless creak. Behind him Oblek swore, long and awed.

It was all small stuff, votive pieces, but there must have been thousands of them. Brooches, rings, bracelets, necklets. Tiny gold daggers, swords, amulets. Images of animals, birds, oxen, intertwining swans. Bending, he gathered a handful out of the sand; small arms and legs, dozens of eyes enameled with lapis, odd letters and folded lead ribbons. Pulling one of these open, he found it was a curse, calling the god's anger on someone called Roton, and dropped it instantly, as if it was hot.

Oblek gathered up handfuls. "In the god's name," he muttered, his voice raw with delight. "We're rich!"

Alexos laughed. He had drunk some of the water; now he was draping bracelets and necklets round his arms and legs, and round the monkey's neck, so that it chattered and screeched.

"Not you, Oblek. These are offerings to the god. To me." He turned. "Isn't that so?"

The albino loomed in the corner. None of them had heard him come back. Now he limped forward, his strange swaying walk, and stood over Alexos. The boy's beauty was almost restored, the bruises fading, the cuts healed. His eyes were dark, his hair black. Next to his vitality the albino seemed a ghost, a pale reflection. "As you say, little brother. All offerings to the god."

"But where did you get them?" Seth said.

"From the Oracle. These are the gifts of those who ask the god questions."

"You robbed the *Oracle*?"

"Not robbed." He grinned. "I don't have to rob. Don't you understand yet, scribe? I am the god's shadow. The gifts are thrown down to me. This cave lies far beneath the Island itself. And *behold, the Oracle*."

He held the lamp up high, as high as he could reach. And they saw in the cave roof a great crack, a fissure that split the rock, a chimney in the stone.

After a second Seth crossed to it, and looked up.

All he saw was darkness.

Rhetia walked quickly and the guards trailed behind. Mirany couldn't help a small smile at their discomfort. It was totally beyond their orders, they'd insisted, to let the Lady Mirany go anywhere out of her room. More than their lives were worth. Absolutely out of the question.

They hadn't stood a chance. Rhetia had been scorching in her scorn. Now, on the emptiness of the road down to the bridge they marched in a sort of aching anxiety, glancing back as if desperate for some superior officer, and at the same time terrified to see one coming.

At the doorway to the Oracle, Rhetia paused. She turned.

"You will wait here. You will not, for any reason, enter the Oracle. Do you understand that?"

The taller guard licked his lips. "Lady—"

She nailed him with a glance. "Is it so difficult to take in? Should the earth split, should the world end, you will not enter the Precinct."

Helpless, he nodded.

Rhetia gave a cool nod in return. "Good. Because the vengeance of the god would be more terrible than anything you could ever imagine. As for the Lady Mirany, she is in my care and I take responsibility for her."

Again the guard nodded. He looked sick. They all knew if Mirany escaped it would be the soldiers who would pay.

Rhetia swept around, and marched up the narrow, winding track.

Considering it was the first time she had ever been inside, Mirany thought, following quietly, she carried it off with complete confidence. But that was Rhetia. Mirany was beginning to see a new side to her. If only she'd made an effort to get to know her before, instead of that giggling, useless Chryse. But then, if Chryse was a spy, she wasn't even really like that. Chryse was someone else she had never known at all.

At the foot of the steps, Rhetia stopped, looking up. Suddenly she seemed unsure, so Mirany walked past her quickly and said, "Come on. If you're going to be Bearer it will be all right."

They climbed the worn, smooth steps. On the top the faint breeze she had felt before had freshened; now it was almost cool, a gusty, flapping wind. Up here must be the only place you could feel anything but heat, Mirany thought, turning her face gratefully toward it, feeling her dress sticking to her back.

But the sea was bare, capped only with a few flecks of foam, and the sky was blue to the horizon, a merciless, burning dome.

"Is that it?" Rhetia stood back warily.

Mirany came over. "Yes."

The pit was black in the stone's shadow. As they looked at it a faint miasma seemed to drift from its mouth, and they saw that no plants grew around it, and that the surface of the rock was coated with a faint glistening of crystal.

Mirany knelt, and after a moment Rhetia did the same. To gain time Mirany said, "You must make an offering. It's customary," and an echo of the terror she had felt here the first time rose up inside her.

Are you here? she thought fiercely. *We've got to convince her I can hear you. Are you even listening to me?*

Rhetia slipped a bracelet off and held it up on one finger, a silver chain threaded with fine pearls. It must have cost a fortune, but she didn't hesitate. Leaning out with it over the pit, she said, "For you, Bright Lord," and let it go.

The jewel fell into the dark. For a second they heard it hit rock, slither, and drop. Then silence.

Rhetia glanced across, her dark hair coming loose. "What about you?" Mirany shrugged, then remembered the scorpion brooch. It was pinned to her dress, so she undid it. Perhaps this time the god would accept it. Silently she dropped it into the pit.

"All right, Mirany, we're here. You say the god speaks to you and you can prove it. Well, this is your chance."

Mirany licked her lips. All the way up here she had thought desperately, but still she had no idea what to do or say. She sat back, brushed dust from her hands and skirt, and looked out at the sea. Whatever happened, she would never see the sea after today, never feel the sun. Whatever happened, her life on the Island was over.

She said, "Rhetia, I have to tell you something."

The tall girl scowled. "If you've lied to me—"

"I haven't lied. It's just . . . how can you prove you've spoken to a god? How can you prove it even to yourself? Maybe Hermia does hear a voice. Maybe she thinks what she's doing is right, just like I do. Just like Oblek did."

In the hot sun the stones beneath their knees burned. Rhetia looked furious. She scrambled up, grabbed Mirany's arm and hauled her to her feet. "In that case," she hissed, "we go back now!"

But it was a small voice in Mirany's mind that answered her.

I'm here, it said. **We're all here.**

The slither made Seth jump back—a small shower of dust came down, a dislodged scorpion that made him gasp and jerk his feet away. The creature scuttled into a crevasse and Kreon grinned. "Hundreds of them. They crawl up there all the time."

And then something else slipped and rattled and rolled

and fell from the high crack with a glitter and flash through the torchlight. Alexos stretched his hands up, and caught it.

Oblek came close. "An offering? Someone's up there?"

It was a pearl bracelet.

Seth glanced up. "Can they hear us?"

Kreon laughed. "Now that's a good question. I've tried speaking, but who knows what they hear. The rock distorts your words. Listen."

There were voices above, but the sense was lost. A strange warped music was all that came down to them, its syllables oddly lengthened, a language filtered through strata and stone, without meaning, translated into mystery. Through it, something else fell, tinkling from rock to rock. It hit the sand at Seth's feet and he knelt and stared at it in utter astonishment.

"It's Mirany!"

"What?" Oblek stared. "Are you sure?"

"She wants us to help her," Alexos said quietly. "She might have a chance."

Far above, she heard him say, *Speak to me. Ask me for a sign. Ask me for water, Mirany, and I can send it. Quickly! Argelin is coming. Argelin knows!*

She pulled out of Rhetia's grip. "All right. You want proof. I'll give you proof."

There was a commotion on the path outside, voices, but she ignored them. Spreading her arms, she spoke.

"Oracle, hear me. Bright One, hear me. Send me water. Send it now, as a sign that I speak to you and you to me. That I am the Bearer. Send it *now!*"

Running feet. Not the guards, but lighter. She whirled round, and Chryse was there, breathless, and Gaia, all of them, and last of all Hermia, her face red with running and wrath.

Furious, the Speaker yelled, "Stand up."

And the Oracle spoke. It scratched and rattled and small stones scrabbled down inside it. In a strange, breathy, gusty murmur it made three syllables.

"Mirany."

Chryse gave a small cry, her hand to her face; Rhetia whipped back, eyes wide.

Inside the dark mouth something moved; Mirany took a step toward it, but Hermia's scream cut her like a knife.

"Keep still! Stay still!" She stepped forward, white faced. "This is trickery! *I am the Speaker.*"

A paw. Small and dirty, it groped out of the hole, and after it a tiny head with two bright black eyes, and then with a leap and a screech that terrified them all, a small monkey with a ruby scorpion pinned to its collar put up both hands and pulled itself out, and they saw it held a cup, a gold cup.

Hermia crouched. Every muscle in her face was taut; she seemed years older.

The Nine knelt hastily, but the monkey ignored them all. Loping to Mirany, it thrust the cup into her fingers, half spilling it, chattering, and she saw there was water in it, fresh and amazingly cold.

For a silent second her own amazement reflected in its surface.

Then Hermia grabbed her; Rhetia was on her feet arguing; someone else was crying. Mirany took her brooch back; the monkey broke away and was gone. Snatching the cup, Hermia threw it down, the water spattering the hot rocks; for a moment she looked almost inhuman with anger, as if she could have killed; then, tugging Mirany toward the path, she raged, swearing revenge, for treason, for the defilement of the Oracle with tricks and lies. At the platform's edge she turned on the others. "You saw nothing," she screamed. "You heard nothing!"

Argelin was waiting at the stone door with a phalanx of men. Hermia hurled Mirany down at his feet.

"Get her to the tomb now," she hissed. "Before I kill her myself."

Alexos was crying silently. Tears ran down his face. He sat down and put his arms round his head.

Seth whirled round. "I have to go. Someone has to do something!"

"And what chance do you think you stand?" Oblek had his arm round the boy.

"More than you think." Seth was shoving his way through the fake furniture. "Stay here. Keep the Archon safe, and if I don't come back—"

"Wait." Kreon stood up, arms folded. "Outside, it will be sunset. That great fire you all fear so much will be setting into the Mountains of the Moon." He stepped forward, and he wasn't limping now, or awkward, but a straight, slim shape. Seth stepped back, wary.

"Who are you?" he whispered.

"The shadow. And the shadow asks is it Mirany you're leaving us for, or Sostris?"

Seth stared at him, numb, face-to-face. "What?"

The albino had lost his smile. "Sostris," he muttered.

Oblek scowled. He heaved his bulk up dangerously. "Who the hell is Sostris?"

She had no mask. Two guards held her tight. The eighth house had been painted black and was totally without decoration. Only one light burned in it, and it was empty. All the hot day the slaves had worked, carrying the furniture, the sarcophagus, the amphorae of food and drink, the mummified cats and hounds, the coffins of the Archon's dead servants, his grain and fans and gaming boards, his clothes and coins and scrolls and horses and chariot, his litter and unguents and perfumes and wine casks and jewels, deep into the secret depths of his tomb.

Now, far below in the tunnels and passageways of the City, the black robes of the Nine dragged through new dust and fresh rubble.

They were all masked; Mirany thought Rhetia was wearing the Bearer's mask, and there must be someone new taking her place, but it was hard to tell. They had made her drink something that blurred her sight and made her legs heavy; the guards had to hold her, and she knew if they let go she'd slump into sleep.

She wasn't afraid. "I'm not," she said, and he answered, **I know. And we'll find you, Mirany,** and that made her smile dreamily. And they were putting strange ointment on her forehead and hands, saying words in the secret language all over her, around her, behind her, but she didn't care, why should she care, she wasn't worried. Two of the girls took her dress off and put a different one on her, a short, gray shift, ragged and rough. And then with a few snips they cut her hair, and she saw it fall on the passage floor and almost laughed, it was so silly and long and there were chunks of it among the dust.

"You are cast out," Hermia's voice was chanting, "into darkness, into the kingdom of the shadow . . . beyond all hope and all time and all light," and that was true, it must be true, because it was getting dark, and the guards had let her go and she was sitting on the floor now. The Nine gold faces were dim but still smiling, and behind them stood Argelin—she saw him clearly for a second and he was mocking and wry, one side of his mouth twisted up, and he watched with one hand on his sword. And then the world was closing, rolling itself shut, a great stone sliding across with a hoarse slither and clang. The light closed up like an eye and went narrower and narrower and finally, went out.

And she was alone, in the darkness.

THE EIGHTH HOUSE
OF THE SHADOW

Where do the songs come from?

From the sun and the wind, and the sky.

They blow past men's faces and men don't hear them. So they have to make these journeys, down, into the dark, through the monsters that come out of their minds, into the deepest places, into death.

The songs, they are certain, are on the other side of death.

Those that set off to find them don't come back. Maybe only a god can bring the songs back, trickling out of his hands, like water.

SIX HUNDRED STEPS IN THE DESCENT
TO THE DARK

Outside, the sun had set in a line of fire.

Through a window high up in the wall, Seth could see the afterglow, and he gathered the dark cloak tight, leaning back. The long corridor was empty. Far down in its silence, a single dim torch smoked on the wall.

Then he straightened. Something had shuffled down there.

"Is it you?"

It had to be them. At the instant of sunset the eighth house of the Archon had been sealed, and the eighth was the House of Shadow. All over the City the lights had gone out. Every door would be locked, the great gates bolted and barred. From sunset until sunrise on the following day, the day of the new Archon, thirty-six hours in all, no one would enter or leave the City, no fires would be lit, no work done, no word spoken. The thousands of scribes and workmen and artisans and slaves would observe a strict fast, mourning the Archon's descent into shadow, the strange uneasy time when the god had left them indeed, before the joy of the ninth house and the new child that would be crowned.

The Port would admit no ships, its hot streets empty.

On the Island, the Nine would be in silent meditation, and the statue of the god would not be tended.

And Mirany, he thought, standing up to face the men, would be dying. A slow suffocation. So he stared at them in negligent arrogance, folded his arms, and muttered, "You're late."

There were five of them. The Jackal, looking at him sharply, the red-haired Fox, and three others muffled up in cloaks; tough-looking men, bronzed, and none too clean, but small, very small, one of them.

"He's the cracksman." The Fox laughed. "For tight spaces. Unless we send you in, that is."

The Jackal said quietly, "Is everything as we planned?"

Seth shrugged, careless. "As far as I'm concerned."

"Rumor is going round the Port about some assassination attempt on the general. Is it true?"

"I've heard something. Some disaffected servant. Argelin was wearing armor."

"Just as well," the Jackal remarked. He was still watching Seth closely. "You seem a little on edge."

"What do you expect!" He'd thought he was being cocky. People always seemed to think the wrong thing. "I'm fine."

The tomb thief's long, amber eyes were thoughtful. But all he said was, "In that case, lead the way."

They were silent, he had to give them that. Like shadows they followed him down from the second level to the third, and then the fourth, the deepest level where the scribes worked. At the top of the great stairway that plunged to the tomb passages they stopped, took off their dark cloaks and stuffed them into an alcove, and he saw the workmen were barechested, glistening with grease, strapped all over with ropes and iron jemmies and strange digging tools. The Jackal wore a dark jacket and a belt lined with small, dangerous-looking implements, pointed and delicate. And several knives, Seth noticed. He licked dry lips. The Jackal looked round at each of his men, then nodded, a jewel in his ear glinting.

"Down then."

There was an ivory gate at the stair top; Seth took out a key and unlocked it, and swung the grille open. If the Jackal wondered how he'd got the key, he didn't ask, and Seth locked the gate behind them, and followed.

There were at least thirty different sets of stairs that led down to the tombs, maybe more he didn't know about.

This one was the nearest to the scribes' quarters. One night last year he'd opened it and gone down at least a hundred steps, the air cooling around him, till some draft had put out the tiny flame of the lamp he'd carried. He remembered that utter darkness. Standing there, he had heard nothing at first; then small noises, droppings and remote echoes, faint as breath. He had managed to bear it only a few minutes, then had turned and climbed hurriedly out, hot, his heart thumping.

Now, as he pushed his way to the front and went down, things seemed different. For a start they had torches, which the Fox had lit; the acrid, smoky flames leaped and danced on the walls. And these men were not daunted by the dead; the two at the back chatted about women, and the one-eyed Fox half whistled a jaunty tune under his breath. Only the Jackal walked silent, at Seth's shoulder.

As they descended, the air changed. It became cool, and then warmed again, a muffling, constant warmth. After two hundred steps they passed the first tomb passages; fairly recent and small, the resting places of important civil servants, chief workmen, clustered close to the Archons.

Seth said quietly, "You must have been this way before."

The Jackal seemed amused. "We don't usually have a key. So no."

"Then how—"

"We dig. Break through walls, infiltrate from above. It takes weeks, sometimes months of secret work, and we can only enter the smaller, more recent burials. So this is something of a . . . special event."

All the better. He had been afraid they would know something of the layout, and guess.

"And you," the Jackal said, his cultured voice echoing. "How much have you explored between your listing and your counting?"

Seth set his teeth. "Not this far."

Three hundred steps. They were passing through soft rock now, scooped and hollowed centuries ago. Seth's legs ached and his eyes were stinging with the smoke; he rubbed them, but it didn't help. Down, and farther down, until he thought he must surely be at the very heart of the earth, inside her hot, beating heart, and he could almost hear it, a thudding, distant vibration that he thought was only in his head and chest till the Jackal caught him and said, "Listen."

Small stones rattled.

Before them was darkness. The men's breathing was loud and wheezy; the Jackal snapped, "Be silent!" and it quieted, and they listened.

There was something. It pulsed and throbbed, barely there, and then as they strained to hear, it had gone, and Seth was sure he had imagined it.

"The god's shadow." The Fox's voice was a rumble.

Seth looked around in alarm; the Jackal smiled. "Our word. Often you hear strange sounds in the tombs; noises of falling or settling. The men like their grim jokes."

He gave Seth a small push. "How many more steps?"

"The plans say six hundred."

Behind them the Fox groaned.

Halfway down, pausing breathless, a pain in his side, Seth asked, "Why do you do this? A man like you."

The tomb thief leaned against the wall. "A man like me," he said quietly. "And what manner of man is that?"

"Rich," Seth said. "Educated. Of the ruling class."

The Jackal laughed; the men coming down the steps looked up in alarm. "I do it for the same reason you do it, my friend."

Seth stared. "My reason is to get water for my sister. That's all."

"Do you believe that? Have you fooled yourself that much?" The Jackal's amber eyes widened.

"There are easier ways to get water, even in these dry days. No, you crave adventure, friend. Danger. The thrill of disobeying. Look at you, planning, exploring, despising those you work for—"

"That's rubbish," Seth hissed, chilled.

The Jackal turned and walked on. "You're tired of lists and inventories. Deep inside, you desire songs now."

Seth stared at his back. The Fox nudged him sharply. "Move, pretty boy. Back in front. If there's a trap we don't want the chief falling in it."

Six hundred steps. Finally they reached the bottom, and only knew it because Seth stumbled.

He took a torch from the men and held it out.

A passage lay ahead of them, straight and neatly cut. On each side the walls were plastered and had once been painted, but the images were dessicated and crumbling away.

He glanced back.

"Well." The Jackal's voice was close to his ear. "You haven't forgotten the way, I hope."

"Of course not."

He began to walk. This was the difficult part. He had learned the plans with Sostris's tomb in mind, not any other; now each crossroads became a challenge, every turn a nightmare. If he lost them they could wander here for days, and Mirany would die. His footsteps were muffled in the soft tufa; every passageway looked the same and the air was heavy with dust, so that he tasted it and breathed it and coughed. On the high rock ceiling, ancient soot stains were black. The men had grown silent; now they closed up, as if in unspoken anticipation.

Left and right, under arches and up great ramps and through narrow sidechambers too small to stand up in. At one place they had to crawl, the Fox complaining bitterly, and at another there was a great pit in the floor which had to be edged round. Seth kept silent, walking grimly ahead, concentrating on the map in his memory, almost unaware of anything but counting the turns, and the Jackal's light tread at his heels. When they finally came out into a small hall with eight doors leading off, he was almost unprepared; he stopped in dismay. Then, before the Jackal could speak, he pointed to a great door sealed with a scorpion. "This is it. Sostris's tomb."

They were silent. The Jackal's voice came out of the dark. "Shouldn't it be deeper than this?"

"We are very deep."

"Surely not in the earliest levels." The tomb thief pushed past him, then raised his hands and felt the smooth hammered metal. "Hold that torch up."

Seth did it, glancing back. In the red light the scorpion of the Archon gleamed and flickered as if its sting was poised to strike. One of the men wiped his dry mouth.

"What do you think, chief?"

Carefully the Jackal's fingers explored the central crack, touched the seal, stopped. When he turned, his long eyes were bleak. "I think this seal is fresh," he hissed.

Stones rattled. The tomb thief's knife flashed out; instantly Seth threw himself forward and grabbed him, arms tight round the man's body, hurling him against the door. *"Now!"* he screamed.

At his back a grid sliced down, shaving his heels. Then another. And another.

With a hiss of fury the Jackal flung him off, scrambled up. "Out! Out!" he was yelling, but the men were already cut off, back to back, weapons ready, spades raised.

Another grid. It rattled down between the Jackal and his men, trapping them; instantly the Fox gave a great roar and hurled himself at the rusty contraption; it creaked and rang, but held.

Seth was fighting for his life. The tall tomb thief was lithe and well trained; he had an arm round Seth's neck and was choking him; "You betrayed us!" he hissed savagely. Seth convulsed, knees up, jerked his elbow back hard. A grunt, and the knife fell into the sand. The Jackal grabbed for it. At the same time a thin white hand came through the darkness and whisked it away; Oblek waded in, roaring, and in a confusion of yells and throbbing in his ears, Seth fell, retching, heard the slither of hoarse metal, blows, a strange, breathless silence.

Then the flame-lit tunnel swam back, and someone put water to his lips and he drank from it eagerly.

Oblek held the flask. "Not too much," he said gruffly. "Are you all right?"

Weak, suddenly shaky, Seth put his hands to his throat. "Sore," he croaked. Then he looked round.

Trapped in their metal cage, the Fox and the other thieves gripped the bars and were silent, till the one-eyed man said, "You can count your life in hours now, pretty boy."

Oblek straightened. "Shut up. Is he alive?"

The Jackal was sprawled against the metal door; Kreon straightened from him. "You were heavy-handed, for a musician with a good touch. But yes, he is."

"Then tie him up."

"What with?"

"His own belt." Oblek fumed. "Archon? It's safe to come out now."

Alexos stepped out of the shadows. He was still wearing the jewelry, and the silver crown of the Temple god, and in the strange light he looked unearthly for a second, poised and remote. And then he was just a boy, with a monkey on his shoulder. He looked wide-eyed at the Jackal, as Kreon hauled the man over and tied him awkwardly. "Is that the thief? He was going to rob my tomb?"

Kreon grunted, "Not while I guard him, brother."

"And not your tomb," Seth said bitterly. "Sostris's."

Alexos looked at him. "I am Sostris," he said quietly.

In the utter silence that followed, Seth knew for a second how deep in this he was, how deep and how dark. Then Oblek stood.

"Right." He picked up one of the torches guttering on the floor, and thrust it between the bars of the cage. The thieves leaped back, swearing. He grabbed a spade and some tools, yanking them out. "I want the rest. Ropes. Everything you've got. Or you rot in there."

They hesitated. Then the Fox began to unravel the rope from his waist.

Oblek watched, cold-eyed.

Seth stood groggily, and walked over to the door. He looked up at it, then felt it as the Jackal had done, the fresh seal, the great lock, the complete impregnable strength of it. "How do we open this?" he whispered. No one answered him.

Then he put his mouth to it and yelled, "Mirany. Mirany, can you hear us?"

THE SCORPION MOVES ON ITS OWN JOURNEY

Time did not exist. It had stopped.

She had lain here forever, curled in a dreamy eternity. This was the place you were before you were born, and she had come back to it. It was nowhere, the darkness behind the sky, hot and musty and full of faintest rustles and murmurs and drips. It was black and crowded.

There were other people in it, but they were still, like men painted or dead or coffinned in stifling layers of gold. This was the place of the shadow. This was her tomb.

She thought about the word, savored it on her tongue. *Tomb*. It was a rumbling, echoing word. Long echoes of a closing door that reverberated all round inside her head. A doom-laden word.

Maybe decades after that, she opened her eyes, or maybe they had always been open, because nothing was different except, deep in her mind, there was a murmur, a rumor. It nagged her. "Go away," she told it sleepily, and turned on the soft pillows of her own bed in her room on Mylos, but the sound wouldn't go; it transmuted to the whisper of the sea, to the slither of a snake, the low throb of a heartbeat. It broke and reformed like waves, and though it annoyed her, she couldn't help hearing it; it was growing louder, and there were three soft syllables in it, repeated over and over.

Mirany. Mirany. Listen to me.

"Go away."

Wake up, Mirany. Please.

A draft. The slightest of movements of air. Like a touch on her face.

Mirany.

Fingers on her face. Or no, something lighter, something that crawled, small and with tiny pincers and a tail that quivered. With a scream of terror she leaped up, jerking and flailing in a spasm of panic, sobbing, crashing against piled furniture, smashing an amphora full of grain that cascaded out with a sinister hiss. In the dark her hands tore at her dress, convulsively flicking, squirming back till she hit the sarcophagus and stopped, utterly still.

Breathless, she fought for control. Still. Keep still.

The scorpion had to have fallen, scuttled away somewhere. If it was clinging on . . . the thought appalled her. Her hand groped out sideways; she found a small round thing, a lamp.

She almost sobbed with relief, but it took an age of feeling, and groping among things that rattled and fell and broke to touch the carved top of a tinderbox; shakily to strike it, all the time gasping odd hysterical little squeals of noise.

The flame sparked and died, sparked and died. Then it steadied. Shakily she brought it to the lamp, let the wick kindle.

Light.

It seemed brilliant, steadying and glowing.

It showed the Archon's gold mask, a chair stacked with food boxes, a propped mirror.

And in the mirror a face, dirty and tearstained, its hair hacked unevenly. It stared, stricken.

After a while she rubbed it with her hand, raised the lamp and turned, looking acutely at her reflection, twisting to see her back. There was no scorpion, nothing clutching itself on her shoulder, poised to sting. It took her a long time to satisfy herself; she turned again quickly, as if to surprise it, to dislodge it.

Then she caught her own eye.

That was the way to go mad. She looked at herself sternly. "Pull yourself together." Her voice was hoarse; she coughed. "Better! All right, so they made a real mess of the haircut. It'll grow again. And the dress is disgusting."

The sound helped. "You need to get some more light," she told herself. "There'll be plenty of lamps. Food, too. Every luxury you need is here, after all." Except water.

As she moved, something hard hurt her bare foot.

Holding the lamp out, she saw it was the ruby scorpion.
After a moment she picked it up, feeling its warmth, puzzled. Then she pinned it on.

The lamps were in a wicker container. She spread them
out and lit them, and the light in the chamber gleamed on
the stacked gold, on the bronze and copper vases, the
painted gilt of the Archon's great coffin. In the shadows all
the thousands of grave goods were heaped, great mountains
and valleys of them, stacked haphazardly, and to the right
the black rectangle that was the door to the next chamber,
where the servants lay in their wooden boxes.

She kept her eyes away from that.

There was food, of course, plenty of it, but she wasn't
hungry. The only water was in three tiny jeweled cups near
the door; perhaps the most precious offering the people had
had to leave. She picked one up, and drank.

There was no point in rationing herself, she thought
calmly, licking a drop from her lips.

The air would run out before the water did.

They couldn't even make a dent in the door. Finally Seth
hurled the crowbar down in an explosion of noise and yelled
with fury. The smallest prisoner raised himself on one elbow
and laughed; the other two had gone to sleep, the Fox lying
curled up in apparent comfort. Breathless, Oblek staggered
back, baffled.

He was hot and frustrated and even turned on Alexos.
"You could help us, old friend!"

The boy shook his head. "I haven't got any muscles, Oblek," he said, maddeningly objective. Cross-legged, he sat and watched, the monkey's tiny arms around his neck.

"Him then!" Oblek raged, kicking the Jackal's foot. "He can help or we cut his men up one by one in front of his so-superior stinking face!"

The Jackal smiled. He had propped himself up against the passage wall, and even though a cut on his forehead was bleeding, he was watching in obvious amusement. Seth felt a deep despair. He had no idea how long they'd been working, or what time it was now. Probably well after daylight. Mirany had been in there for hours. The air must be going. And he was worn out, all the sinews of his arms aching. None of them, except Oblek, had any sort of strength. *Too many years of sitting at a desk,* he thought sourly.

Though Kreon was a revelation. Tough and wiry, he had stripped to his white chest and heaved and levered and pushed with the rest. None of it had worked.

Now they all sat in utter dejected silence.

Finally the Jackal spoke. "You see," he said conversationally, "your problem is that the tomb is sealed. Completely airtight. This keeps the contents fresh for the otherworld. Unfortunately it means that once your little friend has breathed up all the air, she dies. Choking."

Oblek raised a sour scowl. "Shut your mouth."

"I could. But I hate to see you so upset." The tomb thief grinned. "It seems to me you people need the services of a professional."

"God, I'm going to kill him right now." Oblek lumbered up, blear with fury.

"Wait." Seth threw out a hand. "Wait."

He looked at the Jackal. "Do you mean you can get this open? How?"

"Secret of the trade. Can't tell you."

"He's lying," Oblek growled.

"Am I? Wouldn't Sostris's tomb have been sealed, too?" The man's long eyes watched them, then flicked to Alexos and Kreon, sitting side by side. "Why not ask the god?" he said sarcastically. "Or his shadow?"

"It would have been," Kreon murmured, reluctant.

There was silence. Oblek sat down, still simmering. Then Seth said, "What's your price?"

The tomb thief straightened his legs calmly. "First, you let my men go. Second, once inside, whether the girl is alive or dead, I take as much as I can carry from the treasures of the burial. And third"—he glanced lightly at Alexos—"if he ever becomes Archon, which I have to say seems exceedingly unlikely, I receive the highest of civil service posts—say, a lord of the treasury? Or even"—he laughed—"Supervisor of the City of the Dead?"

Seth gritted his teeth. "Done."

"You agree that easily?" The Jackal made a pretense of great shock.

"We haven't got time to bargain. She's suffocating in there."

The Jackal snorted. "She should have thought of that

before she got mixed up with a murder plot." He smiled. "I was right about you, it seems. When you jumped us, I thought you'd sold us out, but now I see treachery of a different kind."

Seth nodded sourly. "It bothers you?"

A strange look came and went in the man's eyes. "Argelin is a tyrant. Everyone knows that. My family more than any."

Curious, Oblek said, "Why yours?"

"My business. You, mad child. Release me."

Alexos came and knelt by him, his thin fingers working quickly. Oblek muttered to Seth, "Are you sure—"

"No. But we've got no choice."

Once free, the Jackal stood and mopped the cut on his face. "Now my men."

Seth looked at Kreon. "Open the outer gate. Not the inner one."

With a nod the albino walked into the darkness. The Jackal opened his belt and took out several small tools. Glancing at Seth, he muttered, "I knew you were ambitious. Yet now you will have lost your career and given up the chance of Sostris's wealth, and for what? These people? Each of them is mad, in his own way, and your friend the priestess, too, it seems. You'll never escape Argelin."

Seth said, "Maybe I'm as mad as they are. Just get on with it. And if you make one wrong move, Oblek will finish you. He's wound up so tight I couldn't stop him if I wanted to."

The tomb thief's long eyes watched him. Behind them, with a rattle and creak, the outer grid began to be raised jerkily. "Get out," the Jackal said. "Wait for me in the usual place."

The Fox said, "You trust them, chief?"

The Jackal laughed, scornful. "They're amateurs, Fox. They need me. We'll make the usual split, as agreed. Everyone still gets their share."

With a sharp nod the Fox turned. The men melted into darkness in utter silence. *What if they lie in wait for us?* Seth thought, but there was little use worrying now. "Right," he said, turning. "Let's see what you can do."

She had washed her face and combed her hair and trimmed the ragged ends. Now she admired the blue and gold robe she had found, turning in front of the mirror. If you were going to die, you should do it in style. Chryse would have liked it.

Chryse! That betrayal still hurt.

She still had the fruit knife. It had been hidden in her belt; now she looked at it. It was sharp enough. You opened an artery and let it bleed. It didn't hurt. Did it? It was slow, but not as slow as suffocating. Because she wasn't going to wait for that.

Quickly she picked up one of the lamps and wandered through the stacked goods, into the next chamber. The treasury.

The whole room glittered. Ivory and gold and amethyst

and emerald. Marble vases of grained stone, exquisitely smooth, green and blue cosmetic boxes with small birds that sang as you opened them. She listened for a while to the chorus, then closed them all up. Silence came back, immense. There were onyx necklets and chalcedony and jet; in one heap of jewels she found an elaborate many-looped necklace of blue faience beads, turquoise and gold; she lifted it out and put it on carefully. It felt heavy round her neck.

She moved sadly round the small tombs of the Archon's animals, the bundled mummies of his cats and hounds.

I'm always closer than you think, Mirany.

She turned, as if he was standing behind her. "I'm going to die because of you," she said fiercely. "Doesn't that matter to you?"

To be a god means that everything matters. Don't lose hope, Mirany. Listen.

A thud. Faint, echoing. Its vibrations made the tassels on a small stool tremble.

Someone was there. Outside. Were they coming to get her out? She ran quickly, back to the great doors, tossed the lamp down, spread her hands against the icy beaten metal. "I'm here!" she screamed, panic rising all at once. "Can you hear me! Help me!"

It took all her breath. She gasped but the air seemed thin, her chest rising and falling to pump it in. Then, from the corner of her eye, she saw the lamp flame.

It was turning blue.

◆　◆　◆

Chryse came in through the door and stared; instantly she turned to run, but Rhetia was between her and the door and kicked it shut.

Chryse was pale. She whirled round. "What's all this about? Does the Speaker know you're all here?"

"Sit down!" Imperiously Rhetia grabbed her, marched her to a chair, and pushed her into it. The others sat around the room, all the Nine except Hermia, variously uneasy and angry and scared.

Chryse bit her lips, taking in the silent threat. "You've got Mirany's place," she said boldly. "What's your problem?"

The tall girl bent slowly so that her face was level with Chryse's. Her voice was a controlled fury. "You are a scheming, treacherous, empty-headed little bitch," she breathed. "Do you think, because you've got no loyalty to the Oracle, that the rest of us can be bought?" She straightened, and Chryse breathed out, face white.

Rhetia turned, as if she couldn't trust herself. Then she swung back. "We all heard it. The Oracle spoke to us all! It said Mirany's name."

"It was probably just the wind." Chryse folded her fingers complacently. "And Mirany's dead by now."

Gaia said, "Don't you even care?"

"No. And you needn't all be so prim and righteous either, because you made fun of Mirany all the time. Mousy Mirany from Mylos you called her. But she's gone now, and Hermia is Speaker, and if you want to stay in your places you know what to do. Keep your mouths shut. And remember that it's Hermia who tells us what the Oracle says." She sat back, smiling her pretty smile. "There's nothing you can do about any of this."

"Isn't there?" Rhetia came so close and looked so dangerous Chryse froze.

"What do you mean?" she asked, her voice uneasy.

Rhetia's smile was icy. "As you say, the Speaker's in charge. The Speaker reveals the identity of the new Archon. *But the Speaker is always masked.*"

Mirany opened her mouth. No sound came. One by one the lamps were going out, and the darkness was webbing her heart, filling her up, a tightness in her chest. She staggered blindly. Objects loomed up, blurred, bruised her. She had the knife in her hand and the veins of her arm were blue and fine; they swam in her sight. But her mind said, "I want to live. You'll have to show me the way out."

It was that simple.

Out of the dark he took her hand and his fingers were cool. All he said was, **We could go to the garden, if you like.**

The door shuddered. The Jackal muttered breathlessly, "Now when I say, push again." He made small adjustments to the metal rods arranged in a bizarre pattern around the lock and hinges of the door. "Now!"

Oblek gave another great shove; beside him, Kreon and Seth heaved.

Something shifted. With an enormous crack the seal broke, the scorpion shattering in two. "Hold it there!"

The Jackal's nimble fingers slid a probe into the lock and turned it, then he crouched and did something else at the foot of the door. Alexos watched at his shoulder, fascinated. The lock slid and whirred.

The door vibrated, a hollow sound. Instantly Seth and the others shoved harder; it moved, slithering inwards hoarsely over the gritty flagstones.

A rush of foul air surged out.

"Mirany!" Seth pushed past Oblek, and ran in. "Mirany! Where are you?"

There were lamps on the floor, all out. Water cups. A gray dress, tossed aside. Scraps of hair. He stared down at them in horror; Oblek was already in the next chamber; the Jackal grabbing jewels, stuffing them into his pockets, into a sack, the monkey screaming at him. Seth ran through the doorway.

"Where is she?"

Oblek thrust the grave goods aside recklessly, whirled round, came back. "In there!" There was a third room, full of head-high jars of oil and grain. In the darkest corner they saw a stone in the wall had been slithered aside, revealing a small dark passageway. Seth put his head in and yelled desperately, "Mirany!"

Behind him someone shouted. Kreon scrambled between the oil jars, a lanky white glimmer. "The Jackal's gone."

"He can rot!" Seth hissed. "*Where is she?*"

The albino grabbed his shoulder and hauled him round. "It's worse than that," he snapped. "*Listen to me*! He's taken Alexos!"

THEY SCATTER

"You'll do exactly as I say." Seth faced Oblek with barely disguised wrath. "I want you with me! All the way through this you've been the thorn in our side. Your stupidity, your reckless revenge! You're the reason Mirany was caught."

"You think I don't know that!" The big man flung another vase over, the crash ringing through the tomb. "You think that doesn't haunt me!"

"Then for the god's sake, listen! Kreon is right; he knows those passageways. He's the one to track down the Jackal. We have to go after Mirany."

"Yes, but the Archon! Why take the Archon?"

"To sell him to Argelin," Seth snarled. "Why else?"

"The Archon is my brother, friend." Kreon was already at the door. "I will look after him."

Oblek stared. "Why do you keep saying that? Of course he isn't."

The albino smiled his crooked smile. "He is. Just as much as he is the old man you loved. He and I are dark and light. The god and his shadow. You find the girl. Leave those who rob tombs to me." Ducking under the arch, he was gone. They heard his loping footsteps race up the passageway.

"Right." Seth flung Oblek the water flask. "Carry that. Let's go."

Without waiting, he crawled into the small square hole in the wall.

At first he wondered if Oblek would even fit; the tunnel was tiny and it barely widened, and in the dust and rubble he could see the traces where Mirany must have crawled through on hands and knees. How had she found it? It was unmarked on the tomb plan. The workmen must have cut it on someone's secret orders, maybe so that years later the Archon's goods could be removed stealthily. Everyone suspected it went on, though no one could prove it. Maybe Argelin had ordered it. Or maybe there were other powers in the City of the Dead that he, Seth, had no idea of. Scraping himself under a jutting stratum of rock, he thought of the thousands of civil servants, the supervisors, the council of the tombs, the whole shadowy bureaucracy. Who planned the tombs? He had no idea.

The tunnel opened abruptly. He dragged himself out and could sit up; there was dust in his eyes and his toes were sore from scrabbling on the rock. Behind him, Oblek shoved. "Get out. I can't breathe."

The tunnel roof was high. Thankfully he staggered upright.

"Mirany?"

There were footprints in the dust. Crouching, he looked at them. Two pairs of prints, both bare. *Who could be with her?*

Once Oblek had squeezed out, they ran through dimness. They seemed to be in a system of natural caverns and hollowed places supported with thin terra-cotta brick, a dim, musty warren of passageways that seemed ancient, the small scurrying things of the god scuttling hastily from the bobbing torchlight.

Turning one corner, Seth gasped, "Someone's with her. Someone got her out."

Oblek grunted. "Not possible."

"Yes, but—" He stopped too fast. The sand quivered. Too late he saw how the footprints hugged the rock's edge, the sides of the passage, that the center was smooth, too smooth. He gasped, tried to jump back, swung, overbalanced.

And with a ripple of treachery the ground cascaded inward. *"Oblek!"* he screamed.

And fell, arms wide.

His hand was on hers and he was leading her, and she knew this was the garden again. It was warm with sunlight, and soft with running water, all the dripping, gurgling music she had heard before. They came to a bench in the shade and rested there. She had a small knife in her fingers; tiny clods of mortar slid from it. She dropped it in the rich soil.

Then she looked at him carefully.

He looked like Alexos, but a little older. His tunic was purest white.

"You're the statue," she said. "From the Temple."

That might be how you see me.

She shook her head. "Am I dead then?"

No. But you are not alive either. He smiled. *You used to think I didn't exist at all.*

"I'm still not sure." She rubbed her face; it felt real. Kneeling, she scooped up water and drank it thirstily. Then she looked up. "I have to go back. But how do we get Hermia to proclaim Alexos as the Archon? Will you whisper it to her? Will you make her point at him?"

Sadly he shook his head. *Mirany, you have no idea. Between what I speak and what people hear yawns a vast divide. But things will work out. Your duty is to take back the rain. I have found the place where it's kept.* He stood. *But we must hurry, before my shadow finds me.*

He caught her hand and ran with her along the path, under olive trees. The hem of her new dress dragged in the sand, the path winding between rocks velvety green with moss, birds fluttering up overhead. And yet, behind that somehow, was a darker world, of stone walls and echoes, an underground labyrinth she remembered. They crossed a small stream on an arching bridge and came to a platform of stone. She stared, because it was identical to the one on the Island. It was the Oracle.

There was a standing stone that leaned, and beside it, shadowy under the trees, a pit.

He knelt, and she knelt next to him, and they looked in. But this Oracle could never speak because it was brimful of water. It was a well.

The water was dark and clear, and in it she saw her own reflection, and his. But his reflection scrabbled its dripping hands out of the water, caught the stone edge, and hauled itself up.

It raised its face and they looked fearfully at each other.

I'm here, brother, it whispered.

The room was cool, with a predawn stillness. Outside, the sea hushed on the rocks. No birds had yet begun to sing. Incense rose from small rose-colored globes; in its fragrance Hermia held out both her arms and her slave slipped the heavy robe on, the glorious robe the Speaker wore for the ninth house, the triumphant dawn of the new Archon.

Crusted with gold, its blue was the blue of the sea.

Hermia turned, admiring it, before the mirror. "Good," she said quietly.

The inner door opened; Argelin came through it pulling his coat on. Standing behind her, he put his hands on her shoulders and they both looked into the glass. "You look like the Rain Queen herself."

She turned, putting one finger against his lips. "Don't provoke the gods."

"Can gods be jealous of us then? I suppose they can."

He stepped back, looking at her. "Now, is everything clear? My nephew will be fifth in the line. Exactly in the center. You know who the Oracle must choose."

Coyly, she turned, looking at her back in the mirror. A cool smile played on her lips. "How do you know I haven't got my own candidate? That I might not please myself?"

The jerk on her wrist jolted her, eyes wide. He was smiling but the smile was the coldest thing she had ever seen. "Hermia," he murmured, "don't joke with me. It's not amusing."

Shaken, she pulled away.

He went to the door, lacing up the breastplate carefully over his bruised chest. "Remember. The fifth in the line."

When he had gone she turned on the slave, furious. "Get out! Get the headdress from its stand and be quick."

The girl ran. Hermia stared straight into the mirror, at her high forehead, her sharp face. She was not beautiful. She had never been beautiful, but she was clever, and she would not be used.

There would come a time when she would make Argelin understand that.

Behind her the door opened and she said, "Hurry. We have to be at the Oracle before the sun rises."

But it wasn't the slave. It was Chryse, with a tray of sweetmeats and a jug.

"I've brought us breakfast, Speaker. It's going to be a long day, after all." She poured the water and brought it over. Hermia took it and drank deeply, then looked at the girl. "You did well over Mirany. I won't forget that. I would say we need to be careful of Rhetia now. She . . . "

A flicker.

A ripple over the surface of her mind.

She put the cup down slowly and tried again. "Rhetia . . . she may . . . "

Her words slurred. They drowned in her mouth, though it was dry. She collapsed into the chair and looked at Chryse and whispered weakly, "What have you done? What was in it?"

"Nepenthe." Chryse's hands clutched at each other. She crumpled. A wail came out of her like a lost child. "They made me do it! They said if I didn't . . . "

But if there was more Hermia didn't hear it. All she saw before the darkness finally blurred over her was Rhetia standing in the doorway, grave and silent.

And the mask of the Speaker was in her hands.

Seth screeched, a howl of terror.

Head downward he fell. The jolt that stopped him wrenched every bone in his body; he swung against the side of the pit, crashing into rock. Pebbles and sand rattled down on him.

He crashed again. *"Oblek!"*

"I've got you." The voice was a gritted effort.

He couldn't see, couldn't breathe. The grip round his ankle was like a vise. The wall of the pit came up again and smacked into his chest. "Pull me up!" he screamed.

"You cocky . . . smarmy . . . little brat." Each word came like a grunt, hugely difficult. "Think yourself so smart. Got a good mind to let go."

Panic flashed through Seth like a spear. *"No!"*

A gruff, odd wheeze. Oblek, laughing. Then the grip on his leg altering, a jerky hauling upward. Arms flailing, he grabbed at anything, soil, stones that gave way. His head was throbbing with dizziness.

Then a great hand had his tunic, his belt, was heaving at it, and his head came level and his body slithered onto stone and he rolled over and crumpled, shuddering, sick.

After a while Oblek said quietly, "All right?"

Seth lay still. Behind his closed eyes the blood-red darkness thudded. "Fine," he whispered.

The musician hummed a few quiet notes. "I was joking."

Seth rolled over. He picked himself up, standing on legs that trembled under him, managed to swallow a drink from the flask and gave it back to the big man. "I knew that," he muttered.

Then he turned and walked on.

Behind him, Oblek grinned.

"I told you," Alexos said calmly, "I won't try to escape."

Breathless, the Jackal clutched his aching side and looked into the three black passageways in front of him. "Really," he said absently, "I wish I could believe you, Lord Archon."

"You can." Alexos curled the monkey's tail. "Because the dawn is coming soon, and I have to go to the ninth house to be chosen. I don't know the way myself, but the god has sent you to take me there. Just like he sent Mirany, and Oblek and the others."

Deciding rapidly on the left-hand tunnel, the Jackal swung the boy up onto his back and ran. "So I'm just a slave of the god then," he gasped.

"Yes. You may not know it."

"I don't."

"Even Argelin is. People think they're far more important than they are. You think that."

The passage forked again. Over each gateway a seated Archon gazed down impassively. The Jackal swore with fury. "How can this be the gate of the second dynasty! We're miles from where we should be!"

The monkey's tail went round his neck and he flicked it aside. Dauntless, it leaped on his head.

"I told you," Alexos said calmly. "And if you think Argelin will give you back your family estates for me, I think you're overpricing me, Lord Jackal."

The tomb thief let him go instantly; with a yell the boy fell, the monkey after him. With one lithe movement the Jackal had turned and grabbed the boy's tunic, his long eyes blazing with wrath.

"How did you know about my family? Who told you?"

Alexos was grave. "I am the Archon," he said. "There is only one Archon. I was Sostris and Pelenot and Amphilion.

A thousand incarnations." His voice echoed in the tunnels, and it was a man's voice, immensely old. The Jackal stepped back. For a moment they looked at each other. Then the boy brushed dust from his black hair and stood.

"If you're the Archon," the Jackal whispered, "get us out."

Alexos shrugged. "My brother will get us out."

"Indeed?" The Jackal sounded wearily polite. "And where will we find him?"

"Behind you, friend," Kreon whispered.

Mirany said, "What do I do? How do I take the water?"

You're the Bearer. In the bowl. The bronze bowl!

It lay by the well. She grabbed it. "But it'll spill! I'll never carry it all that way!"

You must. The people are depending on you!

She saw he was facing himself, face-to-face, hand to hand. On the cave wall his shadow came over him and he fought with it, a strange unwinnable conflict, as if night fought with day, or darkness grappled with light. Without waiting, Mirany plunged the bowl into the well and it filled with water; instantly she ran with it, splashing her dress and hands, slopping over the sides. At a turn in the tunnel, breathless, she looked back. The sunlit garden and the dark rocks flickered and came and went. Arms round each other, light and darkness embraced.

Terrified, she turned and ran.

After only a few steps the tunnel became a sloping

passageway and a flight of stairs; she climbed them, wearily pattering upward till her lungs ached and her legs were in agony. She had no idea where she was. Lost somewhere deep in the tombs, and as she slowed to a gasping walk she felt the drift of ancient cobwebs sweep against her, saw dim, dessicated images of gods and heroes and the great animals of the desert carved on the walls, passed endless doors marked with the sigils of forgotten Archons. Another staircase. Up and up she climbed, along a ramp, around a corner. She came out into a corridor where two great statues sat with swords on their knees. Under one she stopped, crouching. There were voices. A scuffle, as if the struggle was ahead of her, as if she would encounter them again, the light and the dark . . . .

Carefully she put the bronze bowl down. Hands on the crumbly stones, she peered round the vast stone leg.

A man she didn't know was sitting on the tunnel floor. His eyes were strangely shaped; he looked on, exasperated, as the monkey hung on his neck, pulling gold bracelets and brooches and jewels out of his pockets, flinging them away. Standing over him was a white-haired, thin light-starved creature, and it was talking, and the words were strange and yet she knew some of them. The words of the old prayers. The lost language of the gods. A familiar voice answered, high and clear. She leaned out.

Alexos was sitting on the knee of the stone Archon. He waved at her in delight. "Mirany! Here she is!"

◆　◆　◆

Seth leaned down and helped Oblek over the rickety bridge, then crouched, breathless. They were near the surface, but surely Mirany couldn't have come this far this fast. Ahead there was light. The faintest, palest light, but it meant dawn was almost here. Breathless, Oblek leaned on one splayed hand against the wall.

"It's too late. We've lost her. We've failed. They'll choose the wrong Archon."

Seth didn't answer. Instead he straightened and walked to the entrance that opened in front of them, the gate of the scribes, the formal ramped way into the lower levels of the City.

A cool breeze brushed his face as he came up into the open.

Triumphant, up on the ramparts, a trumpet blew, and then another and another. The City was stirring from its mourning.

Out at sea, over the black wall with its seated figures, a pearly line of light broke through cloud.

People were pouring out of the buildings, the barracks, the scribal halls. As Seth and Oblek watched, the gates were opened, and a great crowd swelled in, shouting, limping, pushing, carrying the sick and the old. Small thirsty children wept. Crippled men, veiled women, seamen pockmarked with disease surged toward the plaza. They lined the road from the gates, their noise shattering the stillness, and the misery of their needs rose like a stench on the still air.

Behind him, Seth felt Oblek's utter despair.

"What sort of god lets this happen anyway."

Seth scratched his filthy hair. "One with a sting in the tail," he muttered.

THE NINTH HOUSE
OF THE SPLENDOR
OF THE ARCHON

The struggle is with myself. For generations, I've known that. To link my hands round the world, because both of me are needed.

Sun and moon. Day and night. Joy and sorrow.

As for the Rain Queen, she comes when she will and restores the world. Once, she touched my face with a wet finger. She told me, "They have forgotten our stories. We won't let them forget us."

Last night I dreamed she made a flood that covered all the earth.

But that was long ago.

REMEMBER THE KINGDOM BENEATH

She picked up the bowl and carried it out to them, awkward, careful not to spill a drop. The strange-eyed man watched her approach, awed, as if a ghost walked from the darkness, but Alexos leaped down happily and said, "I told them you'd be here soon. Is that the rain?"

She looked at him closely. "Don't you know?"

The monkey sat on his shoulder, its tail round his neck. He shrugged. "I don't know what I know. Things come and go in my head. Maybe I remember them. Maybe they're dreams."

Mirany turned on the men. "Who are you? Where's Seth?"

The tall one bowed graciously. "Looking for you, I suspect. Call me Jackal."

"He's a tomb thief," the albino said tightly. "He wants to sell the Archon to Argelin." She looked at him; he smiled a lopsided smile. "As for me, you know me, Lady Mirany. You have spoken to me before."

"He's my brother," Alexos said happily.

"Is he?" Confused, Mirany put the bowl down and looked anxiously out at the growing light.

Then she turned to the thief. "Listen to me. I have a way you could help us."

The Jackal folded his arms and said sarcastically, "I should be honored to hear it."

His eyes were long and shrewd. From his voice she knew he was of a high family, and that was what mattered. She said simply, "If you hand him over, Argelin will kill the boy and you, too, just for knowing about him."

"A dirty little urchin like this?"

"The Archon. The true Archon." She stepped closer. "Do you know who I am?"

He frowned. "I can guess. The heretic priestess."

"No heretic." She took a deep breath. "Believe me, it's the truth. We have to get Alexos into the ninth house. I think you can do that, and that's why the god has sent you."

Alexos nodded gravely. "That's what I told him," he whispered. He and Kreon sat together, the albino's arm round the boy's thin back. For a moment Mirany thought of the strange wrestling shapes in the garden. Then she said, "Get us in. If the boy is made Archon, we'll make sure you get your reward. If he isn't, you can hand him over to Argelin on the spot. You'll have lost nothing. And you'll be doing what the god wants."

The Jackal mused, glanced up at the pale shaft of sky, the faint stars, then back at her, taking her face in carefully, the hacked hair, the blue and gold dress. Finally he said, "You people always think you know what the god wants. It may well be just what you want."

She stepped forward. "Do it anyway. You must love danger. This is real danger."

"I have plenty of that."

"Creeping round in tombs? It's time to come out of the shadows, Lord Jackal."

He was silent a long moment. Finally he said, "You were wasted in the Upper House, lady. Have you ever thought of another career?"

She blushed. "What do you mean?"

"Tomb thief. You'd be good. After all, to escape from certain death and then con me into such a crazy idea . . . "

"I've persuaded you, then?"

For answer he stood and brushed dust out of his hair. His voice became crisp. "I can get us in. My family is . . . was . . . important. The boy will be my slave, you my servant, bringing an offering. That bowl. What's in it?"

"Water," she said, but when she turned and picked it up the bowl was dry. She touched it with her fingers, dismayed. It was dry as the desert.

He looked at her oddly, then said, "We'll need something in that. This crazy beast has scattered everything I had for miles along these passageways." Mirany thought for a moment, then unpinned the ruby scorpion from her dress and dropped it into the bowl. It rattled and slid to the bottom.

"Thank you." The Jackal turned. "The brother, though, stays here. I don't trust him."

Kreon stood. "Nor I you, Lord Jackal. So take this warning from the god of shadows." He stepped up close, his white hair long and tangled, his colorless eyes strange. "If you ever come back to the tombs, I'll be waiting for you. The smell of you on the air will drift to me. The bones of the dead will whisper to me. There will be no more theft from my kingdom."

Then he turned and held out his hand to Alexos. "Now I'll show you the way out, little brother."

Alexos gently put the monkey on the man's shoulder where it screeched and bounced up and down, grabbing tiny handfuls of white hair. "We should hurry then. The sun is coming."

They ran for ten minutes, threading a maze of passages. Ahead, the light grew. Mirany could see the walls clearly now, their painted scenes. She could see that the Jackal was well dressed, and tall, and had a strange belt of small tools strapped under his cloak.

But the stronger the light grew, the more Kreon faltered. Finally he stopped under an arch, hanging back in the dimness. "This is as far as I come," he gasped.

The monkey leaped from him; Alexos turned. "The light won't hurt you," he whispered.

"Not you, no. But it hurts me. My eyes." Kreon's

shrug was awkward. "Your world is the bright world, brother, but mine is the darkness. It's too hot out there, too fierce for me. There are places you can come to me, like the shafts that let the sun in, but I can't come out." He backed, head bent under the arch of smooth stone. "When you're Archon, when your shadow lies behind you in the sun, remember me and my kingdom. Because I have a kingdom, too, where everything is a copy of your own. Or is it the other way round?"

Alexos nodded, his eyes dark. "I will remember."

"Come on." The Jackal hustled him by, walking quickly. Beyond the arch the tunnel widened, became a passageway. It looked like the gate of the scribes, Mirany thought. At the foot of the steps to the surface she turned and looked back, holding the bowl tight.

Nothing moved in the darkness.

At the entrance to the Oracle, the Procession stopped. The empty litter was lowered, the phalanx of soldiers rested thankfully on their spears, Argelin reined in his white horse. Far off over the dark sea, the dawn was barely glimmering, a fierce red streak under the clouds.

The Nine paused.

The Speaker, wearing the open-mouthed mask and the tall, elaborate headdress of looped crystal and lapis, turned. Through the eye slits of the mask her eyes were quick and watchful.

"Bearer," she said quietly.

The metal mouth warped the word, hollowed it and made it strange.

For a moment no one moved; then the girl on the end gave the garland to her neighbor and turned, oddly stiff, as if fear had made her clumsy, thickened her muscles.

Together they entered the stone doorway.

Light gathered as they walked the cobbled path, one tall, the other smaller, climbing the steps to the stone platform. A breeze from the sea blew their hair astray. Then the Speaker lifted off the heavy elaborate mask and breathed deep. Her face was tense, full of determination. She turned.

"You know what to do. Pick up the bowl."

"Rhetia please! I can't. I just can't!"

The wail was muffled behind the smiling golden face, but there was no mistaking its horror.

Rhetia smiled sourly. "You will, Chryse! For Mirany's sake, because it's the least you can do for her now." Picking up the heavy bronze bowl, she thrust it into Chryse's hands. "If you were right and she was a traitor, the god will be pleased with you. What have you got to be scared of?"

The blue eyes were wet behind the mask. "I only did it for Hermia."

"Liar." Rhetia turned imperiously to the Oracle. "Kneel down. And pray."

She breathed deep, and then began to speak the words, the words she had learned years ago, as she had learned everything concerned with the Island, every prayer, every ritual. Arms wide, she spoke aloud the language of the gods, and in her heart she was filled with a fierce joy. Whatever happened, at least she would have been, just once, the Speaker-to-the-God and no one could take that away from her.

Head down on the hot pavement, Chryse watched the pit in terror. Sweat ran down into her eyes; she blinked it away with a strangled sob.

Something moved, a few small stones that rattled and fell. A whisper of sound, deep in the earth.

If anything came out, she'd die. Hands clenched in the dust, she stared, forgetting to breathe till her chest hurt. Was that a pincer? *Oh god*, was that a claw! And for a moment her imagination was unguarded, and out of it scrambled one scorpion, and then another, and more, and then a great black, jointed, scurrying horde of them, and she leaped up with a screech.

Nothing.

Nothing.

The Oracle was empty.

Drenched with sweat, she stood bent over the pain in her side. Behind her the Speaker's voice said, "The god is not here. That is a good omen. He waits for us in the house of the Archon."

Chryse turned, surprised.

Rhetia must have put the mask back on. It made her look taller, regal.

Like a queen.

◆ ◆ ◆

Seth edged round the corner of the ziggurat and pushed back into the crowd. He came up behind Oblek. The big man said, "Well?"

"If Mirany is out here, she'll try and get into the house."

"Yes, but where's Alexos! If anything's happened to him, I'll . . . " He stopped, choking off the threat. Then he gave a wry nod. "All right. No more unplanned anger. But has it struck you that the albino hates light?"

It had, but Seth shook his head. He felt weary, worn out. He said, "The whole City is crawling with soldiers. Argelin obviously expects trouble. I've got my pass. Cover your face and take these."

He thrust the great pile of scrolls into Oblek's arms; the musician said, "What are they?"

"Who cares. What I could grab. Ready?"

Oblek juggled the heap, got one hand out and scratched his sunburnt head. Then he said, "All right."

"No stupid moves."

The big man scowled. "I'm cured of all that."

But as he pushed through the crowd, ordering everyone back, Seth could only pray that that was true.

The ninth house was a glory of gold.

Pinnacled and faced with white marble, it was the most splendid building in the City. Inside, every inch of its walls was gilded; even now, in the weak torchlight, they gleamed. The doors were enormous; they made up one whole wall, facing east, and as the attendants unlocked them and folded them back, the people surged forward, impatiently breaking through the cordon, shoving, limping, holding children on their shoulders.

"Back!" Argelin roared in fury. "Keep that rabble outside!"

But even he could see it was hopeless. Like a flood, the mass of bodies surged into the enormous chamber, a noisy, rank-smelling confusion of faces and voices, and their desperation was almost tangible. "The Archon!" a woman cried, and others took it up, shouting, "The Archon. Show us the Archon! We need the Archon!" Bells rang, and hands were clapped; dervishes in the crowd danced wildly, intoxicated with frenzy; lost children screamed for their parents; men held up their arms and howled aloud for rain.

Shoving his way through, Argelin came up to the optio and snarled, "There's going to be riot here if we're not careful. Get a reserve phalanx outside. Stay close to me. If I signal, I want the whole place cleared. Whatever it takes. Do you understand?"

The optio gave a harrassed nod. Then he said, "You think they'll try at you again?"

Argelin was watching the crowd. "Maybe. Look out for the fat man. I want him alive."

"People might get hurt."

"Let them." He turned. "Make some space for the Procession. And get those seats up there cleared. Those are for important guests."

◆　◆　◆

The Jackal glanced imperiously at his slave, who grinned
and flicked a dirty hand over the bench. Then the Jackal sat,
sprawling back, glancing loftily down on the mass of people
in the body of the house. Behind him a servant girl held a
bronze bowl in front of her face, peering nervously round
the side.

"Why don't you put it down, Mirany," Alexos said
kindly. "It must be heavy."

"They'll recognize me," she whispered.

He looked at her, considering. "You look different with
short hair. And they think you're dead. Who'll be looking
for you?"

Uncertainly, she lowered the bowl. Maybe he was right.
And then, with a leap of her heart, she saw Seth and Oblek.
Alexos saw them, too, and he gave a great cry and waved,
but the Jackal grabbed him and hauled him down. "Keep
still, stupid! Do you want to be seen?"

Mirany glanced at the guards; none seemed to have
heard, they were too busy pushing the crowd back. Then
her eyes moved back to Seth.

He was looking at her.

He stared, unbelieving. She looked so different. Older. And
yet it was Mirany, that quick, hopeful smile, the brightness
of her face.

He grinned back, and nodded, and as he turned to
Oblek the grin was still there, foolish; he had to rub his

hand over his face and say gruffly, "Take a careful look. They're up there, in the high seats."

Oblek stared. His small eyes widened. "God! What's he doing here!"

The Jackal waved at them airily.

Oblek shoved forward.

At that moment the trumpets blared. People fell back. A space was cleared and into it walked the Nine, dressed in white.

From her place in the crowding ranks of rich women and merchants and princes, Mirany watched them, their slow stately walk, the golden smiles of their faces.

The Bearer's bowl was empty, but then that was right; the god was with her. She, Mirany, was Bearer. The girl had fair hair. Was it Chryse? It should be Rhetia.

She couldn't see the dark girl, and that worried her. Had Rhetia spoken up for her? Was she in trouble?

The Speaker was splendid in the headdress and mask, the stiff gilt-and-blue robe dragging the floor, tall, graceful as a queen.

Gathered in a half circle, the Nine waited for silence.

Then the Speaker raised her arms.

"We are ready for your coming, Bright One." Her voice was echoing and strange. People turned to face east, a quiet shuffling. No one spoke in the crowded halls; Seth pushed forward, Oblek close behind.

High above them on the gallery, Mirany raised her face,

looking out at the glowing sky. "Come to us," she whispered.

And far out over the sea, shimmering with molten heat, the sun's rim cracked open the darkness.

THE RAIN QUEEN HAS HER WAY

Light.

What was light? How did it make everything different?

At first it burned, a scorching glory that turned all their watching faces fiery red. It began at the top of the walls and inched down, and as the sun rose it transformed and lost intensity, became gold, then blindingly white, and they saw that all the sky was fleecy with rank on rank of rose-tinted cloud.

The people murmured.

Even from the gallery, Mirany heard the word *rain*, like a spatter round the house.

The Jackal was on his feet, sunlight brightening his face. He whispered back at her, "If you want the boy to be in with a chance, it's time to get him down there."

Startled, she nodded, grabbed the monkey from Alexos' shoulder and dumped it in the thief's hands. "Look after him." She grabbed Alexos. "Ready?"

He nodded. In the glowing light his tunic was brilliantly white; the gold in his dark hair shone.

The sun strengthened. As it filled the great house the walls blazed with it, the gold and blue and scarlet of the frescoes, gleaming precious stones studded in the floor, the rich dresses of the Nine. Heat came with it, a wave of warm air so intense that those by the door pressed back into shadow. Birds sang. Scents of flowers drifted. A cacophony of trumpets and horns sounded all along the walls, dimly echoing up from the Port, from the deserted precinct of the Temple. The crowd rippled and pushed and trod on one another.

Mirany and Alexos wriggled through, almost coming face-to-face with the optio. She jerked back, alarmed. At her elbow, Alexos whispered, "This way."

He drew her out of the sunlight, toward a small doorway where a guard stood. The man watched them both suspiciously.

"You can't come in here. The candidates are preparing."

Mirany glanced over his shoulder.

The room seemed full of boys. Actually there would only be nine, each combed and scrubbed, their mothers sent away now. They sat, looking lonely and scared, one with his feet swinging, well off the floor.

She bit her lip.

But before she could speak, an arrogant voice snapped, "Let me through!" Seth pushed past her as if she didn't exist. He had a list pinned to a board; he walked straight past the guard and said to the boys, "Right. I have your names here and you go out for the Choosing in the order I say. Understand?"

The boys stood up, nervous. The guard said, "Wait a minute. I haven't been told about any of this."

With a stare of contempt Seth fished out a piece of parchment and shoved it under his nose. "My clearance. Signed by Argelin himself."

The man looked at it blankly.

There was a moment of utter stillness. Then he muttered, "I suppose . . . "

"Right." Seth snatched it away; Mirany's breath clouded the metal bowl she still clutched. He couldn't read. How could Seth have been so sure of that.

Mirany.

For a moment she thought Alexos had said it aloud. But he was edging nearer to the door. *Mirany. Move away. Quickly.*

"Alexos!" she hissed. He didn't turn. Seth had found the masks of the candidates and was giving them out. He flashed one glance at her.

Now, Mirany. He's coming!

Instantly she turned and shoved through the crowd, but there were so many of them, and they elbowed her and stood on her feet and wouldn't let her through, and then, breathless between a fat woman and an old man on a camp-stool, she felt a hand grab her arm from behind and swing her round. She gave a stifled gasp.

Argelin. His eyes were hard, shocked.

Before anyone could see, he had jerked her head back by the hair. His whisper tickled her ear.

"I'll find out how you did this! Where are the others? Where are they?"

"I don't know . . . ."

"The fat man. The scribe." Then his grip tightened, as if a thought had convulsed him. "*The boy.*"

Trumpets brayed. The crowd jolted against them, and Mirany pulled away, twisted among them and fought her way through, the bowl clutched to her chest.

The boys were coming in. There were nine of them, and they were masked. Each wore a thin silver face, solemn and beautiful, and identical white tunics. Their feet were bare and their hair covered by the flowing dark feathers and crystals of the masks.

Even in height, they were the same.

There was no way of telling them apart.

Desperate, she squirmed, but Argelin had given sharp, discreet orders. Two soldiers converged on her. She stood between their warm, sweating bodies, breathing deep. Where was Alexos? Who would Hermia choose?

The entire house was still. The sun blazed directly into it now, a furnace of heat, and she saw there were mirrors in the roof that reflected the light, the whole circular structure a temple of the sun, an orb of brilliance.

The Speaker moved. Tall and regal, she paced along the line of boys and looked at each one. Some glanced down, others stared back. The fifth boy held his head high. The seventh folded his arms. Had Seth got Alexos in the line? Where was he?

I've told you. Don't worry. Whatever happens will happen as I want.

What about how we want! she thought fiercely.

He seemed to smile. *I can't promise that. So many people want so many different things. You, Argelin, Oblek. In all this crowd, all these minds, so many desires. How can a god choose, Mirany?*

Hermia stepped back. Was it Hermia? She seemed taller, the narrow headdress glinting. She lifted her arms and spread them wide.

The crowd gasped. For sewn into the heavy robe were thousands and thousands of tiny glass drops, and now the sunlight caught them, reflecting a myriad of rainbows deep inside them. The robe of the Rain Queen seemed soaked in a glister of droplets, and the words of the god through the golden mouth were spoken in a voice that trickled and rippled. Mirany stared. Across the room she saw Argelin turn instantly.

It was not Hermia's voice.

The Rain Queen's eyes opened behind her mask. They were dark and strange; they looked at the line of boys, and then beyond, at Argelin. Mirany was shaking; her hands slippery with sweat. It was not Hermia.

And at the door, furious, arguing bitterly with the guard there, she saw Rhetia.

There is no controlling the rain. She comes and goes and descends where she will.

"Who is she?"

The one who will choose, Mirany.

The woman stretched out a white hand. One crystal drop hung from each fingernail. She moved along the line, past the first boy, past the second. The crowd waited, breathless. Past the third. At the fifth, abruptly, she stopped.

No one moved.

She carried on. Boys six and seven seemed frozen in terror. Boy eight faced her bravely. Boy nine looked at his feet.

In utter stillness she walked back to the center. The fifth boy waited. His head was high, his arms at his sides. In the rising breeze the dark feathers at his neck stirred.

The Speaker gave one glance at Argelin. The general's smooth face was taut with tension.

Then she reached out with a crystal fingernail and touched the boy who was fifth in the line.

"Behold!" she said softly. "This is the god. The god has entered the house of the Archon!"

People stirred. Someone shouted. Outside, astonishingly loud, thunder rumbled.

The boy took off his mask, and Mirany went limp with relief.

It was Alexos.

How do you know, the voice asked slyly, *that they were not all Alexos?*

A roar of rage came from Argelin; then it was drowned by the yells and cheers of the crowd; they surged forward, holding out their hands, their sick children. The soldiers shoved against them, spears linked.

Alexos looked pleased and shy; he grinned at Mirany, and then up at the Jackal who was standing in astounded stillness in the crowded gallery. The monkey leaped out of his arms and Alexos caught it with a whoop.

And in that instant everything was confusion. Soldiers poured in, blocking the sunlight. Argelin shoved his way out into the emptiness and grabbed Alexos. *"No!"* he yelled, furious. "This is not the Archon! This boy wasn't even a candidate! Treason, my people! If we allow it the god will be angry with us! Listen to his anger!"

Thunder rumbled. A great flicker of lightning whitened hands and faces, crackling fear through the crowd. Argelin turned on the Speaker. "Lady, tell them. This is not the Archon."

She came up to him close, and her eyes were amused and dark blue behind the mask. "The god has told me who to choose, Lord General. Are you debating his choice?"

Seething, he stared at her, his voice a whisper of wrath. "Hermia, I swear . . . "

She put one crystal fingertip on his lips. "I am not Hermia."

For a second then, Mirany knew he would snatch the mask off her. His hand reached out to it, and in his anger he touched it and then jerked back, fingers curled as if they were burned.

Or wet.

"*Who are you?*" he hissed.

"Who Hermia should have been. I am the Rain Queen."

Then, with a graceful nod she turned, and the rest of the Nine filed out silently behind her. People made way. The crowd seemed cowed, scared, and uncertain. Mirany slid away from the guards; everyone seemed to have forgotten about her, and she saw Seth by the door, waving at her frantically.

Argelin roared, "I will never allow this!"

He still had Alexos, but a great arm slid round his neck and choked him; he grabbed at it with a gasp. Instantly his bodyguards closed in; Oblek yelled, "One more step and I break his neck!"

Quietly in Argelin's ear he leered, "And this time, General, I won't make a mess of it."

Who Else Would Take This Test?

"Oblek!"

Mirany stepped out, clutching the bowl. "Leave him! Alexos is Archon! It's all over."

The big man laughed sourly, twisting Argelin back. "Is he? The god says so, the Speaker says so, but the general doesn't. There are soldiers all round the City. It's Argelin who has taken power here today, lady."

She glanced round. The people watched, silent.

"Don't look to them," Oblek growled. "What use are they? They follow whoever's got the command of the army. Who takes the taxes, controls the wells. I know how the poor think. Get behind me, Mirany. You, too, Archon."

Devastated, she did as he said, and Alexos held the monkey and they sidled to the door, Oblek dragging Argelin back, the optio and his men shadowing their every step.

Someone stepped in beside her; jerking round she saw it was Seth.

"You could have got away," she whispered, surprised.

He shrugged unhappily. "It's too late," he said. He looked up at the gallery; she saw that his father and Telia were squashed in up there, watching. His father's face was bleak with fear.

She only realized they were outside because the wind whipped at her robe; above, clouds massed in the sky, split by the hot flicker of brilliant light.

All across the plaza men were running. On the battlements of the City archers waited, bows drawn. Spearmen thronged the great gates. There was no way out.

"Oblek," she whispered.

He was concentrating on keeping a grip on Argelin, but he flashed her a grin. "Don't worry. This time I'll get it right."

"How? We're all going to be killed."

"That, lady," Argelin said between gritted teeth, "I can promise you."

She turned to him. "You can't defy the god. The people won't let you."

"He is not the Archon. The choice was tampered with and you know that. The people believe me!" He smiled, cold. "Kill me and see what happens."

All at once Oblek stopped. He stopped in horror because Alexos had walked out from behind him into the open and now stood before Argelin, the monkey on his shoulder.

Every arrow and spear swiveled to aim at him.

"Archon!" Oblek's voice was in agony.

"Let him go, old friend."

"What!"

"Let him go. It's time the people saw who I am."

The big man seemed frozen with indecision; it was Seth who gently reached out and tugged his rigid arm down. Instantly Argelin tore himself free; his neck was red, his face suffused with anger. He spun round to the optio's men.

"Kill them!" he roared. "Now!"

Mirany flinched; Seth closed his eyes, then snapped them open, ashamed.

No one moved.

In the stunned silence Alexos said gravely, "I think you'll find they're waiting to see, Lord General. To see if what you claim about me is true. Bring me the bowl, Mirany, please." Startled, she glanced at Oblek, then licked her lips and came forward carrying the bowl, the jeweled scorpion rattling inside it. After a second Seth came after her, glancing nervously at the archers on the wall. All around the plaza the people watched.

Alexos held his hand up high, so the crowd could see. Then he put it, deliberately, into the bowl.

There was a small stir of movement. A woman screamed in terror. Gripping the metal tight, Mirany almost sobbed.

Because over the top of the bowl had come a pincer, small and shining. Then a claw, a rattle of metal.

Calm, Alexos waited.

"It's alive," Seth breathed, but she barely heard him; her eyes were fixed on the jointed, glittering scorpion that crawled up over the rim, along the Archon's thin arm, the deadly thing that hung and fastened on his white tunic.

The monkey gave a screech of horror and leaped down, scuttling to Oblek. Alexos smiled and stepped close to Argelin, who took one controlled step back. The scorpion was alive. Its carapace was jeweled ruby, a living gem; its stinging tail raised, quivering with venom. It made small attacking runs up Alexos's shoulders, then it climbed into his hair, and barely moving, he said gravely, "Do you think, General, the other candidates will come and take this test?" Argelin's face was rigid; Alexos turned to the cluster of appalled boys, far off across the pavement, and beckoned. None of them moved. The scorpion crawled on his face, fell awkwardly onto his shoulder and gripped tight. The crowd groaned in terror. Gently the boy disentangled the gleaming jeweled creature from his tunic and held it up in both hands. "See," he whispered. "I am the Archon."

The people roared. They screamed for him. Mirany felt the bowl tremble, thought she'd drop it, her heart thudding.

In all the uproar Alexos stood still and his eyes never left Argelin's face. "Kneel to me," he breathed.

The general did not move. Mirany lowered the bowl. Behind her Seth watched, and the arrows of the archers were withdrawn, the spears lowered. In the crowd someone was singing, a paean of joy.

Slowly Argelin knelt. His face was set, its hatred barely controlled. He went down on both knees and then bowed his forehead into the dust, and Alexos watched him sternly, the boy's dark eyes strange and unfamiliar.

"*You are the Archon*," Argelin said.

Without looking at her, Alexos said, "Mirany, we should give them the rain now."

The soldiers were closing, kneeling, dropping their weapons. The crowd sank in awed rows.

She glanced down into the bowl; it was filling with water. It grew heavy astonishingly quickly. Water began to slop out, splashing and falling at her feet. She lifted it high with a cry of joy, and over the sides of the bowl a great curtain of water cascaded, sheeting down on her face and arms. Thunder rumbled; great heavy drops began to splat around her, deep in the dust of the plaza, and she opened her eyes and held back her head and drank and drank because it was raining. *Raining*.

In seconds they were all drowned in a steaming monsoon. The downpour was fierce and savage; it sliced down, a great heavy cloudburst that hurt, and all around her people were suddenly alive; they screamed and ran, dancing and sobbing and pouring out from the buildings into the rain that hissed and rebounded and cut off all speech and muffled the world behind a wall of spray.

She was soaked; her dress clung to her. Her hair was sleeked back and water was running from her ears and neck, and someone was yelling, "Put the bowl down, Mirany," and it was Seth, rain pouring in torrents down his face.

She flung it down; he grabbed her. "It's over! We've done it! You've done it!"

Argelin was staggering up, drenched. She said, "Yes," but for a moment all she felt inside was a terrible fear, and then weariness, a sudden giddiness. She was cold and wet and exhilarated, and very tired. People had bowls out, and containers; they were rejoicing in the rain. It lashed across the great pavement, ran in torrents down the ziggurat, all the steps of the mighty pyramid dripping and splashing like one vast fountain.

Far off in the doorway of the ninth house, the Jackal watched, arms folded.

She said, "We've made too many enemies. Argelin will never let him live. Any of us."

"Argelin has no choice!" Seth's voice was strong, rain dripping from his chin. He caught her arms. "You'll be Speaker, and everything will be as it should be. Believe me, Mirany, it will! There's nothing he can do now; the people, the soldiers, they've all seen!"

Thunder rumbled. Oblek clapped one arm round the Archon, and the scorpion rattled and tinkled onto the stones; he bent and picked it up, and it was metal.

"How you did this, old friend, amazes me," he roared, holding out his hands to the rain. "But things will be different now."

"Indeed they will." Argelin's voice was icy calm. He turned, took something from the optio who had brought it

over and walked with it, right up to Alexos, ignoring the
musician's threatening bulk.

Raising his voice over the downpour his words rang for
all the people to hear.

"This is yours, Archon. And you must wear it now.
Because if indeed you are Archon, you must take on what
that means. From this day you must live apart, and speak to
no one. Should the god require you, you go to him. Should
the people ask it of you, you must die for them."

Deliberately, carefully, he fitted the mask of the Archon
on the boy and stepped back. When he spoke again his
words were low, a whisper of venom.

*"And from this day, my lord, the people will never see your
face again."*

Golden and calm, the god's beauty covered Alexos.
Only his dark eyes were alive through the eye slits.

And all they could hear was his breathing.